A QUIET DISSONANCE

POORNIMA MANCO

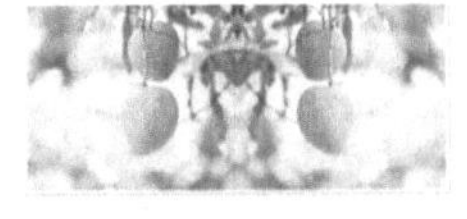

For the friends who stayed. You know
who you are.

*"Close friends are truly life's treasures. Sometimes
they know us better than we know ourselves. With
gentle honesty, they are there to guide and support
us, to share our laughter and our tears. Their
presence reminds us that we are never really alone."*
— *Vincent van Gogh*

If you'd like a FREE story, sign up at www.poornimamanco.com/free!

CONTENTS

PART 1

CHAPTER ONE

It is a strange thing to go through life as an outsider. Anu had never quite thought of herself as one, but the disconnect she felt with her surroundings and with her life was an all-pervasive thing, lodged in her gullet like a dry piece of bread. Something that reminded her she did not belong. That she had never belonged. And try as she might, she would always be found out for what she was - a fraud.

At the school gates, she nodded and smiled at a few mothers, too shy to start a conversation. She watched how they laughed and chatted amongst themselves with ease, finding casual words to describe their days, their children, their lives. Why couldn't she do the same? What was holding her back?

It had been three weeks since her daughter had started at primary school. Neha was no extrovert either, and watching her struggle to make friends reminded Anu of her own difficulties. Would Neha also go through life standing on the fringes, hoping to be invited in? No, she could not allow that to happen to her child. She would do whatever it took to help Neha find acceptance, even if that meant stepping into a circle of women who seemed terribly intimidating.

She inched closer to the group of women who were waiting en masse in the school playground. They were all listening in rapt attention to a blonde woman standing in the centre, talking animatedly, her hands flying everywhere. The story must have been a good one because they were leaning in so as not to miss a single word.

Anu was too far away to hear them, but she watched this woman, fascinated by her confidence and self-assurance. From the sleek bob to her Converse shoes, she was every inch the polished wife of a city broker. Dressed down in her Boden jeans and T-shirt, a patina of wealth still shimmered on her person. The women that surrounded her were not much different. Monied, privileged and very aware of their status in life, they weren't readily accepting of someone new.

When Ravi had insisted on moving into the stockbroker belt of England, she had protested little, even though it had taken every bit of their savings, on top of the sale of their house, to buy a small three-bedroom terraced property in a wealthy area such as this.

"The schools are wonderful," he had assured her, when they'd had to sell her gold jewellery from their wedding to pay the movers. He wanted the best for Neha, and how could she argue with that?

London was filled with pockets of privilege and pockets of destitution. They had sat comfortably in the middle, in an area that was overwhelmingly Asian in its demographic. These were upwardly mobile Asians working in offices, running businesses, having airport jobs of note, and at first, it had felt like the right place to be - amongst her own people. Folk that understood the language, the food and culture of her homeland. Yet Ravi was never at home amongst them, pointing out how different they were from people in India.

"You and I came here in the late '90s, but these guys are stuck in the '60s; that's when so many of them migrated here. India has moved forward in leaps and bounds in the thirty years since they left, but they carry on like they're still stuck in the middle of the last century! Anu, we don't think like them, we don't talk like them, and I definitely don't want my daughter growing up amongst them."

Ravi loved where they were now. This house was smaller than the one they had sold, but he was in his element, chatting to all the neighbours, making friends at their local Sainsbury's. It was she who was still struggling to fit in.

One woman looked over at her and gave her a slight smile. Anu took that as a sign of encouragement and walked over.

"Hi, I'm Anu, Neha's mum."

"Hello, I'm Jill. Are you new to the area?"

"Yes, we just moved in a few months ago."

"It's beautiful, isn't it? Welcome to the neighbourhood. Whereabouts do you live?"

"On Grant Road, not too far from here."

"I know it." Jill seemed to stiffen and back away, turning ever so slightly as if to show that the conversation was over. Perplexed, Anu stood next to the group waiting for the school bell to ring, and for this daily torture to be over.

School was where she'd make friends, Ravi had insisted. Other mothers she'd meet through Neha, women she could chat with about homework and school plays and all such things that women discussed. She didn't have the heart to tell him she wasn't interested in the things that these women discussed. Unlike him, she had no talent for small talk, and she couldn't see a single soul here who would reach out and get to know the real her.

The bell rang, and the doors to the classroom opened. The blonde woman was already there, swamping the teacher with a dozen questions about the pretty blonde girl who stood next to her, presumably her daughter.

Anu waited for Neha to exit the classroom. Neha didn't do things in a hurry, so she knew it would be a while. In fact, her slow-moving ways often frustrated Ravi, but Anu understood it was her daughter's way of reassuring herself that all was well in her upside-down world.

A few minutes later when she came out, her eyes searched for her mother, and upon espying her she smiled so sweetly that Anu's heart filled with a love so painful it threatened to spill out of her eyes.

"Mummy," Neha came and held her hand.

"Hello baby." Anu kneeled down and kissed her cheek. "How was your day?"

They had gone through the phonics book together, mimicking the sounds, laughing at the 'ssss' and 'bbbb'. Now Neha was in the bath, and Anu looked through her school bag for anything she may have forgotten to tell her. A scrunched up piece of paper lay at the bottom and she pulled it out, laid it flat on the table and smoothened it. It was a crude drawing of a stick figure with an enormous head and pigtails. Next to it was a childish scrawl that said 'ugly'.

Anu folded the paper and slipped it into her pocket.

Upstairs, she took Neha out of the bath and towelled

her dry. Combing the tangles out of her wet hair, she asked, "Are you enjoying school, baby?"

"It's okay."

"Have you made any friends?"

"Yes."

"Oh!" Anu felt a sharp relief. "Who?"

"Mr Ferreira."

"Who?"

"Mr Ferreira, the caretaker."

"How... how has he become your friend?"

"Well, he sees me sitting on my own at lunchtime, so he comes and talks to me sometimes."

"But why don't you sit with the other girls?"

"They don't like me."

Neha's tone was matter-of-fact, as though she had come to terms with her reality. Her voice quavering slightly, Anu asked, "Why don't they like you?"

"The girls say I look like a dirty brown puddle, and the boys say I smell like curry."

Anu pulled her daughter into an embrace.

"It's all right, Mummy. Mrs Pellow is a really nice teacher, and she said to me I was very smart."

"Did she, baby?"

"Don't worry, I'll be okay. You don't have to cry."

Before Ravi came home, Anu washed all of Neha's school uniform sets again. Every radiator had something hanging off it, with the heating on full blast.

"What's going on here?" He laughed, looking around. "It's like a Chinese laundry."

"Don't say that!" Anu hissed. "I'm trying to get the smell of cooking out of all the clothes. Can you smell anything on this? Tell me quick! I might have to put it through another wash."

"Only the fabric softener. What's going on, anyway?"

"Neha has no friends. They are calling her brown and smelly. And all our cooking smells are on her uniform." She broke down.

"Hey, hey... it's okay. It's only been a few weeks. It takes time to make friends. All these children have known each other since their nursery days, and Neha is the new girl, so she's the one who has to make the effort. You do too. You know you can call some of her classmates over for playdates, that way they can get to know each other outside of school. My colleagues' wives do it all the time. Now come on, cheer up. It will all work out, I promise." He ruffled her hair and headed to the kitchen. "Something smells good. What have you made for dinner?"

That night, as they lay in bed together, with Ravi talking about his office politics and his upcoming review, Anu's mind wandered back to her own childhood. Mama had been so unlike the other mothers. A statuesque beauty, thrice-divorced and four times married, she had never cared about what people thought of her. Her children had been housed in various boarding schools while she travelled the world with her airline pilot husband. Anu had not adjusted well to the hostel life, was sickly throughout and had been sent to live with her elderly grandparents, neither of whom had wanted to be saddled with the responsibility of a pre-teen girl. So, she'd grown up in a vacuum of sorts. Her basic needs met by the servants in her grandparents' employ. Her emotional needs met by a retreat into art and books.

The few times that her mother breezed into her life, it was like an exotic bird had landed in their midst. All the half-siblings would gather under one roof, some pitying Anu while the others resenting her residence with their maternal grandparents. Their mother would dole out her attention erratically, concentrating on whichever child caught her fancy, while the others watched, hoping they too might get to bask in some maternal warmth. Anu rarely got that chance. As a middle child of five, she felt neither attached to nor repelled by her half-brothers and sisters. They simply existed as an adjunct to her mother's life, and by extension, her own. When they all scattered in their twenties, she felt no grief - it was as it was always meant to be.

When Mama's fourth husband died, she took up with a much younger man, installing him in her Nainital home. Her parents had willed the Delhi property to be sold and shared between the five grandchildren, knowing their own daughter's ways. Mama's anger and resentment against her parents' last wishes overlooked every bit of kindness and understanding they had given their only child in their life-time. Anu hadn't called her in over a month, fearful of the bile she would spew, turning their interaction into a bitter tirade against her deceased parents.

Anu wished she had known her father. He had been a kind man, her *Nani*[1] had told her. Mama was a wilful wife, and he had been patient with her. Perhaps too patient, for after two years of marriage she had moved on to her third husband. He had died shortly after of a heart attack.

"Where are you?" Ravi nudged her on her side.

"Hmmm?"

"You were miles away. I asked you a question, but you didn't respond."

"Sorry, I was thinking of Mama. What did you ask?"

"I was considering booking tickets to India over the Christmas holidays. What do you think?"

Anu's heart sank as she contemplated spending Christmas at Ravi's aunt's house in Delhi. Since his parents had died, his father's sister, a spinster in her seventies, was the one family member he gravitated towards. His brother had migrated to Dubai, and she wished they could go there instead.

"What about Anil *bhaiyya*[2] and Smita *bhabi*[3]? They've been inviting us to Dubai for the last three years."

"Yes, but Varsha *bua*[4] is all alone, and she loves having us stay. We can always go to Dubai over the Easter break."

Anu agreed, but not without the tiniest bit of resentment about once again being made to do something against her will.

As a new driver, Anu tried parking as far away from the school as possible, so that her parallel parking skills wouldn't embarrass her. She always got to the playground car park early to ensure she had a good parking bay. Then she'd sit and read her book until there were just ten minutes to pickup.

Today her mind kept wandering, not allowing her to focus on the murder mystery she was reading. Why had she given up painting? Was it because of Neha? She could remember the sleepless nights, the colicky baby refusing to settle, and Ravi moving into another room to get his sleep. She had packed away all her paints, the brushes and easel to make way for a nursery. And somehow, they had stayed in the attic ever since. Perhaps it was time to resume her hobby. Loneliness didn't bother her too much, but the lack of a creative outlet did.

She glanced at the clock on the dashboard. It was 3:13

p.m.! Just two minutes till the bell rang. She dashed out of the car in a panic, mentally berating herself for her absent-mindedness.

Neha was standing next to Mrs Pellow, looking lost.

"I'm so sorry, Mrs Pellow, I completely lost track of time."

"It's quite alright, Mrs Dhawan, you're only two minutes late. Take a breath." She smiled kindly at Anu, who suddenly felt like a little girl herself, wanting a bit of the maternal warmth and comfort the teacher was exuding.

"Would it be possible to have a chat one of these days about Neha?"

"Is everything okay?" Mrs Pellow's brow furrowed in concern.

"Yes, I..." Anu glanced down at Neha, who was looking at them curiously. "I'd rather not talk about it right now."

"Oh, I see. Yes, of course, I'm more than happy to fit you in next Tuesday afternoon after pickup. Shall we say 3:30 p.m.?"

"Yes, that'll be wonderful. Thank you."

Mrs Pellow smiled before turning to talk to another parent.

Anu and Neha walked back to her car slowly.

"How was your day, baby?"

"Good."

"What did you study?"

"Can't remember."

"Did you make any friends?"

"No."

"Did you finish your lunch?"

"I don't want cheese sandwiches any more. Can I have Nutella instead?"

"But sweetie, they're terrible for your teeth."

"That's what all the other girls have. And crisps, and a Frube. Please, Mummy, please!"

"I'll think about it."

Is this what peer pressure looked like now? Was her five-year-old already subject to it?

Back at the playground, there was an attractive red-haired lady standing next to her car. She looked up and smiled as she saw Anu approaching.

"Hi! I'm Simone. My daughter is in Year 2. I saw you rushing to pick up your girl, and I don't think you noticed this fall on the ground." She was holding up the dog-eared book Anu had been reading in the car.

"Oh no! I hadn't realised... Thank you so much. I'd have been so upset if I'd lost it."

"Looks interesting. I've never read this author before. Any good?"

"It's quite gory, but the storyline is interesting. You're welcome to borrow it once I'm finished."

"Thank you, that would be nice."

They smiled at each other.

"Where's your daughter?" Anu looked around, not spotting a child resembling the slim, pretty woman standing in front of her.

"She's probably on the swings. Dragging her away will be a pain now."

They looked at the playground milling with children of all ages, running around, playing on the swings and the see-saws, climbing to the top of the slide, and squealing as they landed in a heap at the bottom.

"Have you ever taken your daughter in there?"

"No. I just park my car here because it's easier. We are new to the area, so we don't really know too many people."

"I think she'd enjoy a bit of play-time here. Why don't you join us tomorrow?" She smiled down at Neha, who hid behind Anu, staring up at the strange lady chatting to her mother.

"That's very kind of you. Yes, we'd love to join you. What do you say, Neha?"

Neha looked down at the floor as she mouthed a quiet 'thank you'.

At home, Anu gave Neha a snack and allowed her half an hour of television before they tackled the homework. In the meantime, she went through her school bag, pulling out the various notices and drawings hastily shoved in. She sifted through them all, looking for another cartoon like the one before. Much to her relief, there was nothing.

As she was emptying her lunchbox, the phone rang.

"Hello?"

"Hello stranger!"

"Who is this?"

"Forgotten me already?"

Anu hated how some people just assumed she would guess who was on the other end of the line, without bothering to introduce themselves. Did they really think they were that memorable?

"I'm sorry, I can't place you."

"It's Annie!"

"Oh, Annie, how are you?"

Her cousin was just a few years older, but considered herself decades wiser than Anu. Married to a much older man, a professor at the University of Bath, she had assumed all the airs and graces of a Dean's wife. There had been a time that Anu had thought they could be close, but in the last few years it had become increasingly apparent that they were on very different life paths.

Antara had met Richard online, and their relationship had progressed quickly. Before her parents could react, she had declared that she was marrying the shy academic fifteen years older than her. These days it was she who looked older. Richard was still the thin, bespectacled, balding man that they'd first been introduced to. Antara, or 'Annie' as she preferred being called, had ballooned to twice her size.

"Who ate all the cakes?" Ravi had muttered in an undertone when they'd gone up to Bath to see them.

It had been over a year since they had met each other, or spoken. It was no wonder that she had completely blanked.

"I'm so sorry, Annie, I was in the middle of preparing dinner. How are you? How's Richard?"

"We are all fine, but it's been so long since we heard from you. How is the new house? Did you get our card?"

"Yes, yes, we did. I thought I'd acknowledged it. But it must've slipped my mind."

"Not to worry. Anyway, the reason I rang was to ask if you're free next weekend. I'm coming down to London for some work and wondered if I could crash at yours for the night?"

"Uh, yes, ummm... of course."

"Great! That's settled then. I'll text you all the details closer to the time."

"Sure. Uh, Annie, I have to go. The timer is beeping on the oven..."

"Bye! See you soon."

Anu replaced the receiver with a hollow feeling in the pit of her stomach. Antara always made her feel uncomfortable, and she was not looking forward to spending an evening in her company.

❖

Simone waved at them from a park bench, showing that she had saved her a spot. Anu sat down next to her with Neha clinging to her arm.

"Hi! I brought some Indian chai." Anu took the flask out of her bag. "Would you like some?"

"Oh, I love everything Indian!" Simone grinned back, accepting the proffered cup. "By the way, I didn't catch your name yesterday."

"It's Anupama. You can call me Anu for short. And this is Neha."

"Such pretty names. This is my daughter, Kayla. Say 'hi' Kayla. Why don't you show Neha around the park?"

Anu hid her surprise at discovering that Kayla was mixed-race, smiling down at the seven-year-old grinning at her daughter. Nervous, Neha hung back, but upon Anu's insistence she allowed Kayla to lead her away.

"Oh, this is so lovely and aromatic," Simone exhaled after taking a sip. "I bet you're a wonderful cook too."

"I am a pretty decent one, but I wouldn't call myself wonderful," Anu laughed.

They sipped on their teas in a quiet, convivial silence.

"Would you mind if I asked you a question, Simone?"

"No, not at all." She turned herself to face Anu, her body leaning forward slightly.

"Is there something wrong with Grant Road?"

She raised her eyebrows as she looked at Anu speculatively.

"Depends on who you've been talking to."

"What do you mean?"

"Well, let's just say Grant Road is not Millionaire's Row. If you live there, then you probably haven't inherited your money, you've earned it. Or your husband has. But not in the high-flying jobs that a lot of men around here have."

She flicked a bit of lint off her skirt, then looked her in the eye.

"Anu, I don't know you much, but heed my advice. Don't get too involved with the mothers at school. They'll rip you to shreds without breaking a fingernail. I've been there, and I can tell you, it's not pleasant."

Anu digested this silently.

"Neha is a very shy child. I worry about her not being able to make friends, and if I don't reach out to the other mothers, she may end up being isolated completely."

"She doesn't look very shy to me right now."

From a distance, Anu saw Kayla and Neha being chased by another three girls. They were ducking and diving and then giving them the slip, giggling incessantly.

"Kayla has never been a shy girl, so I can't say that I've ever faced your issues. But we don't exactly fit in here either. If you think they look down their noses on Grant Road, imagine what they think of Holly Drive where I live?"

Holly Drive, Ravi had pointed out, was the council area populated by social housing. He had insisted on buying as far away from there as possible.

"I'm a single mother," Simone shrugged. "It was all I could afford."

That night, after tucking Neha into bed after her bath and milk, Anu pondered the irony of making friends with someone from the sort of socio-economic background that Ravi frowned upon. But Simone and Kayla were the first people who had shown them any kindness in their first month at school. She was going to keep it quiet from Ravi for a while. She didn't want him to put an end to a budding friendship between the girls either. It was the first time that she had seen Neha as happily tired as she'd been after her play in the park.

❖

Anu had been wanting to take up jogging for a while. Five years after having Neha, she had still not shed the baby-weight. Although never the slimmest in her family, she had at least been well-proportioned enough to be considered curvaceously attractive. Now, however, her little potbelly, the back rolls and the chafing thighs reminded her daily that genetically she had taken after her father. If she didn't watch out, she could end up obese, diabetic, and prone to cardiac problems.

She pulled up her jogging pants, grimacing at herself in the mirror. A beauty she was not. Her half-sisters looked more like Mama than she did, but Ravi had always insisted that he liked her as she was. She leaned towards the mirror and examined her face. A clear complexion, dark brown eyes, thick hair that fell in waves down her back. She supposed she wasn't all that bad looking. If only she were taller. Or thinner. Well, the first she couldn't do much about, but the second she was going to try her best to fix.

Plugging her earphones in, she took off at a gentle trot. Jogging out of Grant Road, she took a left, running uphill. For a while there were only meadows on either side, with cows grazing on the grass. The sky was a bright blue, and the air crisp as she breathed in and out steadily, pacing herself.

A few miles later, the houses slowly got narrower and more cloistered. This was the less salubrious part of the village, and as she ran past the houses, she saw broken windows patched up with newspaper sheets, a mattress lying abandoned on someone's front lawn, dirty net curtains fluttering in the wind. Further still, a soiled yellow couch gathered dust in an alleyway, with a cat curled up on it. At a distance she spied 'Holly Drive' on a sign that had been overlaid with obscene graffiti.

She did a quick U-turn and jogged in the opposite direction, her breath coming out in little puffs now. Running past Grant Road, she carried on beyond the school and the playground. She stopped and waited for the light at the pedestrian crossing to turn red as she massaged a stitch in her stomach. Then she ran northwards until she reached Grisham Place. Her pace slowed as she ran past the million-pound homes with their gleaming gates and intercoms, their manicured lawns and perfect hedgerows.

Slowing to a brisk walk, her eyes skimmed over the names of the houses - St Anne, Dimbleby, Hawthorne. Then she saw a black Porsche emerge out of the house at the end of the road. The blonde woman that Anu had watched in the school playground not too long ago was driving the car, and she threw Anu a contemptuous look as she laughed with her companion, another mother from the school.

Deflated, Anu trudged home. As she entered Grant Road, she looked at the houses with fresh eyes. They were modest homes, but beautifully kept. The residents took pride in living well, and while it wasn't Millionaire's Row, she was happy she lived here.

The old lady from two houses down was shuffling slowly with her shopping trolley. Anu slowed down so as not to rush her.

When the old lady tripped and fell suddenly, Anu was by her side in a trice.

"Oh, my goodness! Are you okay?"

She looked around to see if anyone else had spotted

them, but at 11 in the morning, the street was quiet. She helped the old lady up, noting that her knee was bleeding profusely.

"I'm just one door away. Do you think you can make it inside? I can take care of you there."

Moaning slightly, she nodded an affirmative, allowing Anu to help her up and take her indoors.

Susan wouldn't stop thanking her for the next half hour. Anu had cleaned and dressed the wound, made her a strong cup of tea and brought all her groceries in.

"My dear, I don't know what happened. One minute I was fine, the next I was on the ground."

"It happens. At least you didn't break anything. Now, are you sure you don't want me to take you to the doctor's? I can drive you there."

"They will not do any more than you have. I am ever so grateful."

"Please stop thanking me. I did what anyone else would have done."

Having taken Susan back home, and after multiple assurances of visiting her soon, Anu sank into her sofa, exhausted. What a day it had been! She couldn't wait to tell Simone all about it.

CHAPTER TWO

Mrs Pellow had the kindest eyes that Anu had ever seen. Typically dressed in a long cardigan and skirt, her entire being radiated warmth and comfort. It was no wonder that they had assigned her the care of the youngest children in the school. Most parents felt comfortable leaving their little ones in her charge, and even the most reluctant child couldn't help but be reassured by her grandmother-like persona.

As Mrs Pellow ushered Anu in after leaving Neha to sit outside the classroom with some crayons and paper, she pointed her to a low stool and laughed.

"I'm sorry there isn't more appropriate seating here. I have the only proper adult-size chair. Everything else is for the children."

Anu looked around the classroom curiously. It was a pretty room dotted with colourful little chairs and stools. Several planters sat on the windowsill, drawings by the children were stuck on the walls, and one corner was filled with stuffed toys. So unlike her own memories of stark classrooms, blackboards and strict teachers who hurled chalk at misbehaving students.

"So what can I do for you, Mrs Dhawan?"

Anu took the proffered seat and examined the floor for a minute before speaking.

"I'm not sure how to put this, but it's been over a month at the school and Neha doesn't seem to have made any friends in class. I'm really worried that she's being excluded."

Mrs Pellow's smile didn't slip.

"You are quite right to be concerned, Mrs Dhawan. Neha is a very quiet girl, and she hasn't been able to break into the little friendship groups that have formed in the course of the last month. But in my experience, these groups dissolve and re-form all the time. She just needs to edge her way in. She's a bright girl, and I don't expect this will be a problem for too long."

"Is there any way that you can help this process along?"

"I can," Mrs Pellow paused for a moment, "I try to move the seating around during story time, and maybe I could get Neha to sit with one of the friendlier girls more often. These things can't be forced, however. You must let time take its course."

"I worry because I've been a loner all my life, and..." Anu was horrified to discover herself choking up. "I... I don't want my child to have no friends either."

"Mrs Dhawan," Mrs Pellow reached forward and patted her arm, "I'm sure you'll discover that you aren't entirely friendless. Nobody is. We just have different ways of making and keeping friends. Neha will be fine. She is finding her own way through it all, and I would let her, if I were you."

"But I want to help!"

"Very well. One way you could help would be to volunteer at school. You could come in and read to the children, or help with the artwork."

"Could I?"

"Most definitely! You'd need a CRB check first. That takes a few weeks to come through. But once you come in and the children become familiar with you, they will open up to Neha as well. Ms Avery, the receptionist will help you with the forms. I look forward to seeing you in school soon."

Driving home, Anu glanced over at Neha.

"How would you like Mummy to come over and help at school?"

"Is that what you were talking to Mrs Pellow about?"

"Well, yes, sort of."

"Are you going to become a teacher?"

"No, baby," Anu laughed. "I'll just come in and do a bit of reading from time to time."

"Oh. Like Sylvie's mum."

"Which one is Sylvie?"

"The blonde, pretty one that everyone likes."

Neha could have been describing the mother, Anu thought to herself, as it occurred to her that Sylvie's mum was none other than the lady in the Porsche.

"What I don't understand, Ravi, is why they send their children to this school," Anu mused while ladling another serving of *daal*[1] into his *katori*[2]. "Surely they can afford to send them to a private school?"

"Yes, but this is their local Church of England school, and it's been rated 'Outstanding' by Ofsted. Why spend thousands a year when you're getting the same quality of teaching and pastoral care for free? Believe me, they'll all head off to private schools for secondary schooling."

"The mothers are all so stuck-up, and the children are no less."

"Come on, Anu! You don't believe that, do you? These are your own complexes talking. There's probably one prima-donna leading the brigade, that blonde one you were talking about. On their own, you'll find most of them are pretty nice and normal. Have you tried making friends with any of them?"

She turned on him furiously, letting her spoon clatter to her plate.

"You think I haven't! Every time I try to start a conversation, it's a dead-end. They look at me as though I smell like a garbage dump, and if I try to make small-talk, they pretend not to understand my accent."

"And none of this is your imagination?"

"You know what Ravi, why don't you drop and pick up Neha for a week? Let's see how you get on. And you can wash up after yourself tonight. I think I'm done here!"

Anu stomped off upstairs, leaving Ravi to himself.

Annie turned up with an armful of packages on Friday afternoon.

"Darling, I haven't seen little Neha in so long and I had no idea how tall she might be. So, I picked up three different sizes of clothes from John Lewis. We can return the ones that don't fit. Also, I went into Harrods Food Halls and bought us some foie gras. It'll make a nice appetiser with this Picpoul de Pinet."

She started unloading everything onto the dining table, not giving Anu a chance to say a word.

It had always been this way with Antara. Supremely confident from a very young age, she had taken Anu's natural reticence as an inability to think for herself, and steamrolled over her at any given opportunity. In her mind, she was decisive and quick-thinking. To Anu, she had always seemed bossy and arrogant.

"Annie, I have a whole Indian meal planned. Foie gras won't exactly work."

"Nonsense! Foie gras always works. I'm sure Ravi will agree with me."

Ravi would, because he was apt to get swept up in the moment and disregard his wife's preference in favour of something new and exciting. No matter how much he complained about Annie's ways behind her back, to her face he was always incredibly amiable. It was no wonder that Annie suspected Anu to be totally at fault when it came to their stop-start relationship, even though Ravi's opinions had never been wholly favourable towards her cousin. In Annie's eyes, Ravi had always done his best.

"I like your little house, it's very homely. So many Indian touches." She looked around at the various trinkets Anu had decorated the room with, all her Cottage Industry buys. "So, how are you finding the area?"

"It's nice. Very green and beautiful, as you can see."

"But...?"

"What do you mean?"

"I can sense a 'but'."

"Well, it's nothing really... just... it's hard to make friends. Both Neha and I are struggling in that respect."

Annie curled herself into the armchair, tucking her feet beneath her.

"Really, Anu, have you tried at all? You know you can come across as quite stand-offish."

That stung. Anu knew she didn't have the friendliest demeanour, but that was more out of shyness than anything else.

"They call it an RBF, did you know?" Annie carried on thoughtfully, "A Resting Bitch Face. Goodness, the terms these youngsters find nowadays!"

Anu grimaced. Is that what her face looked like?

"Would you like a cup of tea?"

"I'd really love a gin and tonic, darling! And do use the Bombay Sapphire. I don't really care for Tanqueray."

She sat across from Annie, sipping on her own G&T. It was a Friday evening and she would not deny herself.

"... all I'm saying is call the mothers over for a nice Indian meal. It's the perfect opening gambit."

"But why do I have to be the one to call everyone over? Surely they can make an effort too!"

"Do you want to get accepted into their circle or not? How do you think I got all of Richard's colleagues to absorb me into theirs, hmm? These things take a bit of effort. Now, what about this Simone woman? I thought you said she was friendly..."

As always, she ended up telling Annie way more than she had intended, even while knowing it would come back to bite her at some later date. Annie had a way of turning from solicitous to supercilious in a flash, and every time she did, it caught Anu by surprise. Because just when she had let her guard down, Annie would slip in a vicious barb that would find its mark. It was a childhood pattern between them that repeated itself endlessly.

"Simone is really nice and friendly too, but when I told Ravi where she lived, he was quite disapproving. He's not keen that Neha mix with children from the council estate."

"Really! Quite the snob, isn't he?" Annie chuckled. "Well, it's perfectly clear to me you must widen your circle, and to do that you need to put yourself out there a bit. It's like dating, only tougher. Women are much more discerning than men, and they can sniff desperation a mile off."

"So, how do I do it?"

"Start small. Invite a few girls home after school. Then take it from there."

Anu stood up to refill Annie's glass while she chatted on in the background. Yes, it was worth trying. What did she have to lose anyway, except her pride, maybe?

Later at the dinner table, Annie looked at them and slurred, "You are both really lucky, you know? Richard and I tried for seven years, but we were just not meant to be parents."

Ravi helped Anu take her to bed, even pulling off her shoes and tucking the covers around her.

"She was plastered! What time did she start on the booze?"

"Do you think she's happy, Ravi? I've always thought that she'd gotten exactly what she wanted in life. But watching her with Neha earlier today, and that comment of hers... makes me wonder..."

"Define 'happy', Anu. We are all unhappy in our own unique ways."

"Are you as well?"

"Oh, come on! That was more of a philosophical observation than a personal one."

"But you'd tell me if you were, wouldn't you?"

"Don't be silly, Anu! Of course I would."

. . .

On Saturday afternoon, as they waved Annie off in the train headed towards Bath, Neha pronounced gravely, "I don't like Auntie Annie. She smells funny."

"This isn't your PE kit, Neha!" Anu looked at the label to decipher the biro markings. "Who's RL?"

"Rebecca Lawrence."

"Why have you brought her PE bag home?"

"It was the last one on the peg. I thought it was mine."

"Neha!" Her exasperation was plain enough because Neha looked up shame-faced.

"Sorry Mummy."

"It's all right, I'll just have to find her mother in the playground and apologise. I might as well launder this and hand it in next week. Now come on, let's finish up that art homework you have."

Ravi came downstairs at noon, yawning and scratching his head.

"How long have you both been up?"

"Since 7 a.m. Some people don't believe in Sunday lie-ins," Anu gave Neha a mock sidelong glance.

"What's for breakfast?"

"It's lunchtime now, Ravi. I've made a *pulao*[3] with *raita*[4]."

"Don't fancy that. Let's go out for lunch."

"And what am I to do with this food?"

"We can always eat that tonight, it won't go off. Let's go get some *dosas*."

Neha visibly perked up at the thought of *dosas*[5], her favourite Indian fast food.

Driving towards Southall, Anu remembered when they had first moved to the UK. For a very short while they had rented a small flat in the area, which was the only place they could afford. Her first few outings with Neha in the buggy had been in the colourful by-lanes of King Street and The Broadway.

It was another version of India. A more raucous, condensed and hyperbolic version perhaps, but a place where people of Southeast Asian descent found commonality and comfort. From food to clothing and groceries to jewellery, anything and everything could be found in Southall. Wembley was its Gujarati cousin in northwest London.

But for all that, Anu was never entirely comfortable in its environs. She did not hail from a *pind*[6]; she spoke English fluently, and she expected that she would have more in common with the English than with the Indians that populated this part of the UK.

If she dressed down though, and she frequently did whilst living there, she attracted no stares at all. Anu blended into the sea of brown-and-black clad young women rushing about their business, while older women comfortable only in their national costume of salwar-kameez, saris or burkas walked sedately along the streets.

She supposed it was a kind of belonging, even if it was only because of skin colour and fluency in an Indian tongue.

They pulled into the busy car park of a large grocery store. Ravi's plan was to eat first and shop later, something they had done over the years. She was running low on her spices, so this was as good a time as any to stock up.

The usual hustle and bustle of the streets was even

more amplified on a Sunday. Cars were being stopped ille-
gally on the double yellow lines, families in colourful
clothes spilling out of them to attend the prayers at the
many *gurdwaras* [7]dotted around the area. Heaving buses
competed for road space with rash young men driving reck-
lessly, without concern for the pedestrians trying to dash
across the road. All semblance of living in Britain evaporated here. A white face was an anomaly, an intrusion even,
on what had been adapted and moulded into a version of
Southeast Asia that the locals were comfortable with. In this
bubble they could speak their language, eat their foods, do
their prayers and be more or less left in peace for their
entire lives.

All of it fascinated Neha, her eyes growing wider with
excitement each time they visited.

"Is this another country, Mummy?"

A year ago they had driven to France. Neha had fallen
asleep in the car, and when she'd woken up, they were in a
different country.

"No darling, this is Southall. Remember when we came
here to attend Shona didi's wedding at the *gurdwara*[8]?"

Neha shook her head, still gazing at everything in
wonderment.

At the restaurant, the service was quick, and piping hot
dosas arrived at their table in no time at all. Breaking off a
piece of the crunchy pancake, Anu dipped it into the
coconut chutney and took a bite. She sighed with happiness
as the familiar flavours of her childhood burst upon her
tongue. There was no disputing it. Sometimes Ravi had the
best ideas.

Later, as they wandered the aisles of the Indian supermarket, exclaiming on all the varieties of *daals*[9], Ravi said to
her, "Anu, we are lucky to be living here in this day and age.
When my uncle and aunt moved here in the sixties, they

felt like they'd arrived in an alien land. Indian groceries weren't available anywhere, they had to make do with the utensils and spices they had brought with them, and their English neighbours constantly complained about the smell of their cooking. It's taken over forty years to build something like this, and we are reaping the benefits of it."

It was true, Anu thought, as she brushed her teeth that night before bed. They were lucky to dip in and out of their Indianness, choosing to retain the bits they wanted and discard the ones they didn't. But this was not an all-encompassing kind of luck, for in the picturesque English village that they lived in, they were still seen as outsiders; interlopers with strange customs and traditions. A curiosity at best, a nuisance at worst.

"You must be Neha's mum," a plump brunette with a sweet face approached her in the school playground, holding what Anu surmised was Neha's PE kit.

"Yes, I am. I'm so sorry about the mixup. Here's Rebecca's kit, I've washed everything in it."

The lady beamed at her. "That's a relief! I've done the same. There you go. Don't worry about these things, they happen all the time. My son is always bringing someone else's kit home."

Anu was taken aback by the woman's friendliness. This was the first kind word any of the class mothers had spoken to her in over a month of Neha attending the school.

"I'm Natalie. And you are?"

"Anupama. Anu for short."

"Anoo?"

"Umm, y... yes."

"Well, Anoo, we meet up for a coffee morning every Friday at the cafe across from the church. Why don't you join us?"

"That... uhh... can... uhh..." Anu felt lost for words in the face of such unexpected kindness.

"So, should we expect you this Friday? I'll save you a place at the table. You can get to know some other school mothers this way. It's hard when you start out at a new place, isn't it?"

Anu nodded dumbly, swallowing the lump in her throat. Natalie touched her arm lightly, smiling as she moved away to talk to the other mothers.

"Natalie's nice," Simone declared, peeling off the wrapper on a sweet as she handed it to her daughter. Anu did the same, watching the two girls skip away together. Neha worshipped Kayla, looking forward to their after-school play in the park far more than she looked forward to going to school. "Her son's in Kayla's class, and she's one of the few mothers who is kind and approachable. But, don't forget, she's still considered one of the elite clique. So, tread carefully."

"Who is that blonde lady that is always surrounded by all the women?"

"Oh, that's Zoe Frobisher, the Queen Bee. Never cross her, or they'll all turn against you."

"I don't think she likes me much."

At this, Simone gave a sharp laugh.

"She doesn't like anyone who doesn't 'fit'. And you and I definitely don't 'fit' around here."

"But why be so mean to people you don't even know?"

"It's in her DNA. Have you not seen girls like her your entire life? The ones who need to be the centre of attention all the time? They always have their hangers-on, their syco-phants. They only mingle amongst their own kind, they only thrive in their own little pond. Try putting them some-where else and they'll create the same ecosystem there."

Anu mulled this over in her mind. Yes, she had seen the same thing in her days at the hostel. Close to breakdown, Mama had had to take her out and place her with her grand-parents. She could never thrive in an environment like that. What did this mean for her chances of survival here?

"And you, Simone? How have you gotten by here?"

"Me?" Simone gazed into the distance. "By being a part of it, and yet not. I say the right things to the right people, but I never let them into my life or my home."

"That must be a lonely life?"

"No, it's not. I have other friends, people who I've grown up with. They accept me for who I am, irrespective of where I live or what I do. Those are 'my' people, not this gaggle of superficial geese."

"Oh."

"Don't worry, Anoo. You'll find your feet soon enough. Make friends amongst your own kind. They are always less judgemental."

"My kind? Do you mean other Indians? But there aren't many around here, and none in Neha's class."

"Why don't you enrol her in some Indian classes? You might meet some mothers there."

That evening, as she tucked Neha into bed, Anu struck upon an idea that excited her. She pulled out her laptop to Google places nearby. When Ravi came home, she was fairly buzzing.

"How about teaching Neha Indian classical dance?"

"Anu, can I at least get a drink first?"

She took his coat and handed him his whiskey.

"Well? What do you think?"

"Neha's only five. Why do you want her to learn Indian classical dance?"

"Think about it, Ravi! It's the best age to start. She'll be exposed to our culture, our tradition, in the best way possible. Besides, it's good exercise, and we can meet some other Indians locally too."

"Locally? Whereabouts are these classes?"

"In a hall in Slough. That's only twenty minutes from here. I'd be happy to drive her there and back. It could be a wonderful experience."

"Hmm, okay, if that's what you want."

What she wanted more than anything else was to belong. To find a community of people who would accept her for who she was, who wouldn't consider her too westernised or too Indian because of the way she looked, behaved or spoke. Was that too much to ask for?

On Friday morning, Anu walked in a little later than she had planned. Finding a parking spot near the church had been nearly impossible. After driving around for ten minutes, she had eventually slipped into a spot recently vacated by a church-goer.

The cafe was busy, with people lining up to buy coffees and cakes, toddlers running through the throng, and tables populated by women she assumed to be other mothers from the school. From a distance she spotted Natalie waving to her, indicating the vacant chair by her side. Anu walked towards the table, her heart sinking a little as she realised that Zoe and her cohorts were seated there as well.

"Hi Anoo!" Natalie exclaimed enthusiastically, pulling out the chair for her. "Everyone, this is Anoo. She's Neha's mum."

There were murmurs of hellos from around the table that Anu responded to shyly.

"So, as I was saying," Zoe continued after flicking a glance in her direction, "we really should have a Christmas Cake Sale. The school needs the money for new Huff and Puff equipment. Mrs Pellow was saying they were all bits donated by parents over the years, but I can't believe the tatty old stuff they've got in there! The skipping rope is almost falling apart! Syl nearly tripped herself on it the other day."

The mothers nodded in agreement. Jill, the woman who had dismissed her summarily, spoke up.

"It's our duty as the more well-off in the community to provide for those less fortunate than us."

Anu looked around the table. Most of the women were impeccably dressed; their nails manicured, the makeup subtle, and hair blow dried to perfection. There were a few like her who looked like they had just had time to wash their hair and rush to school, but they were the ones who sat quietly on the periphery, not vocalising their opinions. Natalie seemed completely at home in this strange confluence of women. Anu wished she had a similar self-assurance.

She looked at the woman sitting on her left and smiled. "I can't really bake. Can I bring Indian sweets?"

"I wouldn't, if I were you. Zoe won't like it. Besides, nobody will buy them." She responded in an undertone. Anu was grateful for her honesty. This woman was one of the lesser entities at the table.

"Whose mum are you?"

"Jacob."

"Oh! Neha's mentioned him to me."

"Really? Well, he's not the brightest spark in the class. He's had learning difficulties right from the start."

"No, she said he was very good at football."

"That he is," she could see the woman swell with pride. "He wants to be a footballer when he grows up."

"That's nice," Anu responded, "I wish I'd known at that age what I wanted to be when I grew up."

"I'm Helen, and frankly Anoo, what we want and what we get are two different things, aren't they?"

"Yes, you're quite right. They really are."

"Do you work?"

"No. In my previous life, I painted, but not anymore. After Neha, I just got so busy being a mother that I stopped all that. Do you?"

"That's a shame. It's nice to have a life outside of all this," Helen glanced around the room. "I'm a part-time receptionist at the surgery. It keeps me sane."

"Do you just have one child?"

"I have three. But two of them are already at secondary school. Jacob's my youngest. I had him when I was forty, my surprise baby." She beamed. "I wouldn't change it for the world."

Natalie leaned over to them. "I was thinking of organising a trick-or-treat walkabout on the 31st of October, seeing as Zoe's already taken over the Christmas planning." She grinned at them. "Interested?"

"Sure," Helen winked back at her. "Better pick up the crumbs before she swoops those up, too."

They laughed together, as though privy to some inside joke. Anu laughed alongside politely, confused by the mild snarkiness on display.

Zoe's hands waved about, the diamonds flashing in the sunlight streaming through the windows of the cafe.

"We must have a mother's dinner, and a parent's drinks night too. Neil was saying it's been a while since we caught up with all the parents. Local pub's being refurbished by the new owners; it'll be fun to see what they've done with it."

"I've heard they've removed the pool table, and it's a wine bar now," chirped the tiny woman sitting next to Zoe, her dark ponytail swishing. "I can't wait to have a decent place to go to. The old place was so grubby and filled with all kinds of people." She gave a delicate shudder.

Zoe's blue eyes blazed. "This place is really going downhill with all sorts moving in. I said to Neil that maybe we should consider moving to another area, but he relies on the train to go to work, so I guess we'll just have to stay and put up with it."

"It doesn't mean that we actually have to mingle with them though, does it?" Jill added. "As long as they leave us alone, we'll leave them alone."

"Yes, but our children have to, don't they?"

Anu's mouth had fallen open slightly. Was all of this aimed at her?

"Don't be shocked, this is their weekly rant." Helen whispered. "Just ignore it."

"Really ladies!" Natalie called out. "Get off your soapbox. We've got some new mums here. What are they going to think of us?"

"Oh, sorry!" Zoe looked at Anu directly for the first time. "Didn't mean to be rude, but this is becoming a nation of scroungers. You just have to go down to Holly Drive to see all the people who are living off our taxes. Anyway, I'll stop here before Miss Leftie here has another go at me."

She said this affectionately; her gaze warming as it landed on Natalie. Clearly they were friends with opposing viewpoints, but friends nonetheless.

Anu wondered where that placed her in this hierarchy of women. Somewhere at the bottom, she surmised. Not white enough or rich enough to belong, but not entirely down-and-out to be completely dismissed either. She guessed she'd have to live with that for now.

CHAPTER THREE

Anu had taken to popping in for a tea with Susan every Wednesday morning. It hadn't taken her long to ascertain that Susan was just as lonely as her. Neither of her children lived close or visited often.

That morning she had taken along a bit of the cake she had baked. It was her very first attempt, a simple sponge recipe she had gotten off the internet.

"Well, what do you think?"

"It's nice," Susan commented, taking a second bite out of the rock-hard cake.

"No, it's not." Anu felt ashamed, realising that the little old lady was only trying to spare her feelings. "I just can't seem to get a handle on this baking thing. The last cake, I had to throw away because it was uncooked in the middle. Ravi just told me to stop wasting my time and all these ingredients."

"Anoo dear, it takes time to master baking. I am no expert, but I used to bake a lot when my children were younger, and I can tell you that the tiniest thing could ruin a cake. For instance, you've probably baked this at a very high temperature and that's why it's turned out this hard. Just keep practising and one day it'll all come together."

"With cooking, I only took a few months to pick it up. I knew the basics, of course, but Ravi likes me to try out more exotic stuff too. I think I'm a fairly decent cook…"

"Better than decent, my dear. Your curries are delicious, although I can't always take the heat in them. Thank you for the last lot you brought over. It tided me over a few dinners. And remind me to give you your Tupperware before you leave."

They chatted for a bit longer before Anu got up to rinse the cups at the sink.

"Do you need me to pick anything up from Sainsbury? I'm headed there this afternoon."

"Oh no, I'm all right. I got my groceries from the Co-op just yesterday."

Anu knew Susan survived on her pension, and Sainsbury's prices were probably beyond her purse. She worried about her though, watching her scrimp and save even on daily necessities.

"Has Jan called recently?"

"No, not really. I imagine she's very busy with all the new children she's taken in after school."

Susan's daughter Jan was a childminder who was always too busy to stop by and see her mother. Lately, it appeared she was too busy to even call. Susan and her son Mark's wife had had a falling out many years ago, and he had cut off all ties with his mother thereafter.

Susan never blamed her children. In fact, she always sought to deflect the blame off them, making constant excuses for their wilful disregard of their mother.

"Have you heard?" Susan brought the plates up behind her. "New neighbours at number 11."

"Oh? When?"

"It just sold, so I expect they'll be moving in in a few days' time."

In their little cul-de-sac, this was news. Populated by pensioners or older working couples, it would be interesting to see who would move in a few doors down. Anu hoped they had children that Neha could play with.

"I've booked them!" Ravi walked in through the front door in the evening, looking smug.

"Booked what?" Anu looked up from laying the plates on the table.

"The tickets to India, of course. Have you forgotten already?"

Anu had indeed forgotten. In fact, she had pushed it to the back of her mind. Now she tried appearing pleased for Ravi's sake.

"I was thinking. Do you want to go up to Nainital to see your mother? We could go just after New Year's for a few days."

"Ravi, school reopens on the 5th of January. I don't think we'll have the time."

"Neha can miss school for a few days. That shouldn't be a problem in Reception year."

"No! I don't want us getting a reputation. They were saying on the radio the other day that Asian parents are the worst for attendance. Apparently the government wants to institute some kind of fine for taking children out during term time. I hope you're bringing us back in time for school?"

"*Arey baba,*[1] don't worry! We'll be back on the 4th. I've booked the tickets from the 21st to the 4th, just a fortnight like we'd discussed."

"Hmm, okay."

"You could show a bit more enthusiasm, you know. You're going to be meeting your friends too."

What friends? Neha wanted to ask. They were mostly his friends, and she had to mingle politely with their wives who, once again, she had nothing in common with.

"What about asking Nonita to come up from Mumbai? Wouldn't you like to catch up with her?"

His words brought an unexpected pang of nostalgia. Nonita had been her best friend, her only friend for the longest time. Now she was a hotshot editor at a women's magazine in Mumbai. They had communicated for a while after Anu's marriage, but that had dwindled to a few cards sent on birthdays every year. It would be nice to catch up with her.

"Can I go to Mumbai instead, for a few days?"

"What?" Ravi looked a bit shocked, but then smiled at her expectant face. "Yes, why not? Varsha *bua* and I can handle Neha between us, I suppose."

With an extra spring in her step, Anu ladled out the biryani onto their plates. It would be nice to revisit the happier memories of her childhood and youth with Nonita. She couldn't wait to call her.

Nonita's squeal was still ringing in her ear as she disconnected the call. Her excitement hadn't been faked in the slightest. She had promised to take her to all the hotspots in Mumbai and introduce her to all her friends, before Anu had reminded her gently that she wanted to spend time with her, not her friends. And she couldn't care less about the hotspots. Nonita had promised then that for two days it would just be them, wine and reminiscing.

Anu smiled as she recalled their youthful forays into fashion. How Noni would sit with the film magazine open to a bi-fold picture of Rekha and copy the over-the-top makeup to look just as glamorous and beautiful as the film star. They had been nine then, and aunty would always mock-scold her when she found her makeup box raided once again. These days, Nonita was drop dead gorgeous even without the acres of makeup, her style credentials impeccable as the editor of a top fashion monthly. Anu wondered what her friend would make of her own drab appearance.

Anu examined her face in the mirror. There were days she forgot to even look at herself, hastily brushing her hair into a ponytail, running out of the door with Neha in the morning. Now she ran her fingers over her cheeks. Maybe she needed to invest in some new makeup. Her Max Factor foundation was so old, it had separated. She looked at her chocolate brown eyes, the irises a lighter brown, the only feature she had inherited from Mama. But where Mama accentuated her eyes with a heavy application of kohl and mascara, Anu hid them behind wire-rimmed glasses, only occasionally switching to contact lenses.

The thought of Mama made her realise it had been five weeks since she'd last spoken to her. Reluctantly, she picked up the phone to dial her mother.

The phone rang for a while before Mama answered.

"Well! She finally finds the time to ring…"

"Sorry, Mama. It's been really busy here. How are you?"

"I could be dead for all you care." The anger always bubbled beneath the surface of their interactions. Why Mama felt abandoned was beyond Anu's understanding. It was she who had done the abandoning all life long.

"Mama, I do care, you know that. Anyway, please don't

be annoyed. I just called to say that we will be in Delhi late December, if you happen to be in town."

"So no plans to come to Nainital?"

"Not this time. Neha's vacation isn't that long, and we have to be back in time for school. Maybe in the Summer?"

"That's what you said about last Summer and the Summer before that, too. I just can't understand what all of you hold against me! Haven't I done my best by you? Sent you to the best schools, provided you with everything you needed?"

Everything except a mother's love, Anu wanted to say, but refrained. Her mother carried on.

"None of my children want to visit me in Nainital. Abhishek doesn't bite, you know. He's a nice man, if only you'd allow yourself to get to know him. But your *Nana-Nani* [2] poisoned your minds against him, and against me too. Oh, don't think I don't know it... I may be miles away, but I'm aware of everything..."

When Anu finally ended the call twenty minutes later, she realised she was shaking. Mama's toxicity had a way of reaching its tentacles out and wrapping them around her heart even now.

"You look pensive," Simone noted as she sat down next to her on the park bench. "Everything all right?"

"Yes. I'm fine, I guess."

"You don't look it, but it's none of my business. If you want to unburden, I'm here. If not, that's okay too."

They sat in silence for a bit. Then Anu looked at Simone and said, "I don't really know much about you. What do you do? Are you married, divorced, single? I don't mean to pry, but we've spoken about so many other things except ourselves."

"You mean you have heard none of the stories they tell about me?"

"What kinds of stories, and from whom?"

"Well, I've been branded all sorts. From a home-wrecker to a pole dancer. What I really do is teach children with learning disabilities. I work half days at a school in London." She smiled at Anu wryly. "Curiosity satisfied?"

"I'm sorry. Did I come across as nosy? I didn't mean to be. But I still don't understand. Home-wrecker? Pole dancer? What do you mean?"

"Brace yourself, it's not a pretty story. And you may decide not to have anything to do with me afterwards. Still want me to carry on?"

Anu nodded, curious about what might emerge.

"Well, when I moved here three years ago, I was getting away from an abusive partner who had been jailed for attacking me." She fingered the long, thin scar on her arm. "I was lonely and vulnerable, but glad to have escaped my past. I had hoped to rebuild my life here and give Kayla the sort of future she deserved."

She looked down at the grass, moving her right foot like a windshield wiper on it.

"As you can see for yourself, there wasn't much of a welcoming committee here from the other mothers. In the beginning I tried really hard, but soon realised that no matter what I did, my sordid past branded me as unsuitable. Perhaps I had spoken too freely at first or confided in the wrong people, and word got around. People started to ignore me or avoid being seen in my company, and some mothers made no bones about the fact that I was unwelcome in the community. I felt even more isolated here, despite all my other friends in London. Remember, I had wanted to establish roots here, start from scratch, but all I got was stony silence or polite indifference. Then I committed a cardinal sin."

She looked at Anu in the eye. "I got involved with a school dad. His name was Daniel, and he was a charmer. The only one who took the time to talk to me, listen to my concerns and give me advice. At first it was just friendly, but it soon developed into more. We had a passionate affair for six months, and then, one fine day, he just dropped me like a hot potato. His wife had found out, and that was the end of that."

"Oh."

"Yes. That's my little secret. So on top of everything else, now these women think that I'll be making eyes at their husbands!"

"Is he... Daniel, still around?"

"No. They pulled the kids out of school and moved back to South Africa. That's where they were from."

"I see. And your partner?"

"Still in prison, as far as I'm aware. I hope he rots in there for the rest of his life, frankly. But Anoo, there was a malicious smear campaign against me for the longest time, spearheaded by these school mothers. I almost gave up several times, and if it wasn't for the fact that Kayla loved being here, I might have left long ago."

Anu looked down at the grass, silent for a beat.

"Thank you for sharing that with me. I'm not here to judge you. If you still want to stay friends, I'd like to."

"Then, as a friend, you need to tell me what's on your mind as well."

As Anu talked about her mother and her own chequered history, she felt the first glimmer of hope; that this could be the start of the friendship she'd been yearning for all along.

Dressed as a little witch, with her broom in hand and a mask complete with a hooked nose and a hairy mole, Neha was excited beyond measure. She hopped from foot to foot, eager to get started.

"Give me a minute, darling, I need to lock up." Anu made sure she switched on the porch light for Ravi as she shut the front door. The air was chilly now, and a faint smell of smoke from a garden fire lingered in the air.

Cautiously optimistic, she had agreed to join the walkabout with Natalie and the other mums. At the very least, she'd have Helen to chat to as they went through the village, trick or treating with their children.

It was the first time both Neha and she were taking part in this Halloween ritual. In their previous house they had turned all the lights off, pretending not to be home. Ravi, in a fit of paranoia, had warned them about the feral gangs of teenagers that wandered the neighbourhood on Halloween. For nearly five years, they hadn't ventured out on Halloween. This was a first.

She met up with Natalie and the other mums at the corner of the school, having parked in her usual spot. All the children were dressed as ghouls, zombies, mummies and witches in scarily effective outfits and makeup. The only drawback to the realism were the coats that the mums insisted their kids wore as they traipsed around the village. Despite their protestations, most were glad for the warmth that the extra layer offered on a cold evening.

Anu waved at the few faces she recognised as she walked towards them. Natalie beamed.

"I'm so glad you could make it. Neha, you make a pretty witch."

Neha's eyes sparkled behind the mask, and Anu could sense her pleasure at the compliment.

"Why don't you join Rebecca and the other children? Your mum will be safe with us, I promise!"

As the group of mothers and children swelled, she found herself wedged next to Zoe and Jill.

"Hello," she mouthed, but they looked right through her, so she moved away to get closer to Helen's group. Here the welcome was a lot less frosty. These were mostly the boys' mums, and as they smiled and exchanged pleasantries, she wondered why the girls' mums couldn't be as relaxed as this.

Their troop set off slowly, working their way through the various streets in the village. There were houses that had gone to town with the decorations. Spider webs hung from the bushes, ghosts floated off trees, carved pumpkins leered from doorsteps, and bells chimed with unearthly wails.

In one house a man stood with an axe in his hand while a wraith-like figure watched from a window above, motionless and creepy. In another, three witches seemed to cackle over a smoking cauldron.

"Wow! I've never seen anything like this." Anu whispered to one mother walking beside her.

"I have to admit this is definitely better than last year, but people love Halloween here. You wouldn't know it's an American festival, the way they carry on."

"Soon we'll be celebrating Thanksgiving too," another mother chimed in.

"Nothing wrong with that. The more festivals the merrier, I say."

"Ummm, do you celebrate Diwali as well?" Anu asked.

"Tivali? Is that the one you do fireworks at? No, not

really. But it's always around Guy Fawkes, isn't it? Gets very noisy, I have to say."

"My poor dog just hates it. I wish they'd outlaw all fireworks. It's just wrong."

Anu looked over at the children to see how Neha was getting on. She seemed happy to skip along with Rebecca, Sylvie and another girl, exchanging sweets out of their pumpkin-shaped baskets.

Helen saw her watching and laughed.

"They'll be trading all evening long. That's half the fun of it. Just be prepared for a sore tummy tomorrow after all that sugar."

At one house, a man stood ladling mulled wine into paper cups for the frozen adults.

"This is always our last stop. Go on, take one; don't be shy. You'll find it helps." Helen chuckled at her reservations. Never a big drinker, Anu accepted the cup graciously, taking a tentative sip. The warmth spread from her core to her frozen limbs in an instant. This was delicious! She nodded happily to the man, who tilted his head in acknowledgement.

Later, at home, as Neha chatted happily about their walkabout and all the sweets she'd bartered, Anu silently admitted to herself that it had been a very nice evening. Barring the frosty duo of Zoe and Jill, everyone else had been pleasant enough. Maybe they were finally accepting them into the fold of the community?

The Autumn leaves drifted down onto the grass in her garden, copper and gold glinting in the pale morning sunlight. November had brought chilly winds and constant rain in its wake. Anu shivered in her dressing gown, nursing her second cup of coffee for the day.

For the first time in months, Ravi had agreed to take Neha into school, giving Anu the unexpected pleasure of lounging at home in her PJ's. Today she felt like doing nothing.

A sadness had been coiling within her all week long. She couldn't quite put her finger on it, but it reminded her of the time that Ravi had come home and found her curled up and sobbing on the floor. Even back then, she'd been unable to articulate why she felt the way she did. It was a sense of being completely and utterly alone in the entire world. Not logical because of course she had her little family, a few friends from her past and the tentative relationships she was building here. But it was a feeling that persisted for days on end.

Today she felt the same feeling rearing its head.

To distract herself, she decided to cook a complicated dish from scratch. But even as she pounded the meat, then spread the *masala*[3] marinade over it, memories pressed upon her, insistent, unwilling to be ignored.

Mama's laughter, cigarette ends ringed with crimson lipstick, memories of Anu's isolated upbringing and her inability to form friendships with her half-siblings, *Nana's* disappointment tingeing everything, *Nani's* withdrawal into her religious texts, a childhood of sorrow and silence - wave upon wave of images, sharp and blurred, crashed into one another.

Exhausted, she went to bed, but lay awake recalling her childhood yearning to belong, to be accepted. Had her life been forever tainted by a past she had no control over?

Forcing herself out of bed at 2 p.m. she showered and changed into a bright yellow jumper and blue jeans. Noni had always told her to wear happy colours when she felt sad. As she stepped out of the house to go pick Neha up from school, she noticed a Removals truck parked outside Number 11. Furniture was being carried into the house by men bustling in and out. A young and heavily pregnant woman came out to supervise. Glancing over towards Anu, she gave her a friendly little wave. The new neighbours were finally moving in. Anu waved back with a smile, then got into her car, reversing carefully into the street.

At school she smiled at the few mothers she recognised now, side-stepping Zoe and her clique. Neha came out holding a drawing and looking happy.

"Mummy, look what I made!"

"What's this baby?" She tried to make sense of the many figures that populated her daughter's sketch.

"It's all of us, on Halloween."

"Oh, of course! I see it now. That's you as the witch, Jacob as a mummy, and Rebecca and Sylvie as zombies..."

"Mummy, can I please call Sylvie over after school?"

"Umm, yes. Sure, we can do that." Anu's mind raced to find an excuse, but settled on nothing. "Has she been playing with you?"

"Yes, mummy. Mrs Pellow made Sylvie sit next to me at story-time and she braided my hair. Look!"

This could be a good thing, Anu thought to herself. Maybe the most popular girl in class could teach her daughter something that Anu couldn't impart: how to make friends in this new and uncertain world.

"We need to stop by Sainsbury on the way back, Neha. Do you want anything as a snack?"

"Are we picking up milk for Susan again?"

"No," Anu smiled at her daughter's recall, "I'm getting flowers for the new neighbours across the street."

• • •

An hour later, having deposited Neha in front of the television with her milk and biscuits, she walked across to Number 11 with a colourful bouquet. Ringing the bell, she hoped this wouldn't be seen as an intrusion.

"Hello!" The young woman from before opened the door.

"Hi! I'm Anu from Number 4. Just wanted to welcome you to the neighbourhood and wish you well in your new home."

"That is so sweet of you! What a lovely bunch of flowers." She smiled at her prettily. "I wish I could call you inside for a cup of tea, but as you can see, the entire house is a mess..."

"Please don't worry about it. I can't leave my five-year-old alone in there either," Anu indicated the partially open front door of her house. "When are you due, if you don't mind me asking?"

"Not till February, but look at me! I'm a whale."

She was anything but a whale. Tall and slender, with waist-length chestnut brown hair and cornflower blue eyes, she could have stepped out of a woman's clothing catalogue. She was that pretty.

"I have such a baby brain! I completely forgot to tell you my name. I'm Cathy, the bump is going to be called Melanie, and my fiancé's name is Andrew. You'll see him this evening. He's just out sorting last minute stuff."

"Well, it's nice meeting you, Cathy. We are pretty new to the area ourselves. I only know Susan two doors down. The rest of the residents are mostly pensioners or working couples, so I have seen little of them."

"Anoo, right? You'll just have to come over for a drink once we're settled in. It'll be nice to get to know people in the area."

Anu smiled as she said goodbye. A weight seemed to lift off in the presence of this happy, pretty woman.

A red maple leaf drifted onto her shoulder as she crossed the street, and she cupped it in her hands, placing it gently on the grass. Looking down her tree-lined street - a riot of green, gold, rust and red - her sadness dissipated just as suddenly as it had descended.

Diwali was late this year, but it also fell on a weekend, so Ravi was home to help her clean up and sort the house out. They had already been to Southall to buy their Indian sweets and the earthen *diyas* [4]she planned to dot around the house. Her grandparents had had a simple tradition of wearing at least one new item on Diwali day. She had bought some colourful bangles for Neha and herself, and Ravi had bought himself a fresh shirt.

As she cooked the vegetarian meal she planned to serve in the evening, Anu hummed to herself. This was the first time they were going to have guests over for Diwali. Cathy, Andy and Susan were coming over for the *Lakshmi Puja,*[5] and staying for dinner and drinks. She so wanted it to go well. If she were honest, she wanted to wow them with a cultural experience beyond their imagination.

Ravi had swooped down on all the fireworks on sale after Guy Fawkes night, the one advantage of Diwali falling later than usual. Anu had taken out her blue silk sari and the kundan jewellery that complemented it. Neha would be in the red and gold *lehenga*[6] they'd purchased in India the last time.

As she draped the sari around her body, she marvelled silently at how it transformed her figure. Plump in her usual uniform of jeans and jumpers, she looked hourglass-like in her sari. Truly, it was a garment meant to enhance and flatter the more generously endowed. She did a twirl in front of the mirror.

"Someone's happy today," Ravi grinned from behind her.

"It feels nice to be celebrating something with our neighbours." She smiled at him in the mirror.

He came over and hugged her from behind.

"I like to see you this way, Anu. Smile more, it suits you."

She turned around and placed a light kiss on his lips.

"I love you, Ravi."

"I love you too-too," he said, using the old code from their early days of marriage.

They stood in a respectful semi-circle around the little makeshift temple she'd constructed on the side table. Cathy, in a black flowing dress with red roses on the hem, had covered her head with the red shawl Anu had given her for the purpose. Susan had tied a scarf around her head as a mark of respect for the prayers. The men stood at the back with their hands folded, as Ravi had shown all of them.

They watched wide-eyed as she conducted the prayers, singing her *bhajans*[7] in a light, breathy voice. Ravi joined in with his baritone, and as she propitiated Goddess Lakshmi to bless their homes with happiness and prosperity, she wondered what her English neighbours were thinking as she performed the rituals of her festival.

Later, Cathy followed her into the kitchen to help with the snacks.

"It's so beautiful... the colours, the singing and all these lights. I love what you're wearing too."

"Thank you, Cathy. I'd hoped you'd enjoy watching something traditional."

"It's fabulous," she breathed, taking the plate of *pakoras*[8] out to the living room. "Thank you so much for having us over. We still haven't settled in, but once we do, you have to come over as well."

In the living room, Ravi was pouring Susan a glass of wine.

"What's your poison, Andy?"

"What are you drinking, Ravi?"

"This. It's an Indian rum and I mix it with Coca Cola." He picked up the bottle from their small bar in the corner.

"Old Monk? Interesting name. Go on, pour me one too. I'll give it a try."

Once everyone had their drinks, Anu passed the plate of *pakoras* around. They sat together chatting and sipping on their drinks.

"I've never been to India," said Susan, "but today I feel as if I'm there."

The Indian flute music playing in the background added to the ambience of the evening. Anu looked at her sparkling home, the guests in their finery, the *diyas* twinkling everywhere, Neha sprawled on the floor drawing and felt a deep sense of contentment.

Andy and Ravi seemed to get along well, discussing work, cars, football and world affairs. She turned towards Susan and Cathy, who were chatting quietly in the corner.

"We were planning to get married, but then I found out I was pregnant, so we postponed the wedding. I didn't want to be waddling down the aisle."

Anu figured that Susan's generation probably found the whole children-before-marriage idea pretty unorthodox, but then heard Susan say, "My dear, it's the most special day of your life. You must do it when you're ready. Right now you have to prepare for this little one's arrival." She leaned forward and patted Cathy's stomach.

Dinner was an unmitigated success. Andy laughed uproariously when he realised that he'd eaten an entire meal with no meat in it and enjoyed it too.

That night as Ravi helped her clear up after their guests had left, she said, "Aren't Cathy and Andy adorable? What a good-looking couple they make. Their baby is going to be beautiful."

"What say we go make a baby of our own?" He dropped the kitchen towel and pulled her towards him.

Their lovemaking was tender, and Anu hoped they had made a baby again. Neha had been a blessing. Could she hope to get lucky a second time?

The next day two thank-you cards sat on her floor mat, having dropped in from the letter box. Happily, she skimmed the messages and then displayed them on her shelf for Ravi to read when he got home from work.

It had taken three months, but suddenly she believed she could belong here, amongst people who may not be like her, but liked her nevertheless.

CHAPTER FOUR

Anu's CRB verification came through exactly six weeks after she had applied for it. The same afternoon she approached Mrs Pellow at the door, after she had finished speaking to another mum.

"Hello Mrs Dhawan. I was hoping to get an opportunity to speak to you. Neha was telling the class about your Diwali celebrations after the girls asked her about the henna patterns on her hand. It sounded wonderful. Maybe someday you could come in and explain your traditions to the children?"

"Actually Mrs Pellow, I wanted to tell you that my CRB check has come through. I can come in to do reading or anything else you'd like."

"Well now, that is good news. You can liaise with Miss Davenport, our Teaching Assistant. I'm sure she'll be pleased to get an extra pair of hands on board."

Mrs Pellow called out to the young, dark-haired woman at the back of the classroom.

Anu got Neha to sit outside the room while she went through the schedule with Miss Davenport.

"Tuesdays at 11 a.m. and Thursdays at 2:30 p.m. are the best times to come in for reading. The other slots have been taken by Mrs Frobisher." Miss Davenport raised her eyebrows ever so lightly, leading Anu to assume that Zoe Frobisher wasn't exactly her favourite person. "Are you any good with artsy-craftsy things?"

"Yes, I was a painter in another lifetime. You know, before Neha and all that." Anu laughed.

"Then I have the perfect project for you! We are going to be making a large mosaic for the outside wall, and perhaps you could help with it?"

"I'd love to!"

"That's settled, then. Do come in on Thursday. I'll put you down in the diary."

On the walk back to the car, Neha stopped to pick up more leaves for her collection. Anu watched her daughter as she bent to examine a leaf. The two pigtails were a bit askew, her shirt had come untucked from the skirt, there was dirt on her pink coat, and she had lost another glove from the umpteenth pair that Anu had bought her. But for the first time in months, Neha looked happy. The knot around her own heart eased slightly.

At home, Neha sat quietly at the dining table reading the book assigned as homework. Anu went through her school bag as normal. She smoothened out a crumpled paper invite, reading it to herself.

"Baby, who is Gina Davies?"

"Oh, that's Sylvie's best friend."

"And she's invited you to her birthday party?"

"She's invited all the girls, Mummy."

"But that's wonderful! Aren't you happy, baby?"

Neha just shrugged, returning to her book immediately.

This was the first birthday party Neha had been invited to, and Anu wanted to make sure that she got the nicest present she could find. She didn't want them being labelled as cheapskates, knowing that excessive frugality amongst her own kind often led to that assumption.

All of Anu's baking experiments had ended in disaster. Even with all the advice and tips that Susan had offered, often being the guinea pig and sampling the varieties of cakes and bakes from Anu's kitchen, she still hadn't mastered this particular skill.

"Susan, the Christmas bake sale is only two days away. What do I do?"

"I think you're getting unnecessarily bothered. Just buy some cakes and take them with you. What does it matter as long as you're contributing something?" Susan poured her another cup of tea, offering her a slice of walnut cake.

"But Zoe is so judgy! She'll just give me one of her looks and I'll want to crawl back under a rock."

"Anoo dear, why are you so worried about that woman's opinion? How does it affect your life?"

"Not my life, but it does affect Neha's. Zoe's daughter is the most popular girl in class, and right now she's being nice to her. So all the other girls are being nice too. If anything upsets that balance then Neha will suffer."

"I see. Well, the only alternative is that I come over and show you how to bake these cakes, if that is all right with you."

"Oh Susan, you're a lifesaver! Please, can you come tomorrow? I'll buy all the ingredients and have them ready."

· · ·

The next day Susan turned up at 4 p.m. sharp and took her through each step of baking the vanilla cupcakes. When the cakes had cooled, she showed Anu how to layer the different colours of icing inside the piping bag so it swirled out rainbow-like on the cakes. Finally, like a fairy godmother, she sprinkled edible glitter on the cakes, making them look even more beautiful.

"Susan, this is genius! Why didn't you tell me earlier that you could bake so well?" Anu sighed with happiness, taking another bite of the leftover cupcake.

"You wanted to learn for yourself, and I let you." Susan leaned forward and patted Anu's hand. "Now that your cakes are done, can I give you a bit of advice too?"

"Of course! Here Neha, take this cake and sit at the table. Don't get icing on the tablecloth, please!"

She turned towards Susan, smiling inquisitively.

"Anoo, I know you want to do the best you can to ease your child's path through life." Susan looked at her gravely. "But let her fall and pick herself up on her own as well. You will not be around her entire life clearing the way for her. Besides, someday, she may turn around and accuse you of being overprotective. I've been there Anoo, and it's been a harsh lesson to learn at my age."

Anu digested this silently, trying to put two and two together. Was that the reason for the estrangement between Susan and her children?

"Thank you Susan, I'll keep that in mind."

She felt proud displaying her beautiful cupcakes next to the assortment of treats and bakes brought in by the other mothers. She had seen Zoe eye her contribution critically and knew that if there had been any fault she would have found it by now. Natalie had asked her to help sell the cakes along with them, so she stood next to her nervously, waiting for the school bell to ring and the children to rush out of their classrooms.

Zoe stood near the cashbox, giving them instructions on the prices.

"The little cakes are 25p each. The large slices and cupcakes will be 50p each. Anything that doesn't sell can be reduced to 10p at the end of the day. Is that clear?"

The mothers nodded nervously. It was a first for many of them. The slender blonde woman standing on her other side nudged her slightly in her ribs, whispering, "Bossy boots, isn't she?"

Anu gave her a startled look.

"Hi! I'm Julie, Will's mum. Haven't had a chance to chat with you, but I've seen you with your sweet little girl in the park a few times."

"I'm Anu, nice to meet you."

The bell rang just then, and the children swarmed out of their classrooms, heading straight to the cake stall. In the flurry of activity that followed, Anu was excited to see how quickly her cakes sold.

"Mummy, I want that pretty rainbow one!"

Within minutes they were all gone, and as Anu kept selling the other cakes, Julie once again whispered to her, "Well done, all your cakes sold really fast. You must be a pro."

"Far from it," Anu laughed, "My neighbour helped me bake them. She's the pro."

"Well, at least you're honest. I just bought mine in Sainsbury, bashed them about a bit and passed them off as home-baked!"

"What?!" Anu faked horror. "Don't say that out in public."

"Or the Queen will shout 'Orf with 'er 'ead'?" Julie giggled, flicking a glance at Zoe.

In between selling cakes, they exchanged little remarks that made them laugh at the uptightness of a certain Mrs Frobisher. Careful that Natalie didn't cotton on, Anu kept her responses brief, but enjoyed just how carefree Julie was.

"Have you ever been to the Friday coffee mornings?" Anu asked Julie.

"Once, but it was unbearable. We've got our own little group, and we do gin luncheons." Julie grinned. "Why bother with coffee, hey?"

Reading with the children had proved to be more challenging than Anu had anticipated. Some children had already gotten a grasp of the alphabet and were racing through the starter books, while others dawdled, insistent on chatting to her about everything except what was on the page in front of them.

"Mrs D," Jacob asked, his hair all mussed up from football, "where do all the grasshoppers go?"

"Jacob, we really need to get through this book now..."

"I think the butterflies eat them."

"What?"

"Pardon! Mum says you should never say 'what'. It's rude!"

"Yes, she's right. Pardon, Jacob? Why do you think butterflies eat grasshoppers?"

Before long, she was involved in a lengthy story of Jacob having witnessed firsthand the atrocities that butterflies inflicted upon unsuspecting insects. Once again, she had been led down the garden path by a wily child trying to sidestep his or her reading.

Zoe Frobisher arrived at the tail-end of the story and threw them both a contemptuous look. She walked over to the bookstand, taking an advanced learning book from in there.

"Jacob, be a dear and call Sylvie out, will you?" Then she looked at Anu and raised her eyebrows. "I'm here to take over. You need to wise up to their tricks, otherwise you'll make no progress at all."

Duly snubbed, Anu nodded silently, before making her way out.

With the November chill leading into a colder, frostier December, Anu tried leaving home earlier in order to defrost her car windows. But Neha had taken to getting up later than usual, burrowing herself under the covers for 'five more minutes, Mummy' thus ensuring that they hadn't made it to school in time for three days running.

Anu yanked the covers off her in annoyance this morning. Neha lay shivering and slightly scared of her mother's uncharacteristic anger.

"Get up now, Neha! I refuse to be late again."

Part of Anu's exasperation stemmed from the look Jill had given her as she ran up to the classroom, slightly out of breath, holding on to a pink-cheeked Neha. It was a look that said - you're a mess! - and her latent guilt went into overdrive.

She had never been the most organised of people. She went through bouts of having it all together, only for the entire facade to collapse when her day-dreaming alter-ego took over. As a wife and a mother, she considered herself just about adequate, but then the example set for her had been less than ideal.

Starting today, however, she planned to be at those school gates earlier than all the other mothers. So she dragged Neha out of bed and placed her under the shower, much against her will.

Ravi had already left for work, but she knew Neha would voice her complaints to him. Sometimes he played peacemaker between his little daughter and her increasingly harried mother. Other times, he just ignored them with a 'sort it out' look at her.

She hurried along with a subdued Neha who refused to take part in any conversation, but as planned, she was at the school gates earlier than most mothers.

She spotted Simone in the distance and waved to her.

"You're early today, Anoo," Simone remarked. "Normally I see you just as I'm driving off to work."

"That's why I never see you here in the mornings!"

"Right. Some of us have to work for a living, missus."

Anu smiled at the mock barb. She had missed Simone's straight talking.

"Where have you been? I haven't seen you or Kayla in the park either."

"I've been around. It's you who's been busy selling cakes and mingling with the high-and-mighty."

"Oh, come on…"

"Just joking, honey. Your cakes were delicious. Kayla bought a couple too. Bet Zoe wasn't best pleased."

"Why not?"

"Can't you guess? She doesn't enjoy being shown up in any arena. Not even cake-making."

"That's ridiculous. The cake sale brought money in for the school. That was the point, right? So what does it matter whose cakes sold the most or the fastest?"

"I'm just telling you to watch your back, that's all."

Anu looked at her puzzled and privately wondered if Simone's past problems had created this chip on her shoulder. Was she to let herself be influenced by someone who was so clearly happy to be on the outside? Especially when she herself was finally making inroads into this tight-knit group of school mothers?

That afternoon, as she scanned the children leaving the classroom, Neha was nowhere to be seen. Worried, Anu approached Miss Davenport, who stood at the door.

"Is Neha still inside?"

Miss Davenport nodded, then indicated with her head that she could go inside.

In the classroom, she saw Mrs Pellow talking quietly to Neha, who was sobbing into her hands.

"Neha! What's happened?" She rushed towards them.

"Nothing to be concerned about, Mrs Dhawan. We've had a bit of a setback, that's all."

"W... what happened?"

"Just a little spat between the girls. I've addressed it, but Neha is still quite upset. Nothing a hot chocolate at home won't sort out." She smiled kindly at Neha. "Now Neha, you can tell mummy all about it when you get home. Don't forget to bring in your homework tomorrow."

As she held a visibly distressed Neha's hand and led her out, her heart clenched. Had rushing her out this morning led to this?

"Baby, did you forget to take your homework in? Is that what this is about?"

Neha shook her head, still refusing to speak.

Anu made her the hot chocolate at home, and they sat down at the table.

"Do you want to tell Mummy what happened?"

Neha looked down, her eyes swollen and red from crying. Anu pulled her into a hug.

"Mummy loves you, baby. I promise I won't get angry, you can tell me anything."

Neha's little body started shaking again. The story came out in fits and starts.

"I wanted to be Mary in the play, but Sylvie got the part... She said... she said that I looked like a camel... all brown and ugly... th... then... the boys started laughing and calling me a c... camel,.." More tears followed. "M... Mrs Pellow made me a wise man. But I don't want to be a man!" Neha ended on a wail.

Anu didn't know whether to laugh or cry. On the one hand, Sylvie's bullying had led to Neha being called names. On the other hand, Mrs Pellow had resolved it in the best way possible. Recalling Susan's words, she just hugged Neha closer.

"It's okay, darling. As long as they apologised for their behaviour, you can forget about it. You know you don't look like a camel, just a furry little teddy bear." She tickled Neha on her tummy, leading to a fit of shaky giggles.

"And the three wise men are major roles, much more so than Mary, who will just sit with a doll in her lap. You'll get to wear a really nice costume, too. Now cheer up!"

The next day she let Neha have the extra five minutes, throwing an equally disdainful glance back at the band of mothers at the gate as she rushed in five minutes late.

Anu wrapped the present in sparkly paper with a pink bow on it.

"Do you think she'll like it, Ravi?"

"I should hope so, considering you've spent thirty pounds on it."

"I just wanted to make sure..."

"I know, I know. We can't be seen as cheapskates. But are you really going to do this for every child in the class? That's 900 quid, Anu!"

She shrugged. She knew she'd gone a bit overboard this time, but her daughter's happiness depended upon it.

They drove up to one of the big houses at Grisham Place and parked on the road outside, as the driveway was already full of cars. Anu noted how old her Ford Fiesta looked next to the gleaming Mercedes and BMWs lining the drive. Just then, Zoe pulled up in her Porsche.

She dashed past Anu and Neha, barely looking at them. Sylvie carried a helium balloon that said 'Happy 6th Birthday Gina' and Zoe held a bottle of wine in one hand and a Christian Dior bag in the other.

Gina squealed in excitement, spotting Sylvie and the balloon. Soon she, Sylvie, Rebecca and Daisy were hugging and jumping up and down.

Anu handed the present to Neha, who waited patiently for Gina to acknowledge her. Gina's mother Dawn, a tall toothy woman, smiled at her and welcomed her in.

"Thank you for coming, Neha. My, what a big box that is! Gina, come here and welcome your guests in please."

Anu took her leave, promising to be back at 7 p.m. to pick Neha up. As she drove home, she hoped Neha would have a good time.

Ravi was brandishing the remote excitedly when she got home.

"We've got two hours! Let's watch that new Hindi movie - 'Om Shanti Om'. I've borrowed the DVD."

"Ravi, Hindi movies are a lot longer than two hours. You'll make me late for Neha."

"Don't be a spoilsport, Anu. I've even got your favourite chilli cashews here. Come on..."

She could never resist his pleas, so she made herself comfortable on the sofa next to him and soon got absorbed in the love story playing out on the screen.

At 7:15 p.m. as the credits rolled, she stood up in a panic.

"Oh, no! I'm late! I knew it, I just knew it..."

"It's not the end of the world, Anu. Just tell them you got caught up somewhere."

"You don't understand, Ravi! I have to go..."

She drove as fast as she could, noticing that only Zoe's Porsche and one other Mercedes remained on the drive.

Ringing the doorbell, she waited a few minutes before hearing movement behind the door. Zoe Frobisher opened the door, wine glass in hand.

"So you finally turned up! We were going to send out a search party."

Dawn came to the door too.

"Don't worry. The girls were having a good time. Neha, your mum's here to collect you."

She slurred over the last sentence and Anu noticed she was holding a wine glass too. Noticing her glance, Dawn said, "Would you like to join us? There's a few of the mums in there. Zoe, you know, and Natalie. There's also Jill, Daisy's mum..."

"No, thank you. Neha's dad is expecting us home for dinner."

"Oh, speaking of which, this little lady didn't eat much.

You need to feed her up. All right, thanks! See you Monday."

Dawn shut the door and Anu heard their steps retreating, a burst of laughter accompanying a comment she couldn't make out.

Walking towards her car she asked Neha, "Why didn't you eat anything baby?"

"I didn't like the food."

"Why?"

"It was all chicken nuggets and chips. I had the jelly and ice cream instead."

"Is that all they served?"

"No, there were crisps and cheese sticks too. And a big caterpillar cake."

"Hmmm, okay. Did you have a good time at least?"

"It was okay. Gina mostly played with Sylvie, Daisy and Rebecca. All their mummies were there too. They are staying for a sleepover."

"The mummies?" Anu asked.

"No, the girls. There were some other girls from class there, and they were being nice to me today. But I mostly played with her dolls' house. It's huge mummy. THIS big. And so many rooms with windows and lights that turn on and off..." Neha chatted about the dolls' house incessantly till they got home.

"How did it go?" Ravi asked.

"Well, someone fell in love with a doll's house is all I can make out."

Anu got to the church early for the Christmas service. Simone had tipped her off that the pews filled up quickly, so if she wanted to get a good view of the proceedings, she would need to get there fast.

Sure enough, within minutes of her finding an empty pew, the church started filling up. She looked around at the stained glass windows and the beautiful and intricate detailing on the ceiling and columns, fascinated. This was her first time in the church, and it was truly beautiful. An old and iconic part of the village, it stood proudly in the centre of a burgeoning community, manned by a friendly vicar and his female assistant whom she'd spotted upon entering the church.

She waited impatiently for Simone to show. It was unlike her to be late. She'd set a bag down on the spot next to her, saving her a place. She needn't have bothered. No one came and sat next to her. She tried sniffing her coat discreetly. Was she smelling?

The numbers in the church swelled, but her pew remained empty. A strange hardness lodged itself in her chest, and she blinked back tears. So this was how it was. Never mind.

Suddenly she heard movement and turned her head to see Julie smiling down at her.

"Shift up. You've grabbed a good spot. Care to share?"

Gratefully, she moved a bit to allow Julie to slip in next to her. She still kept the bag on her right, just in case Simone made a late appearance.

After a few introductory speeches by the vicar and the head teacher, the show began.

Each class presented its own version of the Christmas stories. From a futuristic take on the Nativity play to a modern-day enactment of The Christmas Carol, each year came up with creative ways of retelling the familiar tales around Christmas.

When the children from Reception began their little presentation, Anu couldn't help but smile at how cute it was. Little Sylvie looked every inch the part of Mary cradling baby Jesus. Then Neha walked behind the two other boys, holding the little jewellery box Anu had bought in India. She held it carefully, as though it really carried gold within it.

"That's your girl, isn't it?"

Anu nodded proudly. "And your boy?"

"He's one of the shepherds. Had to use an old sheet for his costume." She giggled. "And a tea cloth on his head."

A man slinked in quietly to join them. Julie introduced him.

"Oh hey, this is my husband Charles. This is Anoo."

Anu smiled and moved further along the pew. It was a shame that Ravi couldn't make it; he would have enjoyed the show very much. They were forbidden from filming it because of privacy laws, but she was sure Neha would give him a blow-by-blow account, anyway.

After the goodbye songs were sung, and the children collected from the front of the church, Anu slipped five pounds into the donation box as she waited in line to thank the vicar. His assistant was gushing over the robot costume on the child in front of Neha. Then she looked down at Neha, smiled politely and looked away. Catching Anu's eye, her gaze hardened, then immediately moved to the next parent in the queue.

Anu's smile remained fixed on her face as she thanked the vicar, who shook her hand warmly.

"A very merry Christmas to you too. Please come again. Everyone is welcome in God's house."

"Where were you yesterday?" Anu asked Simone accusingly.

"Why, did you miss me?"

"I could've done with a familiar face."

"How was the lion's pit?"

"I survived. Seriously, why didn't you come?"

"I did. I just stood at the back, watched the whole thing, then grabbed Kayla and left as quickly as I could."

"And there I was, saving you a seat..." She didn't want to admit the humiliation of sitting on her own until Julie joined her.

"Good show, huh? They always do it well, I have to say."

"Very good show. My first, and I enjoyed it thoroughly. I think Ravi was a bit jealous he couldn't see it, but his meeting couldn't be postponed."

"What did you think of the vicar and the battle axe?"

"He seems nice, but her..."

"Well spotted. She's got her favourites, and you and I will never fall into that category. Wink, wink, nudge, nudge."

"Honestly, I don't care. How much am I going to see of her, anyway? I'm just a little tired of all this covert exclusionism."

"Ooh, big words! Someone's getting all knotted up."

"Simone, sometimes I think we made the biggest mistake coming to this country. We are treated like second-class citizens here, no matter what we do."

"What happened?"

"Apparently the gift we bought Gina was too over the top. It shows that I'm needy and wanting attention."

"What did you buy, and who said that?"

"It was a pretty red coat for thirty pounds from Next. Natalie took me aside and told me I was putting out all the wrong signals. Apparently nobody buys anything over a fiver. Is that true? I thought I was doing a good thing!"

"Anoo, thirty quid? That is extravagant! You should have asked me. Most of these mums buy some crappy rubbish from Primani, wrap it up in fancy paper and ribbons and present it like they're handing over the Crown Jewels."

"How was I to know? They're all so rich I thought that's the sort of gifting they do."

"Haven't you figured it out yet? The richer you are, the more miserly you become."

❖

Finding the hall in Slough wasn't easy, even with her SatNav. Anu drove around for ages with Neha getting testy in the back of the car.

"Do I have to learn dance?"

"You don't have to do anything you don't want to. This is just a trial lesson." She glanced at Neha in the rear-view mirror. "Don't you want to meet other little Indian girls?"

"No," she pouted truculently.

Neha had been in a mood all afternoon, and despite all her gentle probing, Anu hadn't extracted a reason yet.

"Here we are!" Anu sighed with relief, spotting the entrance to the temple car park.

The class had already started when they walked into the hall, so they just waited in the back. Neha seemed fascinated with the quick foot movements of the girls practising Kathak. The teacher was a kindly older lady who called out instructions, correcting girls if they got something wrong and smiling when everyone moved in tandem.

Another lady sat down next to her.

"Hello," Anu smiled at her. "Are you new too?"

She gave her a supercilious look and said, "Those are my daughters in the front."

"Oh, I didn't realise. How long have they been coming for lessons?"

"Nearly four years. They are the best in the class."

The girls were good, but not outstanding, and Anu had to wonder why the woman was being so boastful.

She watched the rest of the lesson in silence, while the woman next to her pulled out a mobile phone and launched into a long conversation in Gujarati. Near the end of the lesson, other mothers trooped in, exchanging pleasantries with each other. They gave her and Neha curious looks, but no one spoke to her.

Once the lesson finished and the girls disbanded, Anu went up to the grey-haired teacher, Mrs Madhok.

"*Namaste*[1], I'm Anu Dhawan and this is Neha. I spoke to you over the weekend about enrolling my daughter in Kathak classes."

"Oh yes," Mrs Madhok looked at her and smiled. "We'll be happy to have Neha join us. As this term has already begun, maybe she'd like to start in January?"

"Yes, that would work out fine for us."

"You are welcome to bring her in for a few introductory classes. The older girls can show her some moves too."

Satisfied, Anu and Neha walked back to the car.

"Mummy?"

"Yes, baby?"

"Daisy said that you speak with a funny accent."

"Oh?"

"She said you pretend you aren't Indian when you talk."

"But baby, this is how I've always spoken."

"Then why don't you sound like those ladies in there?"

"Because some of them have grown up in this country, so they speak English like locals."

"But that other lady didn't speak like Mrs Pellow."

"Neha, accents depend on which part of the world you

come from. Sometimes you could be from the same country and speak with totally different accents. Mummy grew up in Delhi and studied in a convent school, which is why I speak the way I do. The dance teacher is also from India, but she speaks differently from Mummy. Similarly, the other lady probably grew up around here, and her accent differs from Mrs Pellow's."

"I don't like it when they make fun of you."

"I know, baby. Don't let it bother you. Look at me, I don't care, do I?" Anu plastered a big smile on her face as she unlocked the car and put Neha inside.

But she did care, and increasingly, she was finding her self-confidence being chipped at in a million different ways.

"Chilly there and cold here, what's the difference Anu? Just pack as you've always packed. Why is it such a big deal?" Ravi looked annoyed when, for the umpteenth time, she asked him about the suitability of packing boots for their trip to India.

"I'm just trying to assess how much room we'll have in the bags. We have to carry all those presents too." She snapped back.

"Nobody has asked you to carry presents back. Why do you still insist on doing this? Everything is available in India now. It's not 1990, you know!"

"Yeah, I know Ravi. But it's never your problem, is it? If I don't take something back for every single member of our families, guess who'll get the blame?"

"Anu, these are people you barely speak to! Your half-brothers and sisters? Come on! Why are you still trying to appease them?"

"I'm not appeasing anyone. It's just what people expect. You come from abroad, they expect a present or two."

"Then train them not to! After the first few times, I promise you, they won't even notice."

"I can't do that, Ravi. It's just a token anyway, why are you making such a big deal of it?"

"You have become such a people pleaser Anu. Then you complain at the most minor of slights. Like everyone owes you something just because you went out of your way, even if they didn't ask you to."

Anu stomped out of the study and banged the door to their bedroom shut. How dare he! Just because she'd unburdened herself to him and revealed all her insecurities surrounding the school mums? So now he felt he could stand in judgement of her!

"Anu, I'm sorry. Please unlock the door. Listen, I was way out of line there. I'm just stressed about completing this report tonight. Please!"

She remained adamant, refusing to speak to him. But her tears flowed freely, self-doubt creeping up on her again.

India was just as busy as she had expected it to be. Varsha *bua* had prepared a room for them, but as soon as they arrived, she cornered Ravi and left Anu and Neha to their own devices. Anu tried not to resent this, but it was a pattern that had been repeated over the years. Varsha *bua* had never hidden the fact that Anu would never have been her choice for her beloved nephew. Too plain, too ordinary. Ravi should have had someone glamorous, like her sister-in-law in Dubai. Smita was effortlessly charming and never set a foot wrong. Anu, on the other hand, too full of insecurities, had never quite gelled with Ravi's pushy aunt.

A week into their holiday, Anu was already tired of the

party circuit. The men drank into the wee hours of the morning, reminiscing and comparing their successes with each other. The women talked diets and Botox, tearing down the absent ones, while Anu sat quietly in the corner, not sure where she fit in this dynamic either.

The family visits had been stilted and uncomfortable. Her half-brothers and sisters just about tolerated her. They took the presents, thanked her and set them aside without even looking at them. She wondered if Ravi had been right all along.

When it came time for her to fly to Mumbai and see Nonita, Anu was relieved. Even though Neha's crestfallen face was more than she could bear.

"You go, Anu. Have fun! Give Noni our love, okay?"

Ravi kissed her, putting her in a taxi for the airport.

"Look at you! Just look at you!" Nonita always seemed to speak in exclamations. Anu returned her hug just as warmly. She couldn't believe she was here, finally seeing her dearest friend after five long years.

"It's after you had Neha that we lost touch," Noni poured her a glass of wine. Anu looked at the breathtaking view of the Arabian Sea from the apartment and felt happy for her friend. Nonita had done really well for herself.

"This is beautiful, Noni. Did you decorate the apartment yourself?"

"Bits of it, but I hired an interior designer to do the rest. I'm just too busy for such large undertakings."

"How's the big bad world of magazine publishing?" Anu asked, settling into the plush armchair.

"Like any other big bad world, I suppose. You have the wolves in sheep's clothing here too, but I'm a lot wiser these days."

"I'm really pleased for you, Noni, and yes, I'm sorry about the five-year lapse in communication."

"Hey, I wasn't blaming you, *jaanu*,[2] I was just stating a fact. Motherhood is a tough gig. How are you finding living in the UK?"

Everything came tumbling out of her in a rush. The inability to fit in anywhere, the clique of school mums, the disconnect with the other Indians, her fractious relationship with her mother, the constant feeling of being unworthy and unloved.

Nonita listened silently, topping up her wine glass and handing her a bowl of peanuts to munch on. When Anu had exhausted herself, she leaned over and held her hand.

"Firstly, there is nothing wrong with you. You have an artist's soul and you feel everything very keenly. That doesn't make it right or wrong. I could try to psycho-analyse the hell out of you, but you and I both know that you've had a tough childhood. It's no wonder that you are always looking for love, especially a woman's love. Aunty has never really been a proper mother to you. Hey, don't cry! Hang on..."

Noni rushed to the bathroom, bringing back a handful of tissues.

"Here's what I think you need to do. Get your ruddy art stuff out of the attic and start painting again. You were so damn good, I can't understand why you stopped. Also, find your tribe, woman! There will be other mums like you wanting someone like themselves to socialise with. Why are you so obsessed with this Zoe bitch and her posse?"

"I... I guess, I just want to belong."

"Sweetie, do you really want to conform to some outmoded pecking order to belong? You're better than that!"

"Noni, is it me though? Do I give off a bad vibe? Annie said I have a resting bitch face. Is that true?"

Nonita laughed. "Since when did Annie's opinion count? That woman doesn't know her ass from her elbow."

They both collapsed into giggles at that. Nonita was the very tonic she'd needed on this trip.

Her two days with Noni went by in a flurry of shopping, chatting, eating at new and exciting restaurants and drinking copious amounts of wine. She felt light and youthful again. Nonita had made her purchase clothes that flattered her slimmer figure, and suddenly she felt like she'd shed her 'mummy' persona and regained her old self once more.

"Now listen to me, Anu," Noni steered the car with one hand, her other flicking the ash off her cigarette outside the window. "This is how I want you to be when you go back - happy and confident. Don't let anyone knock you down. Do your own thang, girl. Let the haters hate as much as they like!"

Anu laughed at the slang Noni had adopted. Oh, how she wished she could've stayed longer!

At the airport they promised each other frequent phone calls and messages, vowing to never let life get in the way again. Anu walked towards the plane with a little spring in her step. Next year, she would do better. She would live life on her own terms, not predicated on other people's opinions of her.

When she got to Varsha *bua*'s house in the afternoon, she saw her sitting outside and watching Neha play hopscotch on the road.

"Hello!" Anu called out, grabbing her bags out of the taxi. "I'm home."

Neha came running and wrapped her arms around her in a big hug.

Varsha *bua* looked up with a slight smile.

"So soon? We didn't miss you at all, did we Neha?"

Ravi came out just then, his face breaking into a big smile as he spotted her and came forward to take the bags out of her hands.

Sandwiched between her husband and daughter, Anu walked into the house, not bothering to dignify Varsha *bua*'s comment with a response.

PART 2

"You remember the first time I asked you out to lunch?" Julie placed her sunglasses on her head and grinned at her. "You were like a rabbit caught in the headlights."

Anu grinned back. They were sitting in the outdoor area of the new restaurant that had just opened in their village.

"Okay, so remember my treatment at the hands of Zoe & Co. had traumatised me! I really didn't know what to expect from you ladies."

"She's still quite the bitch, isn't she?" Jemima regarded her with her signature perspicacity. "I wonder why she feels the need to behave in such an abominable manner. What does it achieve?"

"I've always believed that you catch more flies with honey than with vinegar," Julie said.

"Well, apparently she was some hotshot executive before she gave it all up for love. Just like you Anoo." Louise dipped her bread in the olive oil and vinegar.

"Me? I was never a hotshot executive, just a lowly

painter. And I haven't given it up. I'm just waiting for the right time to start again."

"Anyway, my point is that she was probably used to bossing people around, and now she's diverting her energy towards terrorising school mothers."

Anu looked around at the three women sitting with her and wondered how she had gotten so lucky. In the last two-and-a-half years they had bonded over lunches and dinners, long walks during which they had poured their hearts out to each other, and movie mornings followed by a dissection of the film over sneaky gin and tonics. They had spent so much time in each other's company that she felt incomplete without them. This was her group, this was her tribe. And she had Julie to thank for it.

It was Julie who had introduced her to Jemima and Louise. She would probably not have run into them other-wise. Louise worked from home and ran her kids to school before rushing back to attend her online meetings. Jemima lived right opposite the school gates, so she crossed the road with her daughter, deposited her at the classroom door and ambled back.

The three of them had been fast friends for years, but they were all so different personality-wise that it made for an interesting mix.

Julie was the happy-go-lucky sort, with a ready smile and a sunshine personality, prone to odd bouts of dark humour. Louise was more no-nonsense, apt to say what was on her mind and take no prisoners. But it was Jemima that Anu had grown to like the most. The most sensitive out of the three, Jemima was also the most culturally aware. It was she who brought up the latest Indian films popular on the festival circuit. She was the one who had cared enough to delve into Anu's past, fascinated by the snippets of culture and tradition that Anu revealed. Someday, she had said she wanted to travel to India, and asked if Anu would be her guide. Anu had agreed happily.

The last few years had seen Anu blossom into the person she wanted to be. Part of this lovely group of friends, and heavily involved in creating the mosaic at school, Anu felt happy and confident, just as Nonita had said she should strive to be. Which reminded her that her call to Noni was overdue.

"Look at the time, ladies! We're going to be late for pickup again." Julie laughed, not budging an inch.

"Clearly you're in a hurry. Come on, or we'll give Batty Betty a heart attack." Louise said, picking up her bag.

Neha's new teacher was so unlike Mrs Pellow that it was a wonder she had lasted that long with the eight-year-olds in Year 3. High-strung and volatile, it took little to set her off, earning her the nickname of 'Batty Betty'.

As Jemima drove them towards the school, Anu looked to see if her new car was still in the spot she had left it in that morning.

"No one's going to steal your car here, Anoo. We're not living in East London." Louise commented, following her gaze.

"It's just an old habit of mine. I left the car unlocked once and have been paranoid ever since." Anu explained, shrugging.

Every so often she felt wrong-footed like this, but chose to ignore it. In the past few years, these women had been nothing less than accepting. They'd made her feel at home in this little village; like a part of the community. While Anu's natural shyness always held her back, in their company she learned to let go of her inhibitions and become more carefree. Whether that was gin luncheons or karaoke evenings with large amounts of wine, Anu plunged herself into every activity whole heartedly, always up for more fun.

If the price was dreadful hangovers and getting late for school pickups, she was more than willing to pay it.

Neha came out of the Year 3 classroom carrying the scruffy brown travelling teddy bear and its little knapsack.

"Mummy, I've got Buddy the Bear for the weekend!"

"Yes, darling. He will be going to Bath with us, won't he?"

Neha nodded happily, chatting about her day and the caterpillars they had collected to put in the mesh habitat in their classroom.

"Mrs Daniels said they'll get real fat first, then they'll go to sleep, and when they wake up they'll turn into beautiful butterflies."

"Is that right? Well, that'll be fun to watch." Anu looked down at her child and marvelled at the contrast from the shy, quiet girl of the first year in school. In her second year, Neha had finally made friends and settled down happily with her little group, one of whom was Jemima's daughter, Libby. Now she talked twenty to the dozen, happy to try out new things and unafraid of speaking up in class. She ignored Sylvie, Daisy and Gina, but had a pleasant equation with Rebecca, Natalie's daughter.

Anu wasn't sure how much of her own influence had steered Neha away from those girls, but she was glad that Neha had chosen a nicer bunch to hang out with. After a few unsuccessful invitations for a playdate, Neha had given up on Sylvie, and privately, Anu had been relieved. During her reading sessions over the past few years she had noticed how those girls, particularly Sylvie, invariably mimicked their mothers' behaviour. Although they were never rude to Anu, it was evident that they didn't think much of her, often calling her out on the way she pronounced certain words, or pretending not to hear her when she corrected them. As a result, she had stepped back from her reading duties, choosing instead to concentrate on the mosaic.

Contrastingly, Neha's new group of friends were a delightful bunch. She'd had these girls over for tea and found them sweet and uncomplicated, just as children that age should be.

"Mummy, can we go to the park today? I want to see if Kayla is there."

"Oh! Sure, if that's what you want, baby, but we can't stay long. Mummy hasn't cooked dinner yet."

"Were you out with your friends again?"

"Yep, guilty as charged!" Anu winked at Neha, who giggled back.

They walked to the park, then Anu let Neha run ahead while she placed all her bags and the teddy bear in the car's boot. She wondered whether Kayla and Simone would be in the park. It had been a while since she'd seen them.

"Hello you!" She sat down next to Simone, who was reading a book.

"Hi Anoo," Simone looked up but didn't smile.

"Everything okay?"

"Sure."

"You looked preoccupied."

"Because I was." She held up her book.

"Hey! Are you alright? What's with the monosyllabic answers?"

"You tell me, Anoo. One minute you're crying on my shoulder that everyone hates you, and then suddenly you're flitting off with a bunch of women and I'm dropped like a hot potato."

"Simone!" Anu looked at her, pained by the accusation.

"I never dropped you. I just never see you around anymore."

"That's because you've crawled so far up their skirts that you can't see anyone else."

"That's not fair! They are my friends, and that was a nasty thing to say. The problem with you is that one unpleasant experience and you've labelled everyone as wicked and horrible. These are nice women. You're not even willing to give them a chance!"

"You go ahead, Anoo. Keep going out with your 'nice' friends. I hope it doesn't come back to bite you."

Anu came home in a foul mood, having yelled at Neha in the playground that they needed to hurry home. Neha had complained all the way back.

"I only got ten minutes to play with Kayla..."

"I have things to do! I told you before we got to the park."

"But that's not fair! You get to spend time with your friends all you want..."

"Neha, that's enough! I won't tolerate back chat from you."

"Mummy, you're hurting me..."

Anu pulled her in by the arm and sat her on the sofa.

"When I say we have to leave, I mean it! Do you understand, Neha?"

Neha crossed her arms and scowled at her. Just then, the doorbell rang, so Anu gave her a look and went to answer the door.

Susan stood outside with a cake.

"Hello Anoo, thought I'd come by and see you. I've baked this coffee and walnut cake."

Anu calmed herself down and asked Susan in.

"Would you care for a cup of tea, or a glass of wine?"

"I'll have the tea. It's a little too early for the wine, isn't it?"

Susan placed the cake on her dining table and turned towards Neha.

"How are you, my little one? You haven't been to visit me in a long time."

Neha cheered up and started chatting with her while Anu prepared the tea.

When Neha had gone upstairs, Anu made them another two cups of tea and helped herself to another slice of the cake.

"This is really delicious, Susan. I must get the recipe off you."

"Anytime." Susan paused for a moment and then, as if making up her mind, said, "Is there something wrong Anoo? You haven't been around for quite a few weeks, and I'm just wondering if I've upset you somehow."

Startled out of her own thoughts, Anu realised she had been neglecting her elderly neighbour for quite a while.

"No, of course there isn't anything wrong! I've just been busy with some school mums. I'm so sorry! I really did plan to come and see you."

Susan leaned back in her seat in relief.

"I'm glad it's nothing more than that. You know, I had started looking forward to our weekly chats. But you're a young woman with a busy life, I cannot expect you to be at my beck and call all the time."

· · ·

Later, when she related the episode to Ravi, he paused while taking off his socks and said, "Anu, she is lonely and you had sort of established a routine there, hadn't you?"

"Yes, but why should I be made to feel guilty? Her own kids aren't bothered about her!"

"That shouldn't affect your equation."

"Ravi, why are you always siding with other people over me?"

"I'm not siding with anyone. You've narrated the episode to me, and I'm just telling you what I think."

"Then I suppose you'll agree with Simone's estimation too?"

He sighed and looked at her.

"What has Simone said?"

"Just that I've gotten so busy with my new friends that I've forgotten her."

"Well, have you?"

"No!"

"Then tell her. Look Anu, first the problem was that you didn't have any friends. Now the issue is that you don't have enough time for all of them. Which situation do you prefer?"

"I just hate being made to feel like I'm being selfish just because I've finally found a group of women I enjoy hanging out with."

"Nobody can make you feel anything you don't want to."

"It's always so easy for you, so black and white. The rest of us live in a world full of grey."

In a mood to make amends, she knocked on Cathy's door the next day.

"Hello there, stranger!" Cathy answered the door with Melanie on her hip.

"Hi Cathy, how are you? I'm sorry I haven't been around sooner. I meant to bring you some of Neha's old clothes, if you'd like them for Mel."

"That's really nice of you. Come on in! Sorry the house is a bit of a tip, but this one leaves me no time for cleaning up."

Anu looked around at the mess and wondered if her house looked this bad when Neha was little. Then she remembered how tough it had been to keep on top of every-thing with a toddler to take care of, and her gaze softened. Suddenly, the overflowing sink crowded with dirty dishes; the clothes scattered everywhere and the carpet that looked like it hadn't been vacuumed in months, didn't seem that important. What was important was how the mother and child were faring, and both of them seemed happy and healthy.

Cathy set Mel down, and the toddler lunged towards her unsteadily. Then Mel grabbed the end of her skirt, looked up and gave her a big smile showing off her baby teeth. Anu laughed and picked her up.

"She's so cute!"

"She's cute, but a nightmare. Doesn't stop for a minute. Sometimes I think I'm going to die in between feeds, nappy changes and entertaining this little Miss."

"Awww! It will get better. Neha was a colicky baby, and I used to have to put her in the car and drive around at night just so Ravi could get some sleep. I thought I'd die at the wheel!"

"Neha is such a sweet little girl. She waved at me the other day when Ravi brought her home in the evening. Why was she wearing bells on her legs?"

"Was that last Thursday? That's when she goes to her

Indian dance classes. She has to wear *ghungroos*[1] on her ankles."

"Sounded real pretty, very tinkly."

"Thank you. Cathy, I was wondering if you'd like to come out to lunch with Susan and me one day? I think Susan is feeling a bit lonely, and I thought it might cheer her up. We could just go to Pizza Express."

"Sure, that would be nice. You don't mind me bringing this little brat along?"

"Not at all. In fact, I think Susan would like it."

Pleased, Anu sent Susan a message fixing the lunch date. Now, she just had to appease Simone.

May was a lovely month to visit Bath. But the traffic, as usual, was horrendous. Still, Ravi was in a good mood, playing the Hindi music CDs that lived in the car, and which they only listened to on their long drives.

"Such a pretty city, isn't it?" Anu remarked, looking out of the window. "Annie is lucky to live here."

"As are we, where we live. Don't knock it."

"I'm not, Ravi. Just saying how nice it is here, and really, we should make more of an effort to come up and explore it properly."

"I don't have a problem with that. But are you sure you want to spend that much time with Annie?"

"We don't have to tell her. We could just stay in a hotel for a weekend and do our own thing."

"Wow, Anu! You'd do that?"

"Why not? She's not my boss! I don't owe her any explanations."

Ravi gave her a sidelong glance and let out a long whistle.

"I didn't realise just how much animosity you hold against her."

Anu just looked outside, not bothering to answer.

When they finally arrived an hour later, Anu texted to let Annie know they were there. Almost immediately, she came bustling out, telling them which bay to park in.

"Does she know I can read?" Ravi mouthed to her. Anu raised her eyebrows, signalling 'just go with it'.

They unloaded all their bags and a sleepy Neha out of the car.

"Finally! How many years has it taken you to come back to Bath?"

"You can blame it on me," Ravi grinned at her, "Long weekends are scarce."

"As if!" Annie flashed him a coy look and then hooked arms with Anu, leading them inside.

"Richard's just popped out to get some beer for the boys. I've got us a nice wine chilling. I hope you don't mind that I've invited some friends over this evening?"

"I thought it was just family time?" Anu asked, at once annoyed at Annie's routine presumptuousness.

"We'll have all the family time we need on Sunday and Monday. Tonight I'd like to introduce my family to my friends."

Why bother? She thought churlishly. It wasn't like they were close.

"I haven't even brought anything formal to wear!" Anu whispered to Ravi in the room allocated to them. They'd put Neha to bed for a brief nap while they freshened up before going downstairs to join their hosts.

"I don't think it's going to be that kind of evening Anu."

"Wanna bet? Annie would never miss out on an occasion to dress up!"

"Honey, she needs it, you don't. You look fabulous as you are."

"Very nice of you to say so Mister, but really, I feel like something the cat dragged in."

"Come on downstairs, a couple of glasses of wine should sort you out."

Richard had already started on the beer when they went downstairs to join them.

"Hello, nice to see you again." His natural reserve hadn't thawed in all the years they had known him. He always seemed ready to take flight, as though being amid people was wasting the time he might have spent buried in an academic journal.

"I've made us some paella for lunch," Annie bustled about, setting the table. "I've saved all the Indian food for the evening. Come in and give me a hand, Anu."

In the kitchen Annie handed her the plates, but before she could head out, Annie put a hand on her arm.

"Are things okay at home Anu?"

Puzzled, Anu looked at her.

"What do you mean?"

"With Ravi, I mean."

"Why wouldn't they be?"

"I know the financial sector's taken quite a hit in this recession, so I just wondered if his job is okay?"

"We're fine, Annie. Thanks for asking." Anu bit out her

reply. She had barely been here five minutes and Annie was already up to her old tricks.

Anu placed the plates on the table and then excused herself to wake Neha up. She sat on the bed for a while looking at her sleeping child and wondered why she'd agreed to come here for the weekend. Was it possible to have grown up with someone, known them your entire lives, and find out you had nothing except blood in common?

As expected, Annie brought out the big guns for her evening shindig. She wore a dramatic black sari with a vivid red border, lining her eyes with plenty of kohl and mascara and plastering on the red lipstick. Anu glanced at Ravi, who with the tiniest flicker of his eyes acknowledged that she had been right, after all.

Anu and Ravi had both changed into different tops, but as they'd only brought jeans for the weekend, they were woefully under dressed. Neha was still in the dress she had travelled in.

"I wish you'd told me Annie, we would have brought something suitable to wear."

"But you all look lovely, darling! Nothing to worry about."

Most guests that showed up were also dressed soberly, letting Anu relax a bit. Annie, in contrast, seemed almost overdressed for the occasion, but she had always enjoyed the attention, and as Anu heard her tinkling laughter in the background, she wondered how quickly she could make her excuses and escape upstairs.

The dinner had been an enormous success with everyone complimenting Annie on her cooking, her ensemble, her beautifully kept home and her 'obedient husband'. Ravi had made up the last bit, whispering it to her in an undertone and almost making her snort her drink out of her nose.

Out of the twenty-odd people assembled in the room, Anu sighed, thinking it was just her luck to get stuck with a fusty old professor of Chemistry.

"Well, naturally I've said to Richard that he mustn't eat anything outside of home-cooked food in India, but he always does. Then he comes back with a Delhi belly." He laughed uproariously at his own joke. "But this is just marvellous. Marvellous." He took another bite of the chicken curry on his plate. Anu wondered whether to point out to him he had a bit of sauce on his beard, but on an impulse decided not to. The bit of orange on his salt and pepper beard gave his entirely lacklustre personality a dash of colour. She chuckled inwardly at her mean-spirit-edness, but it was her only source of entertainment this evening.

The people in the room were at least two decades older than her. Most of them were academics, dry as unbuttered toast, their only cultural exposure to India being the dinners that Annie seemed to host regularly.

She wondered how Ravi was getting on in his corner, where he was in an animated conversation with a skinny lady dressed in purple. From the way he'd tilted his body, Anu could tell that he was bored senseless, but trying to pretend otherwise.

The tedious old professor on her left was still speaking when she got up abruptly.

"I'm sorry, I need to check on my daughter."

She snuck out of the room and joined Neha on the sofa in the little sitting room adjoining the main living area.

"What are you watching, baby?"

"Bambi."

"Can I watch with you?"

Anu snuggled next to her, content to be away from the adult gathering next door.

"That was really quite rude, Anu." Ravi said, changing into his pyjamas.

"I didn't mean to fall asleep, it just happened."

"I think Annie is quite upset. She wanted you to get to know her friends, and you just disappeared on her."

"Oh, please! She just wanted to show how wonderful she is compared to her drab little cousin from London. Couldn't you see it was all a ploy?"

"What's happened to you, Anu? You were never this hostile before. Sometimes I don't recognise you."

To Annie's credit, she had been quick to forgive Anu, but was still clipped in her responses. Ravi had taken them all out for lunch, hoping to thaw the lingering frostiness between the cousins.

Walking around Bath, Anu tried once again to start a conversation.

"Annie, do you miss India?"

"Yes, I do, but we try to go back at least twice a year, so it's not all bad." She glanced over to Anu. "Do you?"

"Sometimes yes, and other times no. Every time I return, I find it changing at a dizzying pace, and I can't keep up."

"I know what you mean," Annie's tone softened. "The India we grew up in was very different. I think there was a gentler pace of life back then and the people were simpler too."

"Do you think it's because of the economic boom?"

"I'm sure Richard could tell you more about it, but the world really has shrunk in the last thirty-odd years. Information is at our fingertips, everything is online. All those foreign goods we coveted growing up are available in India if you have the money to buy them."

"I look at some of Ravi's friends and think that they actually pity us our lifestyle. One wife said to me the last time, 'you have to do all your cooking and cleaning yourself' as if that's a bad thing."

"Don't forget Anu, we grew up with servants too. It's only living in this country that's made us more self-sufficient. Although, I do miss having house help."

"I thought I did, but then one of my friends, Julie, got a Polish cleaner, and she actually cleans the house before the cleaner comes. I can't be dealing with that kind of stress!"

They both laughed together, all tension dissipating.

"Anu, why did you withdraw yourself from me? When you moved to this country, I thought we'd be close. But you barely call, and only after multiple invitations have you made it to Bath."

"I... I'm sorry, Annie. I don't have a reason, except that maybe I felt we've become very different people as we've grown up."

"Blood is thicker than water Anu. Don't ever forget that."

Driving back home, Anu looked at Ravi's profile as he manoeuvred the car towards the motorway.

"Ravi, have you ever questioned your relationship with Anil *bhaiyya?*"

"In what way?"

"I mean, like there are times you couldn't stand him,

and at other times, you know that he's a part of you and that you love him."

"I don't think men think like that Anu. Anil *bhaiyya* and I know that we're there for each other, no matter what. We don't speak for months at a time, but when we do, it's like nothing has changed. For women it's different."

"How so?"

"Well, you need each other in a way that can't be defined. I've seen women being each other's biggest supporters and champions, but I've also seen women pull each other down, backbite, and be insanely jealous. The dynamics are very different among you lot."

"And Annie? Which camp do you think she belongs to?"

"For all her faults, I don't think she's a bad person. You are both very different from each other, but I also see quite a few similarities."

"Such as?"

"Ever heard yourself speak? If I close my eyes, I can't distinguish between your voices. The tones, the inflection - all exactly the same."

"Huh."

Neha, who had been quietly playing on the Nintendo gifted to her by Annie and Richard, suddenly spoke up.

"I like Auntie Annie now. She's kind."

Anu turned around and laughed at her.

"Is that because you got all these toys from her, you little minx?"

Neha just shrugged, her eyes still glued to the Nintendo screen.

❖

"Mama, it's Anu. How are you?"

Her mother coughed a bit before speaking.

"I'm fine. Just have this chesty cough I can't get rid of."

"Have you quit smoking yet?"

"Please stop. I don't need a lecture from another one of my children."

When Kriti, her half-sister, had contacted her out of the blue to tell her that Mama hadn't been keeping well, Anu had felt a sudden dizziness.

No matter that her mother had flitted in and out of her life, she had still been the fulcrum on which all their lives had rotated for the longest time. She couldn't imagine a world without her mother, glamorous and unapproachable, but blindingly incandescent like the sun.

"We're worried about you."

"So I keep hearing. But nobody wants to visit me."

And because she had no response to that, she asked, "How is Abhishek?"

"Who knows? He hasn't been around the last few weeks."

"But Mama, who's taking care of you then?"

"The maid, who else?"

"Why isn't he with you?"

"Well, rumour has it he's met some other woman."

"Have you two broken up?"

"Not officially. But…" Here she went into another coughing fit. "But if this new bird ensnares him, I guess it's over. If not, he'll be back here, begging forgiveness. Seen it all before."

"He's done this before?" She was more shocked by her mother's cavalier attitude towards it all than anything Abhishek got up to.

"Anu, I'm a big girl and I can take care of myself, so you can stop the Mother Teresa act. I'll be fine. If I die, then I've left instructions on what to do with my lawyer in Delhi. As it is, with all of you so far away, it'll probably be Abhishek who'll end up cremating me."

"Mama! Don't talk like that..."

"What? About dying, or all my stuff? I don't have much, my own parents cheated me out of my inheritance. This house in Nainital has been willed to your brothers. My jewellery and saris will be divided between you three sisters. *Bas! Khatam*[2]."

Long after she had finished talking to her mother, her words reverberated in Anu's mind. What events had conspired to create a woman like Mama? Her grandparents had been hardworking, unassuming, and unremarkable people, middle-class in their living and thinking. Into that house, a wilful bird of paradise had arrived. They had done everything they could to tame her, but she had lived her life exactly how she had wanted, not caring about the trail of destruction she left in her wake. Yet, something about her still inspired awe and a strange love in those who were attached to her.

Troubled, she picked up her phone to dial the one person who she thought might be sympathetic to her dilemma.

"Jemima, sorry to bother you, but do you have time to meet for a coffee?"

They sat at their local coffee shop, talking in hushed tones. The tables were set so close together it was easy to eavesdrop on any conversation nearby.

"It worried me to hear her talk in this way. It's unusually morbid of her. Normally, she's always so fierce in her attitude toward life. Now, it's like she's preparing for death, almost."

"Do you want to go visit her?"

"I feel I should, but it's tough in the middle of the school year. Ravi is so busy at work, I can't expect him to be taking care of Neha as well."

"You could have Neha come and stay with us. Libby would be so excited to have her over."

"Oh no, that's too much to ask."

"You didn't ask, I offered! Discuss it with Ravi if it makes you feel better. But honestly, it's no trouble at all. Taking care of one more child, especially one as well behaved as Neha, will make no difference to me. Maybe her manners will rub off on my two monkeys too!"

"Jemima, that is so kind of you. I may be making a mountain out of a molehill, but if something were to happen to her tomorrow, at least I'd know that I'd gotten to see her one last time."

"Absolutely Anoo, I completely understand."

Anu reached forward and squeezed Jemima's hand, too overwhelmed by her kindness to say any more.

That night they scrolled through all the travel sites to get her a reasonably priced ticket for India. Having booked one for Saturday, Ravi turned to her.

"I'm not comfortable with Neha staying over at anyone else's house."

"It's not just anyone, it's Jemima. Libby and Neha are good friends too. Why are you being so difficult, Ravi?"

"Hear me out. I'll go in later to work and drop Neha off at school in the mornings. If Jemima can keep her at hers till 6 p.m. then I'll pick her up from there every evening until you're back. This way Neha's routine is disrupted as little as possible."

She had to admit that sounded fair.

"Will you be okay without me?"

"You're only going for a week. I think we'll survive, even if it's on beans and toast."

"Thank you, Ravi." She went and put her arms around his waist, hugging him tight.

"Don't be silly, Anu. This is your mum, no matter that she is the way she is. You still have to go and see her."

Packing for her trip to Nainital, Anu wondered what it would be like seeing her mother after all these years. For nearly twenty-five years of her life, her mother had been a celestial body her satellite orbited around, whether near or far. Now, as a mother herself, Anu sought to understand why Mama had never given herself fully to any of her children, choosing instead to seek other kinds of love. The kinds that took her far, far away from all her responsibilities.

CHAPTER SIX

Mama's two-bedroom villa in Nainital had been an impulse purchase by her last husband. It was a modest little home, perched on a hillside with a breathtaking view of the Naini lake. Even in the busy month of June, one could wake up to clouds of mist surrounding the house in the morning.

The valley was green but groaning under all the modern, haphazard construction of homes in the last few decades. Yet, its beauty could not be denied. Chilly mornings transformed into bright sunny afternoons only to fade into orange sunsets, home-lit wood fires smoking in the distance.

Little had been done to the house to modernise it, except for the installation of a washing machine and a television. The upholstery on the sofa was a faded red-and-cream design from the '80s, and the mismatched yellow curtains were thick with dust. At some point, Mama had envisioned redecorating the home, but a brushstroke of paint in the corner of the living room was the only legacy of that attempt. Now, accustomed to her surroundings, it was clear that Mama had neither the energy nor the where-withal to continue that effort.

When Anu had first arrived two days ago, she'd been shocked at her mother's appearance. Where had that beautiful, vibrant woman gone? The one who took care to paint her nails and dye her hair, apply her makeup and look nothing less than polished?

Instead, she found an old lady in her place.

Mama had let herself go. She'd put on weight, given up on her slinky turtleneck and trouser ensembles, and chose instead to lounge around in oversized kaftans and sweatpants.

Perhaps she had detected Anu's shock, because her retort had been acerbic.

"I've been ill, Anu. Don't look at me like that."

"It's okay, Mama, but maybe we could go to the beauty parlour one of these days?"

"What for? Whom do I need to beautify myself for?"

And for the first time Anu realised that this supremely confident woman's self-esteem had always hinged on what men thought of her.

A week to get to know a mother that she hadn't fathomed in years seemed much too little. But slowly, Anu tried to fit into the rhythm of her life in Nainital.

Mama had put her in the smaller bedroom, which only had a bed, an armoire which housed all of Mama's winter coats, and a dressing table. Every morning the maid woke them both up with tea and biscuits in bed. Then Mama would sit out on the balcony with her cigarettes and the newspaper, not inviting conversation until she'd had a minimum of three cups of tea.

Anu sat with her, going through her own emails and messages. The dial-up internet was slow and patchy, and kept dropping, but Anu persisted, eager to receive news from home. There were several emails from Ravi, keeping her updated on Neha's and his daily routines. There were also emails from her friends asking how she was. Jemima sent a few pictures of Neha, Libby and Emily, her other daughter, playing together after school. Julie sent her a photo attachment of three gin and tonics, captioned 'missing our fourth friend'. Anu sent them all several pictures of the valley, the lake, and the tiny houses nestled in the hillside. She sent none of Mama.

"Has Abhishek been in touch?"

Her mother looked up from her newspaper, the half-moon glasses giving her an owlish appearance.

"Why do you ask?"

"I just saw that some of his clothes are still in the armoire in my room and wondered if he was planning to retrieve them..."

"He'll come when that latest floozy drops him. They always do once they discover he doesn't have a rupee to his name."

"Why do you take him back, Mama?"

"What am I supposed to do? Live here alone? I need love and companionship too!"

Anu stayed quiet, wondering how her mother couldn't see the irony of searching for love from a man who had none to give.

· · ·

The parlour was only a twenty-minute walk down the hill, in the more mercantile area of the town, but Mama insisted on taking the car, parking at an odd angle behind the other stationary vehicles.

Little shops with leather goods, scarves, wooden necklaces and more jostled for space in the narrow areas assigned to them. In their midst was a glass door captioned 'Rita's beuty parlour'. The girls inside greeted Mama enthusiastically, exclaiming falsely over how slim she looked and asking why she hadn't come before. They ushered them both into a room at the back with the two narrow beds on which they were to receive their treatments.

"This is my daughter Anu from London." Mama introduced her with not-a-little pride.

Immediately they fawned over her, offering her Fanta or chai, and showing her the most expensive treatments on their list.

She let Mama pick, knowing that the bill would still only be a fraction of what she would have paid for this kind of pampering in the UK.

The girl who waxed her legs would not stop asking her questions or commenting upon her appearance.

"How long have you lived in London?"

"How did you settle there?"

"You really don't look much like madam. Taken after your father, have you?"

"Don't you wax your legs abroad? Your hair is too thick from all that shaving."

"Can I get a job in London?"

Anu felt irritated by the interrogation, but was too polite to say so and answered in brief sentences, not inviting any more conversation and not correcting the girl's belief that all of England comprised just London.

She strained to hear her mother's conversation from behind the thin curtain drawn between the two beds.

Mama was laughing, asking the girl applying her face mask about all the news in Nainital, being her delightful self that always led people to fall so easily in love with her. It was a persona she donned for the public, and one that she rapidly shed in the privacy of her home.

With just a day remaining on her trip, Anu was no closer to understanding her mother, although she had observed some behavioural patterns that helped her understand herself a bit better.

Mama's flightiness had led to her own search for relationships that were grounded and real. Mama's vanity and excessive glamour had led to her wanting something beyond the artifice of clothes and makeup. Mama's lack of female friendships had created in her a yearning for a sisterhood that supported and upheld one another.

But for all that, she realised now that she loved her mother deeply. Anu had wanted to restore her mother to her former self, and even though this plumper, more lackadaisical person was not the mother she had known all her life, at least they had groomed her the way she remembered.

On their last evening together, her mother poured them both a rum and coke, and ordered food from the local *dhaba*[1].

"So, what time are you leaving tomorrow?"

"Not until the afternoon. The train is at 3:35 p.m. but I'll double-check the ticket."

"I'll drop you off."

"That's okay Mama, I'll take a taxi."

"I know you are very independent in London, but here we still like to do things the old-fashioned way."

Not sure how to respond, Anu stayed silent.

The doorbell rang, and Mama opened the door to the *dhaba*'s delivery boy.

"Hand me my purse, Anu."

"Mama, let me get this..."

"Nonsense! I'm paying." Anu watched her count out the notes carefully, before adding ten rupees as a tip.

She shut the door and turned around.

"I'm glad you came, Anu," she said, handing the maid the food to serve to them. "I know I haven't been much of a mother to any of you. But this week has meant a lot to me."

Anu digested this silently, knowing this was a rare admission from a woman who had hitherto displayed no remorse over her failings. Could this be the opening she'd been looking for?

"Why Mama, why haven't you been a mother to us?" Anu asked softly, fearful of tipping her mother into another one of her rages.

But perhaps the moment was right because her mother turned contemplative.

"I never wanted children, Anu. If I were to go back over my life, that's the one thing I would change. Everything else - the men, the travel, the marriages and divorces - I wouldn't bother altering. They made me who I am. But motherhood was never for me."

"Then why did you have children, Mama? Surely there are ways to prevent..."

"In India? In the '70s? Anu, motherhood has always been considered the core of being a woman here. Nobody, and I mean nobody, would have understood if I'd said that I didn't want kids."

She took a cigarette out of the pack, lit it and placed it between her lips.

"I had a few abortions too. I didn't tell you about those, did I?"

"When?"

"Oh, much after you. Between marriages, with some of my lovers."

She blew out a puff of smoke.

"I've always enjoyed sex. Such a sacrilege for an Indian woman to state, isn't it? If one man didn't satisfy me, I moved on to another. But sometimes, accidents happened, and I always resented the fact that it was my body that was punished!"

"So you saw motherhood as punishment?" Anu asked in a low voice.

Mama glanced at her face and then placed a hand over hers.

"More as an imposition. I wanted to be free to love, live and leave, as I chose. My gender and the society I lived in wouldn't allow it. Maybe I should have been born a man." She laughed, taking a sip from her glass.

"Did you ever love my father?"

"I loved the idea of him, Anu. He was my second husband, and a very kind man. I thought he could be someone I might have had that loving relationship with - a proper marriage, you know. But, within a year, I realised that that was not the marriage or the stability I'd thought I needed."

"Is that why you left?"

"Yes. I'd hoped that Sunil would find a better partner after me, but he died soon after."

She stated this with no tinge of regret, and suddenly a powerful hatred welled up inside Anu.

"You are a very selfish woman, Mama. You've wreaked havoc in everyone's lives. Look at you today, sitting here all old and lonely, asking us to come visit you because you have no one left. But I don't see one bit of repentance in you. What kind of person are you?" Anu choked over the last words, the tears flowing down her cheeks, years of pent-up anger and hurt finally finding a release.

Her mother let her cry, blowing smoke rings into the air, watching them dissipate. Finally, when Anu had calmed down, she looked at her and said, "I'm not asking for forgiveness or understanding. You asked, and I told you. This is me, this is who I am. Take it or leave it. Maybe someday you will understand."

That night, as Anu tossed and turned in bed, she wondered if she would ever understand her mother. Her own feelings towards Neha were so powerful that she could never contemplate abandoning her. Yet, she was not ignorant enough to be unaware that there were mothers abandoning their children every day. Which was the more compelling force within a woman - the maternal instinct, or the need to establish an identity separate from the one assigned by society?

Mama had been born in the wrong place at the wrong time, and perhaps even in the wrong body. Had she been a man, her behaviour would not have been questioned even back then. Had she existed outside the traditional and patriarchal system of India, she might have had the choice to live life on her own terms. But as things stood, she had botched everything up by trying to straddle society's expectations and her own desires.

Anu's feelings towards Mama remained ambivalent. All she wanted to do was return home and hug her baby.

• • •

The next day, as Anu boarded the train to Delhi, her mother stood on the platform, cutting a lonely figure in her kaftan and sneakers. They had not spoken of the previous evening over their breakfast of *poha* [2]and juice. A strange peace had settled over them, as though the very airing of grievances had somehow begun a healing of sorts.

Anu hugged her mother before leaving, whispering, "Take care, Mama."

Mama patted her head in response, perhaps the only physical blessing she'd ever given her.

As the train chugged out of the station, Anu leaned back, closing her eyes. She was no closer to accepting her mother's behaviour over the years, but at least now, she understood it somewhat. It was all she had, and it would have to do for now.

Back to a grey and rainy England, she stood at the school gates, a little pensive and not in the mood to socialise. In the distance she spied Zoe, Dawn, Natalie and Jill, the first group of women she had aspired to be a part of. Now she knew that she would never have fit in there. They all spoke the same language, lived the same lives, and without ever having vocalised it, they had shunned her right from the start. Except for Natalie, whose overtures of friendship, warm as they were, seemed superficial at best.

On the other side, she spotted Simone, who always stood apart from everyone else. Her demeanour did not suggest unfriendliness, but she clearly wasn't in the playground to make friends, having been burnt once and wary ever since.

Suddenly Anu sensed movement. She turned to see Louise smiling up at her.

"When did you get back, Anoo?"

"Just this morning." Anu smiled back at her. Out of all three, it was Louise she had never been completely comfortable with. There was a certain abrasiveness about her personality that made Anu wary. But as Julie and Jemima were close to her, Anu had accepted her as part of the group.

"How is your mother now?"

"She's fine. I'm glad I got to spend time with her."

"Yeah, one should. I don't see enough of my parents."

"Where are they?"

"Only down the road, two villages away. Not far from here at all. But you know how busy life can get. And honestly, my dad just annoys the hell out of me."

"Oh."

"Anyway, it was good of Jemima to take care of your girl, wasn't it? She's got such a big heart, that one."

"I'm ever so grateful." Anu sighed, knowing her trip to India wouldn't have been possible otherwise.

"What are you grateful for? Welcome back, sweetie!" Julie kissed her on the cheeks.

"Jemima taking care of Neha after school."

"I could have helped too. You should have said." Julie looked at her searchingly. "All went well in India?"

"Yes, thank you." Anu looked around for Jemima but didn't spot her. "Isn't Jemima coming in today?"

"Both the girls are off sick, so, no. But we are planning a karaoke evening at mine on Friday. Can you make it?"

And just that easily, she slipped back into her life at home.

. . .

A pregnant woman was struggling with a stroller and a toddler having a tantrum right outside the school gates.

"Can I help?" Anu volunteered.

"I'm okay," she snapped, turning her back to Anu, still trying to open the stroller and control the toddler at the same time.

Anu shrugged and walked on, holding Neha's hand. Only three weeks after returning from India, her entire trip felt like a distant dream already. It also made her realise that her life was in England now, and much as India would always be a part of her, she had to leave her past behind and move forward with living in the here and now.

She went and stood next to Jemima, hoping to ask her about the new woman who had finally managed to control her child and the stroller.

"She is very pretty, isn't she?" Jemima noticed her looking at the woman. "Her name is Mia, and she's got one child in Reception and two more, I'm guessing, because I hear they have three different fathers."

"What do you mean?"

"All the kids have different fathers, or at least that's what I've been given to understand." She shrugged. "I could be wrong."

"Gosh!"

"She's just moved into the council estate on Holly Drive."

"Is she married?"

"Not sure, but I know she's living with some chap."

"Huh."

"I'd steer clear of her if I were you. She's already got a bit of a reputation amongst the other mothers."

"In what way?"

"Takes offence to the slightest thing. Is ready for an argument at the drop of a hat."

"That explains it. I tried helping her with her stroller, but she nearly bit my head off."

"Don't mess with that type, Anoo. You'll never win."

Neha was on the swings with Kayla, so Anu looked around to see if she could spot Simone. It had been over a month since their last chat, which hadn't ended well, and Anu wondered if it was time to make amends.

"Hello," she smiled at Simone, who was absorbed in her book. "How are you?"

"Hi," Simone looked up at her, still distant but not as cold as before.

"I've brought you something." Anu pulled out the box of Indian tea she had picked up in Nainital and handed it over to her. "As you love the tea I make, I thought you'd enjoy this. It's pre-made tea bags of chai. You can just add hot water and milk; it tastes pretty good."

Simone seemed to thaw visibly.

"Thanks Anoo, that's sweet of you. Do you want to sit down?"

Anu took her place next to Simone.

"When did you go to India?"

"About three weeks ago. My mother wasn't well, and I wanted to spend some time with her. She is fine now, so not to worry."

"I see. Was that why your friend was picking your daughter up from school daily?"

"Jemima? Yes, that was when I was away."

They were silent for a while, then Simone mumbled, "I'm sorry about last time. It's none of my business who you socialise with."

"Don't worry about it, Simone. I still consider you a friend, regardless of whether you consider me one. I just wish you'd give them a chance. They aren't like the other hoity-toity mothers. They are really nice and down-to-earth."

"If you say so."

"No, really, I mean it. In fact, I'll prove it to you. I'm doing a Bollywood movie and lunch afternoon at mine Monday next week. Why don't you join us? You can get to know them as well, and then you'll see that they don't bite."

"Anoo, I don't think I can belong to that group of women."

"How do you know unless you try?"

Simone looked down at the box of tea in her hands.

"I'm not sure that I'm ready to open myself up to these people again."

"Simone, trust me. I know these women. They are lovely and they will accept you for who you are. They've accepted me, haven't they?"

"Okay." Simone nodded. "I'll give it a try."

On Monday, after dropping Neha off to school, Anu went home and cleaned the house from top to bottom. This was the first time in all these years that she was having the entire group of women over at hers, and she wanted everything to look perfect. It had taken her a few years to muster up the courage to invite them over. At first she had worried that her house wasn't up to scratch, her street not posh enough, and her decor not as *au courant* [3]as theirs. But slowly, having gotten to know them better, she had realised that these fears were baseless. So, she'd been excited and grateful when they had accepted her invitation readily.

She had woken up early to cook the chicken curry and

rice she planned to serve as lunch, mindful of not being heavy-handed with the spices. A bowl of *raita* was chilling in the refrigerator alongside a couple of bottles of Prosecco.

She looked around the room in satisfaction. True, her house wasn't as large as any of theirs, but her heart was large enough. She intended to spoil them with her hospitality, having packed little bags of Indian bangles as a gift for each of them. She hoped that this introduction to her culture would show them that even though she was a part of the group, she was also part of a rich heritage that she took pride in. It felt important for her to prove that not all Indians were coarse and unrefined; dismissible as the immigrants whom one availed services from, but never ever considered equals.

"That's a massive chip on your shoulder, Anu," Ravi had pointed out when she mentioned her concerns to him.

"I don't think it's a chip, Ravi. It's reality. Look at the way Asians can be treated here, as though we've just fallen off a bullock cart."

"Yeah, but look at how some of us behave like we have! Have you seen what's happened to areas that are predominantly occupied by Asian communities? Higgledy-piggledy constructions, no consideration for their neighbours or their communities, a mess everywhere. Are you surprised that the English keep a wide berth?"

"But those sorts of people exist everywhere! Look at Holly Drive. That doesn't mean that I want to be lumped with them."

"I don't think you are. This is just your imagination speaking. I don't get treated any differently at work."

"You're a man!"

"What difference does that make? If we're talking racism, that can happen anywhere and to anyone."

"I'm not talking racism necessarily. It's just this way of

sidelining someone who appears different, just because they aren't someone you are familiar with."

"And you're telling me Indians don't do this? Remember when we were growing up in India, how we referred to people from the North East as 'chinkies'. And these are our own countrymen! It all comes down to education and exposure."

Anu thought back to her conversation with Ravi and wondered whether in trying to establish herself as a cultured and educated Indian, she wasn't doing the very thing that had been done to her? Was this just another way to distance herself from those she felt were not on the same social rung as herself?

Simone was the first to arrive. She looked visibly nervous, carrying a bunch of pink carnations.

"I wasn't sure what else to bring?"

"You didn't need to bring anything at all! Come on in. Here, let me take your jacket."

Simone handed her the denim jacket, looking around at the living room.

"This is really pretty Anoo. What a cheerful room!"

Anu had never heard her living room described in those terms, but as she looked at it with fresh eyes, she was pleased to find that the yellows and oranges she'd picked for her cushions lent the room a sunny aspect.

Before she could thank Simone, the doorbell rang again, and she rushed to answer the door. Her friends stood outside, holding bottles of wines and flowers, chatting excitedly. As she let them in, she saw Cathy's curtain twitch from across the street and felt a stab of guilt. Maybe she should have invited her too? But the group was large enough as it was and adding a new mother to the mix might not have worked.

She turned to the kitchen to put the flowers in vases and fetch the Prosecco and glasses for a little toast.

"Welcome to my humble abode! I'm so glad you could all make it." Beaming, she handed the glasses of fizz around.

"Anoo, this is charming!"

"How do you keep your house so clean?"

"Yeah, where's the mess, I want to know! My kitchen counter top is always covered in a mound of paperwork."

She smiled at their compliments, happy that her friends had not turned their noses down at her considerably smaller home.

"Ladies, before we begin, let me introduce you to Simone. This is Kayla's mum. Her daughter is in Year 5."

As they sat and chatted, exchanging notes over the bowl of pistachios she'd placed on the table, she was glad to see Simone looking engaged and happy to be amidst them.

The movie she'd picked was an old one, but one she thought would be a pleasant introduction to Bollywood.

"Does it have a lot of singing and dancing? You know, the screwing the lightbulb, opening the tap moves?" Louise laughed up at her when she was clearing the table.

"I just love the colours," Jemima sighed. "I wish we could wear those clothes here."

"With our weather? Not a chance!"

Simone asked her in a soft undertone, "Why do they call it Bollywood?"

"I'm not sure, really. Someone nicknamed it after Hollywood and the name's just stuck! But the Indian Film Industry actually consists of all kinds of cinema, not just Hindi films."

"Do you watch those other films too?"

"Sometimes, but Ravi doesn't much care for the heavy

duty movies, much preferring the happy endings of these films."

"Do you always do what Ravi likes?" Simone looked at her curiously.

The room had fallen silent, as though the women had sensed that something interesting was transpiring here.

Anu looked back at Simone and smiled. "When you love someone, you do what makes them happy. Ravi does a lot for me too. That's what marriage is about, isn't it?"

"Hear, hear!" Jemima raised a glass and everyone downed their drinks, ready to plunge into the alternative world she was planning to introduce them to.

"How did it go?" Ravi asked her that evening as he dried the dishes in the kitchen while she washed up.

"It was fun."

"But...?"

"Why do you think there's a 'but'?"

"Anu..."

"Okay, okay. There were just a few things that were odd. Julie left in the middle of the movie, giving us some strange excuse. I don't think she enjoyed the film much. Then Simone and Louise got into it over something, I'm not even sure what. But when I came back from the kitchen there was a definite atmosphere in the room."

"And?"

"Well, nothing really. It all settled down, and by the end of the film, everyone was in a good mood again. But I was just wondering if it had been a good idea to bring Simone into the mix?"

"Stop overthinking it, Anu. Sounds to me like you pulled off a pleasant afternoon. Now you can stop feeling guilty about all the karaoke evenings they've invited you to."

❖

Having let her gym membership go to waste long enough, Anu finally went online and cancelled it. She pulled on her tracksuit bottoms reluctantly, readying herself for a run. The last few pounds she had gained could be credited to all the drinking she had been partaking in lately. Never a big drinker herself, she'd soon realised that to be a part of her group, she had to keep up with the girls, who loved their mid-afternoon tipples just as much as their weekend pub jaunts.

She ran past Cathy's house, surprised to see Susan entering just as she jogged out in front. Neither of them spotted her, but she heard Cathy's laugh and Susan exclaiming over Mel.

Their planned-for lunch had never happened because she had rushed off to India to see her mother. But secretly, she had hoped one of them would arrange it for another time. Apparently they had gotten close in her absence, not bothering to figure out another date for all of them to meet. Anu wondered why this rankled?

She ran quietly, her stamina much improved over the last few years of regular running. It was easy to block everything out when she was absorbed in exercise. It was perhaps the only time when her mind rested aside from when she slept. "Over-thinker," Ravi had once called her, and she admitted she was. It was what had given her paintings a depth of emotion that her words could never articulate.

Having pulled the canvas and paints out of the attic, she was afraid to start again. What if all these years of inaction had robbed her of her talent? What if she wasn't as good as she had once been led to believe?

Jogging on, she spied a tiny woman with a stroller just ahead of her on the pavement. Slowing down abruptly, Anu realised it was Mia, the pregnant woman from the other day. Not wishing to cross swords with her, she waited until she could pass her by at a broader juncture.

As she rushed past, she thought she heard a sob. Walking on, she almost ignored it, but then forced herself to turn and face the young woman.

Tears streaming down her face, Mia made no pretence of hiding her distress.

"A... are you okay?" Anu asked warily, waiting for the rebuff. But Mia just shook her head, sobbing openly.

"Here, let's just go over to the park, shall we?"

She led the strangely compliant woman over to the empty park, getting her to sit on the bench with her. The toddler remained asleep in the stroller.

"Now, you don't have to tell me anything, but I'm just going to sit here with you if that's okay?"

They sat together quietly, Mia staring into the distance, still sobbing. Anu could feel the waves of distress coming off her person and wished she could say or do something to alleviate it.

Finally, after nearly fifteen minutes of sitting this way, she quietened down.

"T...Thank you," she muttered, not looking at Anu.

"I have done nothing, really." Anu responded, wondering how else she could help. "Can I call someone for you? Would you like to go over to the café for a cup of tea?"

Mia stood up abruptly.

"I have to go now. Sorry for the trouble."

She walked away, her back ramrod straight, leaving Anu deeply perplexed by the entire episode.

•   •   •

Choosing not to relate her morning encounter to anyone, she wondered if there was a way to reach out to this young woman who was obviously in some kind of pain.

"What if," she asked Julie as they waited together for their children to emerge from school, "you knew that someone was unhappy, but you didn't know why or how to help them?"

"Who is it?" Julie raised her eyebrow at her. "Come on, spill the beans."

"No one you know… "

"I know everyone, luv!"

Anu laughed, but deflected it once more.

"I'm just 'asking for a friend', that's all."

"Okay, don't tell if you don't want to. But the way I look at it, if this person needs your help, they'll ask for it."

"What if they don't know how?"

"Anoo, seriously, if this is an adult we're talking about, they'll know how. I wouldn't worry too much about it, all right?"

Anu nodded, swallowing her misgivings.

"Now listen, you know my birthday's coming up next month, right?"

"Yes. Are we still going out to lunch? I've blocked that afternoon off."

"Actually, I've had a better idea. I was thinking we could all take off to my parents' place in Ashmore."

"Where's that?"

"In Dorset, sweetie. Jemima and Louise have been before. It's absolutely beautiful, and as Mum and Dad are away in Spain, they're happy to let me have it for that weekend."

"That sounds lovely, but I must check with Ravi if he's okay with me going away so soon again?"

"You don't ask, you tell. Tell him Julie insisted."

The strange morning faded from Anu's mind as she realised how far she'd come in the last couple of years. From having no friends to being invited for a weekend away, she felt a strange satisfaction once again at having finally found her feet in her surroundings.

CHAPTER SEVEN

Anu had avoided going into the dance class for the past year. She would wait in the car park after dropping Neha at the door of the dance hall. She had tried to make friends initially, but her natural awkwardness and her inability to find common ground with yet another segment of mothers, albeit from a similar cultural background, made her retreat to her car, eventually. None of the women had seemed friendly to begin with, although a few had smiled at her once or twice. But the first mother she had encountered, the boastful Gujarati one with the two daughters, seemed to be the Queen Bee around here with everyone else kowtowing to her. Anu had felt quite disheartened upon realising that she would not be making any friends in this place either, unless she was willing to submit to another version of the hierarchy she'd encountered at school. But by the time this realisation dawned on her, Neha had started to enjoy the classes much too much and didn't want to quit. So, Anu decided it would be prudent to wait out the length of the class in her car, a book in hand.

Today Neha insisted she accompany her inside.

"Everyone's mummy comes in and watches."

"Daddy and I watched you at the show last year, baby."

"But I've learned some new steps and I want you to see!"

Anu allowed herself to be persuaded.

Inside, a few mothers stood clustered together. The Gujarati lady with the two daughters bustled around importantly, ticking off the giggling girls even as Mrs Madhok, the teacher, took attendance.

There was something about the self-importance that the woman emanated that was off-putting and intriguing at the same time. Riddled with self-doubt and insecurity, Anu just couldn't fathom how anyone could be so naturally aggressive as to be totally blind to how she was being perceived. This woman had intimidated not just the other mothers but also the teacher into submission. Everyone, and that included all the girls, looked to her for direction. Anu wanted no part of that drama.

Standing quietly to one side, she watched the girls perform the opening sequence. Neha was not a naturally gifted dancer, but what she lacked in talent, she more than made up for in enthusiasm. After her initial reluctance to join the class, she had taken to the lessons like a fish to water, enjoying the cultural bonus of learning the ancient language of Sanskrit frequently used in the description of the movements and hand gestures. It gratified Anu to see that her daughter's shyness had all but disappeared, and she mingled and laughed gaily amongst her friends here.

"Is that your daughter?" said a curly-haired woman with a heavily made-up face and a thick accent she couldn't quite place.

"Umm, yes." Anu smiled at her.

"She looks so much like you."

"Thank you. And your daughter?"

"In the blue. She's just joined, but isn't enjoying it much. Jigna's daughters are making life hell for her."

"Jigna?"

"That one there, the bossy one."

"Oh."

"The girls go to the same school as my daughter, and they are just like their mother."

"Can't you do something about it?"

"What? I've tried talking to the head teacher, but it's only made things worse."

"Then why send them to the same dance class?"

"My husband insists that they stay connected to their culture. I'm from Kenya and he's from India. Arranged marriage, you know. He's not happy that I don't speak Gujarati to my children. So, he wants them to come here and mingle with other Indians. As if the school doesn't have enough of us already."

"We aren't particularly good about speaking Hindi to Neha either. I guess we're just comfortable conversing in English."

"That's what my parents did too! They were trying so hard to fit in here that they stopped conversing in Gujarati to us at home, hoping we would assimilate more easily."

"And did you?"

"I'm neither here nor there. My own people won't accept me because I'm too westernised, and to the English, I'm still that Kenyan Indian with an accent. What to do?" She shrugged.

"What about your children?"

"Another generation of confused Indians. Do you know what they call us in India? BBCD. British born confused *desis*[1]."

"That's terrible!"

"It's true. I agreed to marry my husband because I

thought that through him I could rediscover my roots. But all I've discovered is the joy of being bossed around by a chauvinist." She gave a wry laugh.

Anu looked at her, shocked. How could this woman divulge all this private information to a complete stranger?

"Why do you look so shocked? You think all these women are happy in their marriages? They are caught between two worlds: one of their western contemporaries, and the other of their heritage. Both promise happiness, but neither delivers."

"Surely not all of them?"

"Maybe not all. I did exaggerate there. Jigna is definitely the one who rules the roost in her household, but if you saw her husband you'd know why."

"What do you mean?"

"He's such a wimp. A real wet rag, a dishcloth, you know? It's Jigna who runs the business alongside her father-in-law. If it weren't for her, their household would fall apart."

"You sound like you admire her?"

"I can't stand her! But them's the facts."

Anu digested this silently, not sure how to respond to this deluge of information. The start of the dance lesson rescued her from formulating an answer. She watched the performance, her mind in overdrive. Who knew what forces moulded people? Her aversion to Jigna was only mildly erased by the knowledge of her background. They would never be friends, but now she understood her bossiness a little better.

At the end of the lesson, the woman collected her daughter, waving to Anu as she left. Neha was still chatting with her friends while unwrapping the long string of bells around her ankles. Anu waited patiently for her to finish. Suddenly Mrs Madhok came up to her, smiling.

"Did you enjoy watching Neha dance? She is doing very well."

"Yes, I did. All the girls dance so beautifully together. I'm amazed at how you get them to synchronise their movements."

"But that is my job, no?" Mrs Madhok glanced up at her, a quizzical look on her face. "Mrs Dhawan, Neha tells me you are a painter?"

"I was. I haven't really done much in the last few years though."

"Well, as you know, we have a performance coming up in October, around *Dussehra*.[2] Would you be able to help with the backdrop?"

"Help in what way?"

"Well, we were hoping to have a scene of *Vrindavan*[3]. Could you help us paint it?"

"I could try, but I've never done anything on that scale before."

"Thank you, Mrs Dhawan. We'll start work in September, so please look out for an email from me."

Bemused, Anu led a chattering Neha out of the hall.

"What did you think, Mummy? Was I good? Did you like the last bit - the Bollywood dance? That's my favourite!" She shook her hips to mimic the moves and laughed delightedly at her mother's expression.

The mosaic at school was coming along well since its inception nearly three years ago. Over time the project had grown, but that didn't bother Anu much as she found herself getting lost in the pure pleasure of creating something with her hands once again. The few mothers that occasionally helped were polite if not too chatty, and oddly this didn't affect her at all. Anu felt at home, gluing, sticking, pasting - creating. Her mind emptied itself and instinct took over, guiding her fingers. She came away from these sessions feeling strangely satisfied and removed from the daily stresses of life. It was always a wrench to return to the reality of being a wife and mother.

When the doorbell rang the next morning, Anu was in the middle of kneading the dough for the evening *chapattis*[4]. Her hands still covered in flour, she opened the door to Cathy, Mel slung casually over a hip.

"Hi Anoo! Susan and I are heading over to the café for some tea and cake. Fancy joining us?"

"I'm a bit of a mess right now Cathy," Anu pulled a rueful face, brandishing her flour-covered hands.

"Then clean up and join us in a bit, why don't you?"

"Okay. Give me fifteen minutes."

"See you there." Cathy said, walking towards Susan's house.

Anu washed her hands quickly, putting the dough into the refrigerator for later use.

Running a comb through her hair, she wondered whether to apply a bit of lipstick, but decided in favour of spritzing some perfume instead. There was no point in even trying in front of Cathy, who was so drop dead gorgeous that everyone else paled in comparison.

Anu was slightly envious of how quickly Cathy had bounced back to her figure after Mel was born. And now that Melanie was a little older, Cathy was venturing out more often, each time looking more glamorous than the last. Anu had done her own share of curtain twitching, watching her neighbour go on dates with Andy, dressed in slinky, figure-hugging dresses and quite content to leave their three-year-old with a babysitter. Stop judging, Anu repri-manded herself internally many a time.

Now, as she flung a scarf around her neck, she wondered whether they had invited her as an afterthought?

Susan and Cathy were already sitting at the table with a pot of tea and two slices of cake in front of them.

"There she is!" Cathy waved her over.

"Hi ladies, what are you having?"

Two cups of tea later, she dipped in and out of their conversation, noting how close they seemed.

"... and then there was that time when Mel swallowed a button... "

"I told you not to worry, my dear. It all came out the next day, didn't it?"

"You can't imagine how wonderful it is having Susan to turn to, Anoo. She's like my substitute mum."

Susan looked at her fondly, and Anu's heart clenched. What had happened to her own burgeoning friendship with Susan? Had she been so caught up with her new friends that she'd completely neglected her?

"Cathy, did you tell Susan about our plan to go to Pizza Express?"

"Oh, we went Anoo. You were in India at the time, and we thought, why not? I was gagging to get out of the house."

"We should do another lunch," Susan added thought-fully. "You could join us, if you're free, Anoo?"

"I'd like that." Anu smiled gratefully at Susan, still smarting internally at being replaced by a younger, prettier woman. But whose fault was that, anyway?

. . .

In the park that afternoon, she sat with Simone talking about the latest book she'd been reading, when suddenly she noticed Simone's gaze following someone.

"What are you looking at?"

"That new mum, Mia. She's here with her man."

Anu looked over to see a muscly tattooed man with a shaved head next to the petite woman.

"They look so out of place here, don't they?"

"What, amongst all us yummy mummies you mean?" Simone looked at her, one eyebrow raised ironically.

Anu shrugged.

"You have to admit, you don't see a lot of this kind around here."

"What does 'this kind' mean, Anoo? Don't tell me you've become a 'them' and 'us' person as well?"

"You know me better than that, Simone! I'm just stating the obvious. You were looking at them too."

"Out of curiosity."

"I don't think she's particularly happy," Anu blurted out.

"What makes you say that?"

The entire incident from the previous week came spilling out of her. Simone listened quietly.

"Did you try to find out why she was crying?"

"She didn't want to say."

"But did you try?"

"I could have tried harder for sure, but she's so defensive that I was a bit afraid to, honestly."

"Anoo, when I was going through domestic abuse, I put a brave face on it daily. Just once, if someone had reached out to me, it probably wouldn't have come to this." Her gaze fell upon the scar on her arm as she said this. "Kayla was young, but she saw it all, and it's traumatised her ever since."

They sat in silence, each lost in their own thoughts.

"Do you suggest that I approach her now?"

"I'm not suggesting anything, just saying that sometimes people find it hard to ask for help."

That night as Anu tucked Neha into bed, she wondered whether her disregard of Mia stemmed from her own fear of involvement with others' emotions, or a need to distance herself from a particular kind of person? Perhaps the kind deemed 'unsuitable' by her friends. What would it have cost her to offer sympathy or help? Then she felt a flash of resentment towards Simone. Why was it that with her, Anu always felt herself coming up short? Her other friends hadn't been mean to her, but Simone had refused all future offers of getting together, citing one lame excuse after another. Even with Anu, it seemed that her friendship was one she granted as a favour. One that she could withdraw at any time, pulling up the drawbridge to fortress herself against the outside world. With detachment as her fallback position, how could Simone point a finger at Anu for being inconsiderate?

The next morning as she approached the school gates, something seemed amiss. There were little groups of women talking excitedly amongst themselves, barely glancing her way as she passed them.

None of her friends were around so she went and stood next to Helen, Jacob's mum.

"What's going on?"

"Gossip, my dear. The one thing that keeps these women fuelled."

"Gossip about what?"

"A school mother, but I'd rather not be the one to pass it on, if that's okay by you."

Her curiosity piqued; she didn't push Helen, but wondered what the kerfuffle was about. She hadn't seen this kind of excitement in all the time that Neha had been attending school.

After seeing Neha off, Anu wandered over to Julie and a few other mums.

"... and that's the shocking bit!" As soon as she approached them, the mousy-looking woman stopped talking. Julie looked at her and smiled.

"Let's get a coffee, Anoo."

They walked together to the café, with Julie complaining about how hungover she felt and how desperate she was for an Americano.

"Why did that woman stop talking as soon as I got close to you?"

"Debs doesn't really know you, so I guess she thought better of speaking in front of you."

"Julie, what on earth is going on? Everyone is whispering to one another, and Helen said something about gossip that she didn't want to pass on... "

"It's the scandal of the year, hun." Julie yawned before taking a sip of her coffee. "Zoe Frobisher's husband has left her for their nineteen-year-old au pair."

"What?!"

"Oh yes. They'd been having a rollicking affair right under her nose. Of course, Zoe's nose is so high up in the air that she didn't suspect a thing."

"My goodness, the poor woman!"

"Don't waste your sympathy on her. She's going to take him to the cleaners, you watch. She'll keep the house, of course, and he'll soon be regretting his little peccadillo when she's finished with him."

"But still... "

"Did you see the relish with which the women were passing the news on to each other? Zoe's made a lot of enemies in her time, so people are happy to see her fall flat on her face."

"How did the news get out?"

"How else? Through one of her friends, I'd imagine."

"And little Sylvie?"

"She hasn't been in to school. Zoe'll probably keep her off for the week."

"Should I say something when I see her?"

"What for? Trust me, the bitch-o-meter will be intact. I wouldn't bother if I were you."

It was the first time in years that Anu felt like painting, so she placed the canvas on the landing where the light was at its best, and slowly unscrewed the various tubes of paint, mixing the colours on her palette. As she daubed the first bit of paint on the canvas, she tried examining her feelings about Zoe's situation. She couldn't deny a certain glee upon hearing the news, something that was probably mirrored in the school playground. But simultaneously, there was an underlying unease because instead of the sympathy that should have been extended to Zoe at a time like this, people were behaving like vultures over carrion. Picking over the details, picking apart her marriage, and probably blaming her for its demise too.

"A nineteen-year-old? What a bloody cliché!" Nonita laughed at the other end of the line.

"I know, but that's not the worst of it. It's like no one has any sympathy for her. I mean, I know she was vile to many people. She was absolutely horrid to me most days, but I can't help feeling sorry for her."

"You're too soft, Anu. This is just Karma biting her on the ass."

"Arse." She responded distractedly.

"What?"

"They say 'arse' here. Anyway, I'm sorry I just launched into my story. What's going on with you?"

"Not much, except the usual. Oh, there's one little thing I've been meaning to tell you..."

"What?"

"I'll be staying in London for two days in September, on my way to the US for a show."

"Noni! Why were you keeping this a secret?"

"Haha! Okay, you can stop screaming now. I just wanted to surprise you with the news, that's all."

"You're staying with us, of course."

"Actually, the company had organised a hotel... "

"Noni!"

She heard an exaggerated sigh down the line.

"I turned it down. There's no way I'd stay in a hotel without getting into serious trouble with you. I am so excited to see you again, Anu. And Ravi and Neha, too. Can't wait, my love."

"That's a pretty dark piece up there." Ravi said after changing out of his work clothes.

"Sorry?"

"You've started painting again, but I noticed the crimson and the brown on the canvas. Quite dark and depressing."

"I've just started it, Ravi. You know it will change as I work upon it."

"But why so dark?"

"Just the mood I was in when I started." She went up to him and put her arms around his waist. "Guess what? Nonita's coming to visit in September."

"Oh, no!" He placed his hand over his mouth in mock horror. "Double trouble!"

"Stop it! I'm so happy. Finally, she's making it here after all these years."

"I'm happy for you too, babe. Now, why were you in a dark mood earlier?"

❖

"Have you broached the subject of Dorset yet?" Jemima asked her as they bent over the mosaic together.

The school mosaic which had become larger and more intricate in the past three years and seemed no nearer to completion, even though they had been working on it regularly. Anu's initial vision of showcasing the landmarks that represented the village on one panel had grown beyond the original plan. Now, with input from several teachers and students, it had turned into a gargantuan task. Over the years Miss Davenport had enlisted more recruits from the mothers, Jemima amongst them. Despite the challenges of trying to represent their village through the medium of mosaic work, Anu found the mornings she spent working on it deeply fulfilling. The bonus was the time she got with Jemima.

"No, I've been a bit distracted lately. I will ask tonight." Anu answered.

"Do you think this mosaic will ever be finished?" Jemima grinned at her.

"I think Miss Davenport might have been excessively ambitious with this project."

"Wasn't it meant to cover a panel on the side wall?"

"It's the size of an entire wall now."

They giggled together in complicity. With Jemima, it never felt hard. Anu felt accepted, admired even, and she reciprocated the sentiment wholeheartedly.

Jemima was like that lovely older sister who gently guided one past life's pitfalls, always encouraging and never pushing beyond one's limits. But Jemima also had a mischievous side that popped up from time to time, giving her just enough of an edge to not make her entirely saccharine-sweet. Besides, she always smelled of blackberries.

"I've been meaning to ask you. What perfume do you use?" Anu said, sniffing the air appreciatively.

"I don't. Paul is allergic, so I just stick to soap and water. And the occasional Jo Malone." She winked.

"I wish I could smell as good with just soap and water." She smiled at Jemima. "I'd probably smell of chicken curry if I didn't spray myself every day."

"Anoo, you need to stop apologising about your food, which by the way, is absolutely delicious! If I could cook the way you do, or had access to all your spices, I'd think I had died and gone to heaven."

Anu chuckled at this. Jemima was a terrible cook, and she cheerfully accepted it. Neha had complained about having to eat pizza every day after school while Anu was in India.

"I wasn't much of a cook when I lived in India, but here I've had to learn per force. And Ravi likes variety, so I've had to diversify too. Let me tell you, if we were to go back and live in India, I'd never set foot in the kitchen again."

"Would you, though?"

"Would I what?"

"Go back and live in India?"

"I'm not sure. Ravi loves his job here, so unless he gets an even better offer there, chances are we won't."

"But from what you tell us, your lifestyle there was much nicer than here."

"Only because household help is so affordable. Things are changing there too, I hear. Reliable servants are hard to come by."

"That's such an awful word though, isn't it? Servants. Why would one human being call another one that?"

"You're right. I've never really thought of it that way. Maybe because my grandparents treated them more as family than anything else. They'd been with the household for over forty years. These days it's a miracle if they last four."

"It really is quite fascinating to hear all your stories. Promise me that someday we'll travel to India together."

"Of course! I've already said that we will."

Jemima looked over at her and winked.

"But first, can you speak to Ravi about Dorset?"

"I am beyond tired today!" Ravi kicked off his shoes and fell back onto the sofa.

"What happened?" Anu took his jacket and briefcase before handing him a glass of water.

"Just some HR stuff that I really shouldn't have had to be involved in, but got pulled into unwittingly."

"Oh?"

"Yeah, sometimes I tire of all the political machinations at work. Why can't we just do what we are meant to without being dragged into stupid controversies?"

She let him unburden, only half-listening, but nodding and commenting in the right places. When he was in a mood like this, he was not likely to be receptive to new ideas, but time was running out and she had to let Julie know whether or not she was planning to join them in the next few days.

"I'm going to make us a couple of rum and cokes."

"That sounds good! Let me change and say goodnight to Neha. Be back in a sec."

She had made Ravi's favourite lamb biryani, hoping it would soften him up.

"Anu, what a treat! *Gajar halwa* [5]as well? How come?"

"I just fancied doing something different. Do you like it?"

"Delicious! I'm stuffed, but I'm going to take another helping."

"Ravi... ?"

"Hmmm?" He was sighing blissfully while spooning more of the rich *halwa* into his mouth, eyes half-closed.

"Julie has invited me over for a weekend stay at her parents' home in Ashmore, Dorset. Would you be okay with me going?"

He opened his eyes and looked at her in a measured manner.

"You want to go?"

"I'd like to, yes."

"Anu, this friendship of yours... " He paused, as if deciding whether or not to proceed further.

"Yes?"

"I'm just... Look, you've only known these women for a short time, and it's almost like you live in each other's pockets now. Don't you think it's all proceeding at a rather breakneck speed?"

"I've known them for nearly three years, Ravi! You've

met them, you like them. What's the harm in a weekend away?"

"No, no. That's not what I meant. There is no harm, it's just that sometimes it's nice to give each other a breather too. This constant intermingling can create friction. I see it at work amongst the women."

"So, you're telling me that men never argue?" She asked coldly.

"Anu, you're taking this the wrong way."

"You weren't even happy with me being friends with Simone!"

"But I didn't stop you, did I, when you insisted that she's nice? Now, you're upset with her and distancing your-self. I just don't want a repeat with these women."

"Ravi, I'm a grownup! With Simone, it was a different scenario. I always felt I had to live up to some unattainable ideal. But with these ladies, I can be myself."

"And which self is that, Anu?"

Furious with Ravi, she slapped on brushstrokes of crimson and brown to her painting, still not sure in which direction she was headed with it. They had barely spoken the previous evening after his last comment. She had washed up in silence and he had retired to the bedroom, falling asleep with his book on his chest, the bedside lamp still on when she'd finally joined him upstairs. She had taken the book out of his hands, turned the light off and slipped under the covers noiselessly. Later that night, when he had turned and hugged her in his sleep, she'd stayed stiff and unyield-ing, still upset.

He had left early that morning, giving her a quick kiss

on her forehead as she rushed about organising Neha's lunch.

Now, she stood back and contemplated her canvas, her mind still gnawing on their conversation. Was he shielding her from hurt, or not allowing her to spread her wings? And was she just a subservient housewife who took his word for law in every aspect of her life? Had the inability to work robbed her of more than just her financial independence?

In Delhi, much before they'd met, she had created a bit of interest around her paintings, selling a few through the modest gallery that had agreed to house her. In time, the curator had said, she would build enough of a reputation to command decent prices for her works. 'Audacious', 'daring', 'provocative' were the adjectives they'd assigned to her abstract art. Yet, she herself was none of these things.

Ravi had been the first serious match proposed for her, and her grandparents had gently nudged her towards settling down, weary perhaps of caring for a grown grand-daughter. She was much too timid to have sought men for herself. Her mother's reckless lifestyle had made her even more cautious with affairs of the heart. So Ravi, who seemed to fit all the criteria of a suitable life partner, was someone she'd agreed to marry without too much thought or hesitation.

In the ten years that they had been together, he had never treated her with less than tender consideration, loving and pampering her to an extreme sometimes. However, there was no doubt about who was the boss of the house-hold. She had always deferred to him, even when she hadn't agreed with him. But now, at thirty-five, a streak of rebellion was rearing its head inside of her.

She daubed a bit of green on her palette, considering where she wanted to add it. Her painting reflected her turmoil. Was it worth sacrificing the peace of their household over something as insignificant as a weekend away? But it was the principle of it that made her hackles rise. Why did she have to seek permission every time? Why did everything need a stamp of his approval?

Still in a dark mood, she walked towards the school with her head bowed, hoping to defer Julie's questions for another day.

"Excuse me," a shrill voice behind her called out. "Excuse me… "

She turned around to face Mia, the pregnant mother she'd sat with on the bench.

"Yes?" Her tone wasn't particularly inviting, but she figured that if this one could dish it out, she could take it as well.

"I just wanted to say thank you for the other day."

"Oh." This stumped Anu for a moment until, regaining her composure, she responded, "No need to thank me, it's quite all right. Is everything okay with you now?"

"I'm fine. It was just a bad day."

"Yes. I'm having one of those myself." Anu grimaced, not sure why she had said that.

"I'd be happy to sit with you on a bench if you like?" Mia gave her a shy smile that Anu couldn't help but return.

"Not today. But someday, maybe?"

They walked into school together, noticing that all the parents had gathered in front of a wall.

"I wonder what's going on. Let's check it out… " Anu looked at her petite companion, who shook her head and hung back.

"You go ahead."

· · ·

"Would you look at this?" Natalie was beaming at her. "It's absolutely beautiful."

The mosaic was finally up on the wall, displaying the scenic beauty of the countryside and all the village landmarks, put together painstakingly with bits of stone, glass fragments and tiles. Miss Davenport was standing next to it proudly. Upon spotting Anu, she called her over to stand by her side.

"This piece of art wouldn't have been possible without Mrs Dhawan's help. It was her vision and artistic sensibilities that have created this masterpiece!"

Anu felt herself blush as the head-teacher, Mrs Fulton, led a round of applause for her. From the back of the crowd she heard someone whistling and clapping and looked up to see Jemima cheering wildly for her. Then Miss Davenport started reeling off the names of all the helpers, and the mums came and lined up next to the mosaic wall, happy to be associated with a project that the children and they had created together.

She smiled at the ladies, happy that their community project was being appreciated thus. It had felt wonderful to work alongside the other mothers and children, even though she'd spent much of the time in silence, too shy to take part in their banter. Aside from Jemima, she hadn't really gotten to know any of them too well. Still, she had been a part of something that would now be a part of the school forever, and that gladdened her heart.

That evening, as Neha described how the handymen had installed the mosaic on the wall, and the children's excitement on seeing the finished product, Anu poured herself a glass of wine.

She refused to be the little woman in the marriage any longer. It was time to assert herself, and she would begin by informing Ravi that she was going to Dorset.

CHAPTER EIGHT

"I thought you'd never make it," Julie looked at her in the rearview mirror of her car. "It took you long enough to decide."

"Yeah, sorry about that. We were just trying to figure out the logistics of it all." Anu didn't want to tell them about the blazing row she'd had with Ravi just before leaving.

"You're here now and that's what matters," Jemima interjected kindly.

"Remember Tracy?" Louise turned around from the front passenger seat and looked at Jemima. "What a flake she was!"

"Oh God, I do remember...!" Jemima giggled. "Always making excuses and never on time. Where do you find them, Julie?"

"Ignore them Anoo. They call me a 'people collector' like I'm picking up strays all the time. Tracy just always seemed so harried that I felt sorry for her. Then I started inviting her out. She came a few times and then completely flaked on us after that. So, eventually I gave up on her."

"What happened to her?"

"What happened, girls? I can't remember." Julie turned left down a country lane.

"Wasn't there a husband whose foot was amputated because of gangrene or something?"

"And the older son was absolutely vile to her, as was the husband?"

"I think she was losing it at that point, anyway. Nutty as a fruitcake, that one... "

"But then our charitable Jules called her over for a weekend getaway!"

"Remember? She spent half the time crying and the other half on the phone apologising to her husband."

"Wasn't much of a weekend at all."

"Most depressing birthday I ever had."

"We got piss drunk just so we didn't have to listen to her anymore."

They laughed together.

"Where is she now?" Anu enquired tentatively.

"Divorced, dead, beheaded... who knows? It was a family of crazies. They moved up north somewhere."

"You won't believe this, girls!" Julie added excitedly. "She sent me a friend request on Facebook recently."

"So, not dead evidently?"

"Did you accept?"

"I'm not stupid! Of course I didn't."

"Anoo, we need to get you on Facebook."

Anu nodded dispiritedly. This was a new side she was seeing to her friends. She knew nothing about this Tracy woman, but clearly she had been in some sort of distressing set up. Why had she become the butt of their jokes?

It was dusk when they arrived at Julie's parents' house in Ashmore. Down a narrow lane, the detached house stood proudly within its plot. To the front there was ample parking for several vehicles approached through a gated entrance over a brick paved driveway that also led to a double garage. The attractive front gardens had pretty flower beds flanking the front entrance.

Julie parked her Range Rover in front of the garage.

"Dad's Jaguar and Aston Martin are in there. They are his pride and joy. So, we have to park here in the open. Leave nothing in the car, ladies. It's really safe here, but why take a chance?"

They took their bags out of the boot and headed into the house. The large entrance hall led into an elegant formal sitting room with a newly fitted log burner. Adjoining it was a beautiful Oak frame conservatory. There was an open plan, farmhouse-style kitchen with integrated appliances and French doors leading to the rear garden. The Aga in the kitchen lent a toasty vibe and the entire downstairs had been decorated in an old English country home style with plenty of plaid and plush velvet. Slate and oak flooring covered most of the ground floor with rugs of various sizes adding to the cosy atmosphere.

"It's lovely, isn't it?" Louise remarked. "Wait till you see the view in the morning. It's breathtaking."

Anu nodded. Mama would have loved a house like this. Maybe this is what she'd set out to achieve in Nainital, but hadn't had the energy to complete. At any rate, it was a beautiful home, and she complimented Julie on it.

"Oh, save that for the visitor's book, Anoo. Mum and Dad will be so pleased to read your comments."

"Did you know that our Jules was a rich bitch Anoo?" Jemima laughed.

"This is Mum and Dad's home, Jem, not mine!"

"Yeah, but you'll inherit it someday. Bet Charles is already licking his lips in anticipation!"

"Oh, shush!" Julie flicked a glance at Anu, then back at Jemima. "Right Anoo, let's give you the tour upstairs."

Dinner had been bread, cheese, salami and wine. It was pleasant to sit in front of the wood fire watching the flames dance together while they chatted.

"That movie you made us watch Anoo!"

"I loved it," Jemima said. "Why that tone?"

"Well," Louise drawled. "You'd think there were no problems in India, the way they dance around and wear those fancy clothes. And one minute they are in Mumbayy and the next in Switzerland. Where's the logic in that?"

"It's not meant to be logical. Most Hindi movies are just escapist fare." Anu retorted, a little stung by the unexpected attack.

"I much prefer movies like 'Slumdog Millionaire'. That shows the reality of India. The poverty, the grime… "

"I'm sorry," Anu stared at Louise. "All of India isn't poverty and grime! There's plenty of wealth in India, too. Some of the richest people in the world are from India. The Ambanis, Lakshmi Mittal…"

"Yeah, but it isn't equitable, is it?" Louise challenged her.

"Can we stop with all the socialism now? Drink up ladies, it's my birthday tomorrow!"

As Julie topped up their wine glasses, Anu felt a simmering resentment towards Louise, which she suppressed because she was sharing a room with her for the next two nights. But she was miffed enough to only mutter a short 'good night' and turn her back on her before falling into a deep, dreamless sleep.

❖

"Wellies on, ladies!" Julie shouted cheerfully after a quick breakfast of marmalade on toast. "It's time to work up our appetite for din-dins."

Anu had resolved to stick close to Jemima, even though it was obvious how close Julie and Jemima were. Louise had patronised her the entire way over, and last night too. It was bad enough that she had to share a room with her.

Julie had said upon arrival, "Dad doesn't like anyone staying in the master bedroom, Anoo. So, Jem and I will share, and you and Lou. That okay, luv?"

But this morning she'd had no shower gel in her toiletry pack, assuming that bathing soap would be provided. Louise had given her a look before handing over her shower gel to Anu. Where were these unwritten rules, Anu wanted to ask? Why hadn't anyone told her? Why was it assumed that she'd miraculously know this stuff?

As she slipped her feet into her brand new Wellington boots, she noticed the women glance over at her.

"Ooh, nice pattern." Julie whistled appreciatively.

They were all dressed uniformly in their Barbour coats and Hunter wellies, and there she was, in her bright pink Wellington boots and navy jacket that had seemed like a good idea when she'd bought them. Now, she felt out of place and as though she was speaking a different language altogether.

"That's a lovely colour on you, Anoo!" Jemima remarked kindly. "Look at you - always so glamorous."

Anu smiled back, trying to rev up her spirits. She'd be damned if she was going to let her insecurities ruin a perfectly good weekend.

. . .

The walk across open down-land with views across Cranborne Chase was a varied and circular one. It began on the west side of Ashmore, continuing through Halfpenny Lane before entering Ashmore Wood. Descending downhill to a rough tarmac, they turned left and followed the lane uphill until they found a gateway marked with a yellow Dorset County Council marker. They walked through the woodland, keeping the field on their left, and when they reached a 'Y' junction they followed the right-hand fork.

"This is so beautiful," Anu remarked, slightly breathlessly to Jemima.

"Oh yes, it's our annual tradition to come over here for Julie's birthday."

Anu looked at Julie and Louise striding ahead.

"Can I ask you something, Jemima?"

"Sure."

"What have you bought her as a present? No one said anything, so I just picked up a little something for her."

Anu still hadn't forgotten the sting of her last present faux pas, and so had erred on the side of caution by buying Julie a scented candle from John Lewis.

"That's sweet Anoo. I'm sure Jules will be pleased with whatever you've gotten her." Jemima pulled her boot out of a boggy part, grinning as her wellies squelched in the mud. "We just got her a few bottles of champers, you know. What else do you get a girl who has it all?"

Julie had never come across as anything but nice and down to earth, so it had surprised Anu enormously to discover that she came from an exceptionally wealthy background. But then, Jemima and Louise weren't short of a bob or two either. Jemima's husband Paul worked in the City, and made more than enough for them to have a vast house, a cleaner and a second home in Devon. Louise was a highly placed executive who had the option of working from home and occasionally going into her office in London. Even though she constantly complained about the stresses of her job, the salary more than compensated for all the difficulties.

Anu wondered how she had ended up in their gilded midst. Even though they were nowhere near as loaded as Zoe and Co., the very fact that they lived where they did placed them several rungs above their contemporaries. Ravi and she were well off, but they still had to watch their costs as they paid for their gigantic mortgage.

A part of her was excited to belong to this set. Her being accepted as one of them was a fillip. Maybe she wasn't the fraud she had always thought herself to be? Maybe she had finally found her place in the Universe.

"These are my kind of women!" She'd shouted at Ravi before leaving. "Well read, well spoken and worldly wise. I'm done with hanging out with losers! I'm done with being a loser."

Over dinner that night at a nearby Michelin star restaurant of Julie's choice, the server brought out two bottles of champagne.

"Girls! Not again!" She exclaimed delightedly.

They drank gallons of Veuve Clicquot, barely glancing at the bill when it arrived, divvying it up carelessly between them. Staggering home, Anu pulled her little present out for Julie.

"Oooh, whaz dis?" Julie slurred, tearing open the packaging. "Pretty! I love smellies." She pulled her close, giving her a hug, planting a sloppy kiss on her cheek.

But the next morning before they left for home and as Anu wrote her thank-you note in the visitor's book, she noticed the candle still half in the wrapping, abandoned on the window sill.

She never told Ravi the entire story. To him, it would always be the best weekend getaway she'd ever had. But her own mind wouldn't stop worrying over the tiny details of the mini-break. Then again, she reprimanded herself; it could be her own over-sensitivity to everything. As an Indian woman living abroad, there were bound to be differences between her understanding of things and theirs. She was a stranger in their world, and it was she who had to work harder to be accepted. They were just being true to themselves.

Unpacking after her trip, she put her mud-encrusted wellies outside, as if they were unwelcome visitors left to languish on the doorstep. It was time that she set herself the task of not just learning the subtext of their interactions, but also the uniform of it.

As she walked towards the school, she saw Zoe Frobisher's car pull into a vacant spot. She was the last woman Anu wanted to run into, but at this point it seemed unavoidable. She wondered if Zoe would acknowledge her or ignore her. She hadn't been spotted in the playground ever since her husband's infidelity had become public knowledge, but you wouldn't know anything was remotely wrong by looking at her. Sunglasses perched on her sleek blonde bob, she exited her Porsche, one leopard print-clad leg after another. Smelling of some exotic perfume, she looked over at Anu and smiled. Oh, so it was going to be an acknowledgement kind of day.

"Hellooo! How are you? Aren't I lucky to have spotted this parking space? Where do you park?"

Anu explained her fear of parallel parking to the willowy blonde, expecting to be made fun of. Instead, she listened gravely and remarked, "I had a deathly fear of parallel parking too. I even failed my first driving test because of it. But in this car, everything is automatic. I can even park the car after getting out of it through my phone, but I daren't try that!" She laughed. Anu smiled politely, not knowing which way the conversation was headed.

"So, how's your little girl doing? I heard she did very well in the SATs. My Sylvie was just a whisker behind her. But you Indians are so smart, anyway. All techies, right?"

"Umm, actually I'm a painter."

"Yes, I heard about your wonderful mosaic too. You must be so proud." And with that she sashayed away to join her usual group of friends, leaving a bemused Anu in her wake.

"What was that about?" Helen sidled up to her. "Blondie being all friendly with you?"

"I'm not sure. It was a very strange interaction."

"She's probably being uber nice to everyone, hoping she'll be viewed a bit more kindly. All the gossip must have gotten back to her."

"I would think someone like her wouldn't care."

"But we all have to live in this village, don't we? And our kids go to the same school. She can't possibly sit on her high horse feeling superior to everyone now that her husband's run away with the au pair."

Anu giggled at this, and Helen rolled her eyes.

"Do you know why that lot is so intimidated by her?"

"No, not really. I've always wondered though."

"She's like the fifth cousin twice removed of some minor member of the royal family."

"Oh. But how does that matter?"

"Anoo, that matters enormously. Anyone with the

remotest connection to our royal family is automatically elevated to another plane. We are still such a classist society."

"And you don't like this because?"

"Well, the likes of me come from humble backgrounds, and the likes of her never let us forget it. She may play Lady Bountiful to the hilt, but not before rubbing our noses in it."

"But all of you meet up for coffee mornings and all that?"

"All a facade. Have you ever been invited inside her house? No? Didn't think so. There is a definite hierarchy with people like her, and to her credit, she's never been a hypocrite about it either. She likes who she likes and the rest of the world be damned!"

That evening while tucking Neha into bed, Anu got in with her on a whim.

"Are you sleeping here tonight, Mummy?"

"No, darling. I just thought I'd lie here with you for a bit. How's school?"

"Okay."

"What did you do today?"

"Can't remember."

"Neha..."

"Hmmm?" Neha was busy flipping through her story-book, her eyes already looking drowsy.

"Are you getting on with the other girls in your class?"

"Yes, Mummy. Daisy has joined our group too."

"That's nice. Is that Jill Smith's daughter?"

"I don't know her mummy's name, but her name is Daisy Smith."

"Wasn't she best friends with Gina and Sylvie?"

"Yes, but now she's our friend. Mummy, can you turn the light off now, I'm sleepy."

With everyone ready to scatter for the summer holidays at the end of Year 3, Anu felt a sudden sense of disquiet.

"Why don't we go somewhere too?"

"Where?" Ravi was busy typing away on his laptop.

"Dunno. Somewhere in Europe? France? Italy?"

"Haven't you left it a bit late? It's mid-July. Everything will be booked up now."

"But how can I plan anything when I don't know what's going on with your work?"

"Hmmm, that's true. All right, let me see what I can find. Does it have to be abroad?"

"No, but it would be nice to have a vacation. Everyone else is going away."

"You mean your friends are going away? Many people do stay here and enjoy Summer too."

"What Summer? It's going to be a washout, apparently. The Met Office is predicting record levels of rain."

"Ha! This is England, darling wife. Of course it'll rain."

"Ravi, for once, can you not mock me?"

Ravi shut the laptop and looked up at her.

"I am not mocking you Anu. What's making you so antsy? I said I would look into it and I will."

"I'm sorry." Anu snuggled up to him on the sofa. "That was uncalled for."

Neha came downstairs and seeing her parents sitting together came and plonked herself between them.

"Libby's taking Buddy to Portugal with her."

Buddy? Ravi's eyebrows went up questioningly.

"Buddy's the travelling bear. Remember the one that went to Bath with us?"

"Well, that's one lucky bear!" Ravi tickled Neha's tummy.

"Daaaaaddy stop!"

"Jemima and Louise are going to Portugal for the Summer, and Julie is going to her parents' home in Spain." Anu volunteered.

"Good for them! Shall we go to Delhi?"

"In the heat? No way. Somewhere more pleasant would be nice, Ravi, and you can stop teasing me now."

He grinned at her, pulling them both close.

"Anything for my lovely ladies."

In the end they went to Stratford-upon-Avon. Anu had never been, and Ravi recalled a whirlwind visit in his student years, so that didn't count. He had booked them into a lovely Heritage Hotel set in acres of parkland and only a few miles from the centre of the famed home of Shakespeare.

They gazed in awe at the beautiful paintings and friezes decorating the hotel.

"This is wonderful, Ravi! How did you get such a good deal so late in the day?"

He tapped his finger to his head, but then grinned at her. "Last-minute cancellation. I just got lucky, I suppose. Come on, let's freshen up and go into town."

Once in the market town, they wandered the streets planning their expeditions for the following day.

"We have to see Shakespeare's house."

"Oh, and his mother's farm. Look, it says right here that Mary Arden's Farm is a working museum. We'll be transported to the Tudor times there."

"Anu, do you think this little one will sit through a performance at the Royal Shakespeare Theatre?"

Anu looked down at Neha skipping excitedly next to them and shook her head. "Doubt it. We'll have to save that for another day. But let's visit Anne Hathaway's house."

"The actress?"

"Don't be silly, Ravi. You can see right here that she was Shakespeare's wife!"

He winked in response, and she laughed back. When Ravi was in one of his silly moods, she loved him the most.

They spent their entire Saturday walking in the Bard's footsteps, with even Neha getting engrossed by the mini performances put up by costumed actors in his house.

"Why do they call him a Beard if he wrote stories?"

"It's not Beard baby, it's B-A-R-D. And he didn't write stories, he wrote plays. Very famous plays."

"And poems," Ravi supplied.

"In fact, he may be the most famous writer of all time."

Neha looked at them both and said, "But I thought it was the man who wrote 'Winnie the Pooh'?"

They burst out laughing and ushered her outside.

As they sat in a local restaurant eating their fish and chips, Anu commented, "It's really so sad that Shakespeare spent so much of his time away from his wife and children. Do you think it was an unhappy marriage?"

"Are you thinking of his bequest of 'the second best bed' to Anne?"

"Well, yes, sort of. I know little about the Tudor times, but that is a strange thing to leave in his will."

"Don't worry, Anu. I'll leave you our best bed!"

"Ravi!"

"Okay, okay." He put his hands up. "We don't know the context so we don't know if that was meant to be an insult, an afterthought or just the pragmatic thing to do."

"And here we are, four hundred years later, trying to solve the puzzle of his marriage... "

"True. But you know, what I find really fascinating is how well the British preserve their history. Every little detail is researched and documented, the monuments are taken care of, there is a genuine sense of pride in their past." He looked around the café. "All these tourists get a proper taste of the time period they've come for. Nobody is spitting or putting graffiti on buildings. No one is begging or pestering them here. This is how it should be, no?"

"Yes, but if you're comparing this to India, don't you think that's an unfair comparison?"

"In what way?"

"You can only instil a sense of responsibility and pride in people once their basic needs are met. How can you tell a beggar-child who is scrounging for his next meal that he shouldn't defecate next to a historical monument? What does he care about its significance?"

Ravi paused in his chewing and goggled at her.

"I'd never thought of it in that way, Anu. That is very true."

"I'm usually the first one to recognise the shortcomings of India, but let's try to understand how far behind we are developmentally as compared to the first-world countries. And imperialist powers like Great Britain bled us dry. It will take decades to recover from that."

"Yet, here we are. Living in the very country that bled us dry."

"It's a different time. We are working... well, you are anyway, and we are paying our taxes. So, we are giving just as much as we are receiving, right?"

"Fair point, well made."

Neha yanked at Ravi's arm. "Can we get some ice cream now?"

❖

The rest of August whizzed by so quickly that it was a mad scramble getting Neha organised for Year 4.

"Noni *masi* [1] is coming next weekend."

"Is that your best friend, Mummy?"

"And my oldest one."

"Like Libby."

"Well, if you and Libby stay friends all your lives, then you'll be able to say that too."

"But Libby is playing more with Daisy these days."

"Darling, how is that possible? The schools have been closed for vacations, haven't they?"

"Libby told me that her mummy and Daisy's mummy were going to the same place on holiday, so she would be playing with her more."

"But Libby's family went to Portugal, baby."

With exaggerated slowness, Neha said, "Aaafter Portugal."

Jemima had omitted mention of another holiday, but maybe Neha had gotten it all wrong. Anu was sure she would hear all about it when they met up on Friday. Julie had already been texting them about the new restaurant she had picked out.

On Friday, she parked outside the Italian restaurant, running in a bit late and breathless. Julie, Jemima and Louise were already sitting at the corner table with their drinks.

"This place is so cute!" Anu remarked, dropping into the empty seat. Red-and-white checkered tablecloths covered all the tables, and waiters dressed like Venetian gondoliers floated between them.

"A bit kitsch, but I heard the pasta is to die for." Julie remarked. "And how are you Mrs D? Did you manage to get away?"

"Only to Stratford-upon-Avon, but it was wonderful. Haven't got a tan like any of you."

"Don't need it either with that complexion." Louise commented dryly. "I mean that as a compliment, Anoo."

"Thanks. How were your vacations?"

They talked for a while about Spain and Portugal, and the difference between Porto and Tavira.

"We went to North Portugal and Louise to the south. She was in Eastern Algarve. Such a pretty town, isn't it? I thought you'd like it. We went last year," she explained to Anu, "and when Louise was looking for recommendations, I suggested it to her."

"Loved it! The hotel had a fabulous pool and we could barely get the kids out of it."

"Those are my favourite kinds of holidays, where the kids are busy occupying themselves."

"Well, mine got a bit mad for awhile!" Julie declared, having placed her order. "Guess who turned up at the villa?"

"No!" Jemima looked at her askance.

"Who?" Both Anu and Louise asked in unison.

"Only my worthless brother!" Julie exhaled, her cheeks reddening in anger.

"Wasn't he supposed to come after you'd left?"

"Apparently, he got his dates all mixed up!"

"And did he bring some unsuitable little tramp with him this time?"

"Thankfully, no! But Charles was so angry, he spent the

next two days in some pub avoiding the whole 'dysfunctional' lot of us."

This was the first that Anu had ever heard of Julie's brother.

"Do you not get along with your brother?"

"Get along? I despise him! He's done nothing but sponge off dad all his life. Never held down a job or had a single decent relationship. He's a mess, Anoo! I try to avoid him as much as possible. Wouldn't want my boys being influenced by him in any way!"

They spent the rest of their lunch swapping stories of their vacations and complaining about their husbands.

"I couldn't wait for mine to go back to work," Jemima giggled. "He keeps talking about taking an early retirement, but God forbid!" She crossed her fingers. "I think I'd end up strangling him."

"Oh, Paul isn't too bad, Jem. Bob is such a lazy arse I could barely get him to change out of his shorts! He just lay by the pool like a beached whale, drinking beer after beer, complaining about the terrible Wi-Fi. I think I need a holiday after that holiday."

"Ravi, ummm, he's such a workaholic… "

"Shut up, Anoo! He's such a lovely guy, and he adores you. Stop making up things just to elicit sympathy. No, none for you, Mrs, and I'm having that last cannoli!"

Ravi had dropped her off early at Heathrow so she could welcome Nonita when she arrived, while he searched for a good parking spot. Barely five minutes later Noni walked out, looking impossibly glamorous as always. Her hair was cropped short, giving her gamine figure an elfin look. Huge sunglasses were perched on her nose, and as she pulled her trolley behind her, she looked every inch an Indian Audrey Hepburn.

"Noni!" Anu waved excitedly.

"Hellooo *jaanu*! I'm here. I'm finally here!"

"I know!" Anu gave her a tight hug. "Is this all your stuff?"

"No! The rest of the stuff has gone with the team to New York. I just needed enough for a weekend here, that's it. One quick interview tomorrow, and I'm all yours the rest of the time."

"I like what you've done with your hair."

"It's so much easier than the bob I had. But look at you! My, my. Is that Chanel I spy?"

Anu blushed. Her recent partiality to designer goods had taken Ravi by surprise, but he'd indulged her few extravagant purchases with good grace.

"I thought since I'm mingling with a fashion editor, I'd better look the part, *na*?"

"Rubbish! You've never bothered before. What's going on, hey?"

Just then Ravi came up to them and enveloped Nonita in a big hug.

"*Saali,* I haven't seen you in years!"

"Now, whose fault is that? And look, everyone thinks you're cursing me!" She laughed.

Most Indians standing in the Arrivals area had looked around at his salutation, which could be interpreted as an abusive term, but in reality meant 'sister-in-law'.

"And is this Neha? My goodness, how tall you've gotten! I last saw you when you were this high. Mummy tells me you're in Year 4 now. Is that right?"

Neha nodded and smiled shyly, handing over the bouquet of yellow roses they'd picked up on their way.

"Welcome to the UK, Noni." Anu felt her heart swell with happiness.

Later in the evening, long after they'd eaten and chatted and caught up on all their news, Ravi and Neha retired upstairs, leaving the two friends to reminisce.

"How is aunty anyway?"

"The same. Abhishek is in and out of her life. Kriti calls to complain sometimes, but I don't think any of my other siblings really care what happens to her. Noni, your family was always so close knit. Even now Uncle and Aunty are happy living with your brother and his family in Sydney. Why did mine have to be so splintered?"

"Who knows why any of us are given the destinies we are. I miss my family so much, and I don't get to see enough of them. But then, I chose to live in Mumbai and do what I do, so I can't complain."

"Have you met anyone yet?"

"No one serious, but I'm not even looking. I'm happy being footloose and fancy free."

"It suits you! I swear you're getting younger by the day."

"And what about you, *jaanu*? Suddenly I'm seeing this very grown up, very polished version of the girl I remember in pigtails..."

"You wore pigtails too! But no, I'm just trying my best to assimilate."

"By chopping off all that lovely hair and buying designer goodies? What kind of assimilation is that?"

"Look who's talking!" She eyed Noni's stuff littering the room.

"Yeah, but that's my job and I admit, I like the good things in life too. But this was never you. Not that I'm saying you're not entitled to nice things, just that are you doing all this for the right reasons?"

Anu shrugged. It was difficult to explain her reasons when she barely understood them herself.

"Have you started painting again?"

"There is one piece I've been working on. I'll show you tomorrow. Ravi finds it too dark, but I'd like to know what you think... "

They talked a bit more over their Cognac until Nonita looked like she would fall asleep right there if she wasn't shown up to her bedroom at once.

"Sorry about my mess," she yawned loudly. "I'll clear it up tomorrow."

"Don't worry about it. Just get to bed now."

Kissing her lightly on the cheek, Anu wished her goodnight and shut the door before making her way back to her room.

Ravi looked up from his book as she came in.

"Did you have a pleasant chat?"

"Ravi, am I becoming a very superficial person?"

"In what way?"

"By buying all these designer bags and shoes?"

"If they bring you pleasure, then it's fine. You know that I don't see the point of them, but I wouldn't stop you unless it was prohibitively expensive."

"Noni said she'd detected a change in me."

Ravi drummed his fingers on the book.

"Do you agree with her?" Anu asked.

"Not exactly, not completely. But sometimes I do wonder if you're trying to keep up with the Joneses."

The next evening, Nonita and Anu went to a restaurant for dinner. Neha had pouted at not being allowed to accompany them, but Ravi had pointed out reasonably that she wouldn't like Mummy tagging along on her playdate with Libby either.

"This is nice!" Nonita exclaimed upon being led out to the alfresco terrace.

Anu had chosen this restaurant for its ambience and acoustics. Whilst buzzing on a Sunday evening, it still allowed enough privacy for an intimate conversation.

"How did the interview go this morning?"

"Oh, he was a pompous old ass, but I think I charmed him enough to get some decent copy."

"You've never lacked charm or chutzpah Noni!"

"And you, *jaanu*, have never lacked in talent. I love the new painting! It's quite dark and different from anything you've done before. How long before you finish it?"

"It's a work in progress." Anu said thoughtfully, knowing full well that she hadn't examined her feelings about this piece at all.

"And what will you do with it once it's finished?"

"Not sure. Ravi definitely doesn't want to display it. He says it gives him the heebie-jeebies!"

"That's not nice!"

"I know, right?" Anu grinned. "But it scared Neha, too. So, I might just hide it in the attic after it's done."

"Don't be silly! There must be a gallery you could approach?"

"And why would they take on an unknown artist?"

"Why not? How will you know unless you try?"

"Hmmm."

"Anu, there's another thing I've been wanting to talk to you about... " Nonita sipped on her cocktail before setting it down and looking at her square in the face.

"These women you're hanging out with, do they get you?"

"Get me? In what way?"

"I feel you're trying to change yourself to fit in. Don't lose who you are in the process."

"We all have to adapt to our environment, don't we Noni?"

"Yes, but not at the cost of our individuality."

"Noni, it's taken me long enough to find a tribe. Remember, it was you who'd said I needed to find women similar to myself?"

"But are they? Are they really similar? Do they want the same things out of life?"

"I don't even know what I want out of life."

"Then you need to find out. Anu, life's too short to dance to other people's tunes. I'm happy you have these friends and that you aren't lonely anymore, but I want you to expand your horizons, not allow them to shrink."

PART 3

"The fabric panels are quite large, Mrs Dhawan. Will you be able to paint them all in time?"

Anu leaned over the sketches she had drawn for Mrs Madhok. They'd been a composite of her ideas and the pictures that Mrs Madhok had sent her over their email correspondence. The result was a verdant backdrop of trees, flowering shrubs and deer that depicted *Vrindavan*, the mythological playground of the Hindu deity Krishna.

"Perhaps you could add a lake with some swans too?" Mrs Madhok suggested tentatively. "And a few peacocks?"

This project was growing by the minute, and Anu groaned internally at having agreed to it.

"I think I will need a bit of help with these or it will not get done in time."

"Yes, yes. I will get some other mothers to give you a hand."

"If I sketch the entire picture on the muslin panels, I'll just need a few people to paint the colours in. Then I can add the details of the leaves, etc."

"How many days will it take?"

How long is a piece of string, Anu wanted to ask?

"Well, if I come in every day, I should complete the sketch in a fortnight. Then it depends on how long the ladies take to paint it, only after which I'll be able to finish it. So, we are talking at least a month."

"Ohh, that long?"

"Yes, I'm afraid so."

"You know what's really annoying, Ravi?" Anu stirred the *daal*[1] in the pressure cooker, balancing the phone between her ear and shoulder. "She thinks I can wave a wand and have it done in a week."

"Anu, she probably doesn't realise the amount of work it entails. Have you got the time for it though?"

"Just about, but we're cutting it close. And she's given me that awful woman Jigna as a helper."

"The bossy one?"

"Yep! Who is now recruiting a rag-tag team to help with the painting."

"So, you're getting the help, and you're getting to know some new mums. Isn't that what you wanted, anyway?"

"Oh, I don't know. It seems more trouble than it's worth! Besides, these women haven't bothered with me in all these years. What makes you think it'll be any different now?"

"Well, at least Neha is excited that you're helping."

"Yeah, I think she's even more excited with her role of a cowherd. I don't think she's figured out that it's a bit part. The major roles have gone to Jigna's daughters, of course."

"Sour grapes, Anu?" Ravi laughed at the other end of the line.

. . .

Were they really? Anu wondered as she squatted and placed the fabric over wooden boards laid under plastic sheets. She taped the fabric securely onto the boards to prevent movement. Then placing the approved sketch next to her, she took her pencil to draw the horizon line. With slow, tentative strokes, she started outlining the scene. The more she drew, the calmer she got. Her mind stopped flitting about in irritation and instead focused itself on transferring the scene painstakingly on to the fabric. The few times she went wrong, she swore under her breath, correcting the trajectory of her pencil but working with utter concentration.

When her phone alarm rang, she nearly jumped out of her skin. How quickly the two hours had passed! It was time to leave, so she locked the door behind her, handing the key to the old man at the reception.

Driving home, her mind went back to worrying about whether she really was envious that Jigna's girls had been given major roles in the show. But it wasn't the girls she resented as much as the mother. All her life she'd been subjected to being pushed and shoved around by people like Jigna. Bullied at an early age for being too quiet and shy, she'd taken a natural aversion to aggressive, bossy women like her. To Anu, assertiveness did not come naturally, but it was more the complete disregard of other people's feelings that the likes of Jigna displayed that she found off-putting. To go through life barrelling along and stomping on people was an anathema to her.

"So we need to write you off for the next month?" Julie asked her in the playground.

"I'm sure I can take a bit of time out here and there, and my evenings are free."

"I meant for Louise's birthday lunch that I'd planned."

"I can't make the lunch because I'm committed to this project now. I'll explain it to Louise whenever I see her next."

Julie shrugged. "Let us know when you're free again."

"I will." Anu wasn't sure whether she was reading too much into it, but it seemed almost as though something had miffed Julie.

"Is everything okay, Julie?"

"Yes, why wouldn't it be?"

"No, nothing."

The door to the classroom opened just then and Julie moved off to collect her son, leaving Anu standing alone and bemused, wondering what she had done to give offence.

The sketch was very nearly complete when Mrs Madhok came in to look at it. She had Jigna with her.

"This is looking very nice, Mrs Dhawan. Very nice." She stood next to it, nodding her head approvingly.

"It's nowhere near complete. We still have to add the colour, and then I'll paint the details in to add the depth and dimension."

"So talented you are! Mrs Parekh has organised three other mothers to come and help you from tomorrow."

"Romaji[2]," Jigna looked from the fabric on the floor to Mrs Madhok, her eyebrows raised in disbelief. "We will have to go and buy the paints today. Don't you think this project is going a bit over-budget? This is a very large backdrop."

She flicked a glance at Anu, not bothering to hide her dislike of her. Anu returned the glance coldly.

"The background is exactly in the dimensions you

requested, Mrs Madhok. I have all the receipts for the materials right here."

"Of course, of course! That is no problem." Mrs Madhok looked at Jigna before continuing. "We will get a discount on the paint as my brother-in-law owns the shop, so budget is no problem Jignaji."

"Well, in that case you had better give us a list of the things you need."

As Anu reeled off the items - latex paints, rollers, stencils and brushes - she wondered how exactly was she going to work with a woman who was so clearly hostile towards her?

Being as busy as she was with the dance-backdrop project, Anu had been rushing Neha home after school every day. Today she dug her heels in.

"I want to go to the park!"

"Baby, Mummy is tired. I'll bring you on the weekend."

"No! I want to go today. All my friends are here."

Sighing with fatigue, Anu agreed reluctantly. There was a little bench free on the side of the park and she went to sit there on her own, letting Neha run off and join her friends on the swings. Today she just wanted a bit of peace and quiet.

She watched how the children played, happy and carefree, running from the swings to the merry-go-round and up to the slides. The little ones made castles in the sandpit, crying as another child carelessly knocked them down. Shrieks of happiness filled the air as children swung each other higher, while their mothers called out to be careful. Women congregated in twos and threes; mothers of classmates, friends or not. A merry, sociable spirit pervaded the entire park. There was a beauty to this part of the world; an innocence to this time that she felt like soaking up, instinctively aware that it wouldn't last. As their children outgrew the park and its swings, so would the mothers. These carelessly formed social bonds would disintegrate just as quickly as they had developed, leaving perhaps a lingering memory of days spent in the sun.

"Is this seat free?"

Snapping out of her stupor, Anu looked up to see Mia shading her eyes and pointing to the space next to her. "Yes, do sit."

Mia lowered herself with difficulty, parking her empty stroller next to the bench.

"Where are your little ones?"

"Poppy is on the swings and Ollie is In the sandpit. He loves it there, but I'll have to bathe him as soon as we get home or there'll be sand everywhere."

"I can imagine." Anu smiled at her. "Thankfully, Neha's too fastidious for the sandpit. She hates getting messy."

"She's such a sweet little girl. She's been very kind to my Poppy."

"Oh?"

"Some older girls were picking on her and your daughter told them off."

"I'm glad! Neha was bullied a bit when she started school, so I'm sure she understands perfectly."

"It's beautiful around here, but not everyone is very nice, are they?"

"It takes all kinds, I suppose."

"They've tried it with me, but I'm not having any of it." Mia spoke, a slow flush rising from her neck and spreading to her cheeks. "Who are they to judge me? They don't pay my bills!"

Anu recalled Julie's words about how combative Mia could be and stayed quiet. After a few minutes had elapsed, she asked, "When are you due?"

"Next month, but I have a feeling this one wants to arrive early." She patted her stomach. "Poppy and Ollie were early too."

"They are beautiful children," Anu said, looking at their white blonde heads. "But it must be hard work to have two little ones and another on the way."

"It's nonstop. I'm constantly exhausted and look at my ankles!"

Anu gasped to see how swollen her ankles were. Mia laughed and said, "It'll subside. It always does. Harry, my partner, is taking three weeks off to take care of me when the baby arrives. I'm going to put my feet up then."

Anu remembered the muscular, tattooed man who'd accompanied her to the park the last time. Then she wondered if he was the one who'd made her cry.

"Ummm, that day when you were... errr... upset, is... has... I mean, is everything okay now?"

Mia kept rubbing her stomach and looking into the distance.

"I'd just heard that my dad had died that day."

"Oh, no! I'm so sorry. I really didn't mean to pry."

"No, it's okay. I can talk about it now. In fact, you're probably the only person I would talk about it to at this school."

Anu stayed silent, waiting for her to continue.

"I hadn't seen him in many years. He left my mum when I was fourteen and moved in with someone else. Then he just drifted in and out of our lives as he pleased. I hated him for most of his life, which is why when I heard he'd died, I didn't expect to feel anything. But I did." She looked at Anu and smiled sadly. "How do you explain that?"

"Blood."

"Maybe. But men don't feel that way, do they? Their father didn't." Mia looked towards the park at her children. "He moved on from me too."

"And Harry?"

"Says he's loved me a long time. I've known him since we were little. Lived down the street from me. When their dad left, he found out and came looking for me. Hasn't left my side since then." Mia sighed. "You wouldn't know it from looking at him, but he's a real softie."

Anu felt ashamed of herself for judging them both, knowing nothing about them. It had been easy to assign labels because of how they looked and spoke, yet they were just normal people living through their own heartaches and life's little dramas.

She put her hand over Mia's.

"If you ever need anything, any kind of help, please don't hesitate to ask."

Mia patted her hand and stood up. "That's Ollie crying. I'd better see what's happened. Thank you for our chat. I'll see you around?"

Parking in her drive, Anu felt a subdued sadness. How right Simone had been! One could never tell what was going on in anyone's life, and a bit of understanding and kindness wouldn't ever go amiss. Sitting with Mia on the bench that day may have meant very little to her, but to Mia it probably meant the world. Yet, how little she had done to follow up on it. And when Simone had mentioned it, she had slowly severed her ties with her too. Had she really become so self-centred in the last three years that the very things that had upset her about her treatment at the hands of the school mums, had become her own blueprint?

"She's going to be ready for pre-school any day now." Anu remarked as she saw little Melanie chasing butterflies in the garden. They were sitting together in Susan's house, after a hastily cobbled get-together plan that had been arranged and rearranged several times over.

"I know! I can't believe where the last few years have gone." Cathy sighed happily. "And I'm sorry I've cancelled on you so many times. No one ever told me how often children get sick."

"That's how they build their immunity, dear. The sicker they are in childhood, the stronger they are as adults." Susan supplied.

"I certainly hope so! Was Neha a sickly child too?"

"Not really, but we did have a terrible time with the colic and the teething. Things settled down after that. She's had the usual colds and coughs, and the ruddy norovirus comes around every year."

"That's the vomiting bug?"

Susan refilled their cups of tea as they chatted about their children.

"Jan is visiting this weekend."

Both Cathy and Anu fell silent. In all the years they'd lived in the neighbourhood, Jan had only visited Susan twice. Each time she had either needed money or needed to borrow something.

"She keeps talking about getting me to release equity from the house."

Cathy frowned.

"Why? The mortgage is paid off, and you don't need the money that desperately, do you?"

"No, but she does, and when I protested, she got annoyed and hasn't visited since."

"But Susan, this is all you have aside from your pension. Does she not understand that?"

"She thinks that since it is all coming to her anyway, why not have some of it in advance?" Susan sat down, her eyes filling with tears. "I've only ever been a cash cow to her."

Cathy exchanged a glance with Anu, then went over and hugged Susan.

"I guess she feels a sense of entitlement as she is going to inherit the house someday."

"Her and Mark. They are both my children, even if one of them doesn't wish to speak with me. How can she just assume that everything belongs to her?"

"Then you need to tell her, Sue. She can't just bulldoze over you, don't you agree, Anoo?"

Anu nodded, completely appalled that Jan had the temerity to even broach the subject. It would break her heart if in the future all she represented to Neha was the amount she stood to inherit.

"No wonder these old people leave their money to dog and cat charities," Ravi exclaimed angrily when she recounted the episode to him. "Their kids don't deserve it!"

"Jan hardly bothers to visit... "

"And she'd probably be the first one to stick Susan in an old people's home."

"We are bringing Neha up in this country. Will she be the same?" Anu asked, her voice quivering.

"It depends on the values we instil in her. I have an

English colleague who is absolutely devoted to her parents. They are quite old and infirm, and she's moved them closer to her home, and takes really good care of them as far as I can tell. I don't think we can tar everyone with the same brush."

"No, you're right. But it's just so sad to see old people completely ignored in this manner. Where is the respect for age and wisdom?"

"It's being eroded the world over. Young people are too busy living their lives to be concerned about what happens to the older generations."

"But one day we'll all get old... "

"Yes, but who realises that when they're young?"

When Neha came out of the classroom on Thursday looking upset, it immediately brought back the early days of school when it had been a regular occurrence.

"Everything okay, baby?" Anu asked, concern lacing her voice.

Neha nodded, gulping hard. She held her mother's hand, tugging her out of the school.

Once in the car, everything came spilling out.

"... and then Daisy said that she was Libby's best friend, so I needed to stop bothering them when they were playing... "

"What did Libby say?"

"She didn't say anything, Mummy. She just kept drawing in her book without looking up."

"Maybe you need to talk to her on her own?"

"How, Mummy? Daisy is always with her! She even goes to her house for sleepovers now."

Recalling Mrs Pellow's advice from years ago, Anu reassured Neha.

"Baby, sometimes friendships change for a while. Then everything goes back to normal. Libby has been your friend for such a long time, I'm sure she won't stop being one all of a sudden. Let's just give it time, okay?"

Privately, Anu decided she'd try to have a little chat with Jemima about it. It couldn't hurt to bring Libby's mother into the picture.

Still busy with painting the backdrop, Anu hadn't seen Jemima in weeks, rushing off after dropping Neha at school each day. But the next morning she lingered at the gates, hoping to see Jemima saunter in with minutes to spare, as she usually did.

Sure enough, most of the mothers had already left when Jemima crossed the road with Libby and Emily. Only Jemima could look as unperturbed while running late. Depositing her children at the gate, she said, "Run along, you two." Then she looked at Neha and smiled slowly. "Well, hello you. Haven't seen you around lately."

"Hi Jemima, sorry I have been busy with painting that backdrop for the dance show. I thought Julie would have told you."

"Hmm, now that you mention it, she did say something."

"Anyway, listen. Really quickly, I don't know if Libby and Neha have had a falling out, but they aren't playing together lately. I wondered if Libby had said anything to you?"

"No, can't say she has." She shrugged. "But it's kids. They fall in and out of groups all the time, don't they? I'd just leave them to it if I were you."

"You're right." Neha nodded. "That's what I thought

too, but I just wanted to mention it to you, seeing as the girls have been such good friends."

"Ah, don't worry, Anoo. They'll sort themselves out in time." She made as if to move off. "Aren't you in a hurry?"

"I am! But before I go, I was wondering if you were doing some sort of group present for Louise's birthday. I won't be able to make the lunch, but I'd like to contribute to it."

"Oh! Sorry, but we've already bought her a spa afternoon. Jill chipped in as well, so we got her some nice treatments."

"Jill, as in Daisy's mother?"

"Yes, Jill Smith."

"I thought she was one of Zoe Frobisher's gang?"

"There are no gangs! Gosh, Anu, you make it sound so ghetto." Jemima snickered. "Anyway, I'll pass your wishes on to Lou. Take care, sweetie. We'll catch up soon, okay?"

Jemima crossed the road, waving back to her.

The day of the show dawned bright, albeit a bit chilly. Anu had gotten to the hall a few hours earlier than everyone. Jigna and her army were assembled there too.

It had been an uncomfortable few weeks supervising the mothers recruited by Jigna to do the painting. On the one hand, they had been excited to take part in the backdrop's creation, exclaiming over the sketch, happily following Anu's paint-by-numbers guidelines on what colours to put where. On the other hand, they were afraid of showing too much enthusiasm in case it put Jigna's nose out of joint. Anu herself had felt she was walking a fine line between being assertive in her vision and trying not to appear as pushy as Jigna.

In the end, she felt she had pulled it off. Over the last four days she had put in extra hours painting in the final details and stitching on the eyelets manually. She knew that she was going far beyond her remit, but it was important that she did a thorough job so that no one, least of all Jigna, could accuse her of being shoddy.

Now, as Mrs Madhok supervised the hanging of the backdrop in the theatre, she felt a surge of pride. The scene had brought *Vrindavan* to life. From every blade of grass to every peacock feather, her brushstrokes had created a colourful feast for the eyes. Even Jigna stood back, admiring the scenery, whispering to one of her friends.

Mrs Madhok beamed at her.

"This is beautiful. Truly amazing! I did not think it would be this good."

"Thank you." Anu stood next to her, simple satisfaction coursing through her. Whilst working on the backdrop, she had realised that nothing gave her quite as much pleasure as being immersed in her art. Which had led her to question why her incomplete painting still languished on the landing, a sheet thrown carelessly over it. She resolved to start work on it as soon as she had recovered from this entire venture.

Ravi and Neha arrived an hour before the show was to begin. He joined her in the auditorium after dropping Neha backstage for her costume change and makeup.

Letting out a slow appreciative whistle, he said, "So this is the finished product."

"What do you think?"

"Incredible. When you put your mind to something, it always turns out well."

"Really? I've never thought of myself as a determined person."

"Ask me. I've seen the determination and the doggedness, both. Anu, you just need self-belief."

"I'm exhausted, Ravi. I could sleep for a week after this."

"Don't fall asleep now. Our daughter will never forgive you for missing her star turn as a cowherd."

She giggled and poked him in the ribs.

"To think of the fuss she'd made being a wise man in the Nativity play."

"Oh, but here she gets to wear lipstick, so the length of the role doesn't matter!"

Mrs Madhok had choreographed the dance drama perfectly, and even the littlest ones did their best. When they went ever so slightly wrong, they just turned and copied whatever the child next to them was doing, lending the entire show a guileless, unaffected innocence. Neha seemed to enjoy herself, herding her invisible cows across the stage several times during the show.

"Is she really meant to make that many appearances?" Ravi whispered to her in the darkened auditorium.

"I didn't think so, but Mrs Madhok has probably extended the part as a sign of her gratitude."

Jigna's daughters played the roles of Radha and Krishna so well that Anu momentarily forgot quite how much she loathed their mother, immersing herself in the age old ballet of unrequited love.

At the end of the show, when the children had been given a rousing round of applause, Mrs Madhok was called on stage by the compere. The older girls brought out a large bouquet for her, which she accepted graciously, joining her palms together. Then she turned and whispered something to the compere who approached the microphone.

"We would also like to thank all the mothers who made this lovely backdrop, chiefly Mrs Parekh and Mrs Dhawan. If you two ladies could please come up to the stage too."

Shocked, Anu shuffled out of the aisle and walked towards the stage only a few paces behind Jigna. As they reached the stage, Jigna's daughters came out with another enormous bouquet of flowers, which they handed to their mother. Another round of applause emanated from the hall. Anu stood next to Jigna, her hands empty, the clapping bouncing off her like little pebbles. Her eyes caught Mrs Madhok's who looked dismayed and helpless, as though this hijacking of credit was something she had not foreseen.

Then she looked out into the audience and saw the curly-haired woman who had once chatted with her. Her expression was one of disbelief, mirrored on the faces of many other women who had been witness to just how much effort Anu had put into creating the backdrop. Holding her gaze, she walked up to the stage and took the microphone out of the compere's hands.

"I think there's been some mistake. It was Mrs Dhawan who designed and executed the backdrop. Mrs Parekh and the rest of the mothers were just the assistants. Jigna*ji*, maybe you'd like to hand the bouquet over to the person who really deserves it?"

As Anu stretched out on the sofa with a glass of wine, Ravi remarked, "I can't believe the cheek of it! She was planning to take all the glory, and the dance teacher was letting her. Thankfully, your friend spoke up."

"She's not my friend Ravi, I barely know the woman. But it was brave of her to take Jigna on, especially as her daughter goes to the same school as Jigna's girls."

"Still, I think there was a lot of support for you tonight. I heard so many murmurs in the audience. People will only take so much shoving around before they retaliate."

"You know, I'm so exhausted I don't even care. But if this incident has taught me anything, it's that bullies come in all guises. My natural animosity towards the woman probably didn't help my cause, but my instinct had always warned me against her."

"Always go with your gut."

"Ravi... ?"

"Hmmm?" Ravi's eyes were closed as he reclined on the armchair.

"My gut is telling me something's not right with the school mums."

"What, that blonde one? Zoe something-or-the-other?"

"No, Julie and Jemima. They've been kind of offish with me lately."

"Has something happened?"

"That's the thing. I've racked my brain thinking of what may have started it, but nothing. Absolutely nothing."

"Then don't overthink it. It's probably a combination of your nerves and exhaustion that you're reading too much into it."

"I hope so Ravi, I really do."

"I know so, love. A good night's rest will make everything better I promise."

❖

"Anu, you have always been hyper-sensitive. You take after your mother, you know."

Annie's call had come a week after Anu had left her a voicemail message. Maybe it was the need to get a female perspective on the situation at school that had made her reach out to her cousin, but she was regretting that decision already.

"My mother had been against the marriage right from the start, you know." Annie was on a mission to dredge up ancient history. "She'd told *mamu*[3] that your mother was all wrong for him, but he wouldn't listen, he was that besotted. But not for the reasons everyone else goes on about."

She took a deep breath, and Anu resigned herself to another half hour of hearing about all her mother's faults. Her father's side of the family, particularly Antara's mother who was his first cousin, had never forgiven Mama for her abandonment of him.

"*Mummyji* always felt that your mother was a lost soul."

This was new. Anu held the receiver closer. No one had ever said this about Mama before. She'd been called many things - a nymphomaniac, ruthless, cruel and calculating, a slut. But a lost soul? This she had to hear.

"It was like she wanted something out of life that it couldn't give her. She searched for it in all the men she was with. And even though I couldn't understand it then, I think I understand it now. Look at her Anu. Do you think she's happy? She may talk about liberation and feminism, but how has her life contained any of those things? And look at you. Why have you never found fulfilment anywhere? Now I'm going to say something you will not like."

Anu bit back her comment, thinking to herself that Annie had never spared her feelings before, so why the disclaimer now?

"You have a wonderful family - a husband that loves you and a daughter that adores you. What are you lacking that you keep looking for some kind of approval from outside? Why can't you be content with what you have?"

Anu bit her lip, unsure of how to answer.

"Don't turn into your mother, lurching from one place to another, frantically searching for something illusory. You'll never find happiness that way."

Annie's words had hit home. Much after she'd steered her away from the topic of her mother and chatted about various other things, her mind stayed firmly latched on to what Annie had said initially. Mama had always seemed so callously sure about her choices that it was strange to view it all from an altered perspective. If, as Nonita had pointed out, Anu was looking for a feminine presence in her life because of Mama's absence for most of it, then what on earth had Mama been looking for in her own?

It had been over a month since she'd spoken to her mother and Anu glanced at the clock, wondering whether she had the time for a quick phone call before picking Neha up from school. But she then decided that for the chat she really wanted, she needed more time.

On her way to school she saw Simone just ahead of her, hurrying against the icy wind, her shoulders hunched under a khaki puffer coat. Another person she'd been meaning to talk to.

Anu caught up with her, mouthing a breathless 'hi'. Simone turned around in surprise, said a quick 'hi' and kept walking.

"Are you free to go to the park this afternoon, Simone?"

"I wasn't planning to." Her tone was cold and forbidding, as though she hadn't invited this conversation and had no intention of carrying it on.

"I know it's chilly, but I just wanted to have a little chat with you. The girls could play together for a bit too."

Simone looked at her in an assessing manner.

"All right. I'll see you at the bench then."

From a distance Anu spied Julie, Jemima, Louise and Jill standing together. A few yards away Zoe, Dawn and Natalie stood chatting. She wondered about Jill's defection, but hung back instead of joining the first group. When Neha came out clutching her drawing, she smiled at her daughter.

"What's this then?"

"I won first prize!" Neha beamed.

"In what?"

"Design-a-poster competition. Mine's been picked for the school Christmas poster."

"That's fantastic, darling! Let me have a look. Oh, this is very good."

"Mrs Fulton showed it in assembly today."

"I'm really proud of you, baby. Well done! Fancy going to the park today for a little play with Kayla? I think you've earned it."

Anu felt a bit disingenuous selling it this way to her daughter, but watching her face light up, the guilt receded a bit.

Simone was already sitting on the bench when Anu arrived. Neha ran to join Kayla at the swings.

"They're pleased to see each other outside of school," observed Simone.

"I've been meaning to speak to you for a while, but just haven't had the chance." Anu said.

"What about?"

"Just," Anu paused, trying to formulate an answer. "You were right about Mia, and maybe about some other things as well."

"Oh?"

Anu laughed, a bit shamefacedly. "I'm trying to apologise, I guess, for being so remote over the past few months."

"No need. I figured you were busy with your friends."

"That's the thing, I wasn't, really. It was something else entirely. But now, I feel like I'm being frozen out by them, and I'm not even sure why."

Simone said nothing, staring into the distance. Kayla came running up to them, her hair having come loose on one side. She handed her hair band over to her mother, pulling the other one off too. At once, her hair puffed up into an afro.

"You have such pretty hair, Kayla."

"Thanks, Anoo!" She grinned before running off again.

"So they've dropped you." Simone commented dryly.

"I didn't say that."

"But that's what I heard. And now you need an ally again."

"You're jumping the gun, Simone. I just wanted to chat."

"Am I jumping the gun, Anoo? Am I?" She turned towards her, suddenly furious. "All these months you've ignored me, pretended you haven't seen me sitting on this bench when you've come to the park, swanned off with your shiny friends for lunches and dinners and who knows what else. And now you tell me I've got it wrong?"

She paused, drawing in a deep breath. Then she spoke softly.

"I'm not stupid Anoo, nor am I some kind of counsellor you can come to dump all your angst on. For a while there, I'd thought you were different. I'm sorry to say you're exactly like the rest of them. Vacuous, superficial and empty."

With that, she stood up and called Kayla over. As mother and daughter walked out of the park together, Anu's vision blurred with tears that had come unbidden.

"Mummy, why are you crying?" Neha touched her cheek with a frozen hand. "Did you and Kayla's mummy have a fight? Don't worry. It will all be okay soon."

Anu pulled Neha close, letting her tears drop to the ground. She didn't have the heart to tell her that adults were often more unforgiving than children.

CHAPTER TEN

A week had gone by since Anu's talk with Simone. She'd tried catching her eye several times since then, but Simone had studiously avoided her, leading Anu to believe that their disagreement wasn't just temporary. At a loss for how to navigate this strange and uncertain time in her life, Anu had taken to arriving later for drop-offs and pickups, occasionally even asking Ravi to take Neha to school.

The few times she had seen Julie and Jemima in the distance, they'd waved to her but never called her over to stand with them. Louise had completely blanked her the one time they'd passed each other in the school grounds. But with Louise always preoccupied with work, Anu wondered if her own imagination was playing tricks on her.

"My dear, you need to find a job." Susan said, while making her a cup of tea. She had gone back to her weekly afternoon sessions with Susan, craving the simple companionship their relationship offered.

"I can't do a job, Susan. Who will take care of Neha? Ravi is not in favour of au pairs and childminders. He believes that it's our job as parents to take care of our children."

"He's not wrong, my dear. But childminders aren't a bad thing. My Jan is one. Neha is what, nine now? She's old enough to stay with a childminder after school for a few hours. I think it would do you and her a world of good."

"But what kind of job could I do? I'm not qualified for anything except art. I have a degree in Fine Arts, but no experience. What kind of job could I get?"

"Why not start small? Sainsbury is looking for staff. Apply there."

Anu shuddered.

"Work at a grocery store? Can you imagine if any of the mothers from school walked in and saw me behind the checkout?"

"So what? There is dignity in all kinds of work."

"I don't think they'd see it that way."

Susan sighed.

"Anoo, the problem is that you're looking for friends in the wrong places."

That evening as they lay in bed together, Anu turned towards Ravi and said, "What would you think about me looking for a job?"

"You want to work?" He put down his book and looked at her.

"I just think I need something to occupy my time. Neha is older now and doesn't need me as much."

"I've never said you can't work, but how is it possible, logistically, with the working hours and the travel that my job entails? Neha needs the stability of at least one parent at all times."

"I'm not disagreeing there. It's just that Susan said it

might be an idea to expand my social circle a bit, find some new friends that way..."

"Oh, so we're back to the friends issue again?"

"You don't have to sound so bored, Ravi. I'm the one who is living this lonely life, not you. You have your work colleagues and friends, you still go for your drinks and dinners. It's me who has to sit at home and wait for you."

"I've never stopped you from going out. What about all those karaoke evenings at Julie's?"

"It's been a while since they invited me to one of those."

"Why don't you just ask them what's going on?"

"I've tried, but no one gives me a straight answer!"

"Then call them over for an evening here. That way you can figure out where the problem lies."

"That's a good idea! I could do a little pre-Christmas drinks evening. Call a mix of ladies and that way it won't be so apparent."

"Do it, Anu. I'll take Neha out for the evening, maybe go see that Narnia movie with her. That way we'll be out of your hair, and you can have a proper ladies' evening."

She leaned over and kissed Ravi on the lips.

"You're so good to me."

He turned over, placing his book carefully to one side.

"How about showing me just how good?"

She giggled and locked their bedroom door before getting back into bed with him.

"Guess who's stalking me on Facebook?" Cathy laughed while picking up Mel's toys from the floor. Anu had just parked her car in the drive after dropping Neha off at school when Cathy had called out, asking her to come in for a cuppa.

"I'm not even sure what Facebook is? I keep hearing about it."

"You're not on it yet?"

"Nope."

"Oh, come on! I have to get you signed up. But first that cuppa I promised you."

Cathy had the kettle boiling in the background while she placed a few biscuits on a plate. Anu played with Mel, looking through her well-worn story books and exclaiming at exactly the right places.

"So, this chap I used to date much before Andy asked me out contacted me out of the blue. And now he comments on everything I put on there. It's kind of funny but also annoying."

"What is this about?"

"Oh, it's like a platform where you can connect with old friends. You can put pictures up, what's going on in your life, stuff like that."

"Sounds intrusive though, with this chap from your past able to see everything."

"Oh, no! It's great fun. Let me show you."

Cathy pulled out her laptop, signed into Facebook, and immediately a screen popped up with pictures of her and Mel laughing into the camera.

"Everyone is on it, Anoo. It came out a few years ago, and like you, I was pretty leery about signing on. But I promise you, you'll never be bored if you do."

"Okay. What am I meant to do?"

Cathy talked her through the process, and Anu created an account for herself.

"You can add a profile picture later. Just remember your password, okay?"

"What if I don't find anyone on there?"

"Here, I'll be your first friend. I'm sending me a friend

request through your account. Once I'm signed into my account, I'll accept it. I bet you'll find plenty of friends on there. It's a great way to reconnect with your folks back in India too."

"Oh, let me check if Noni's on here!" Anu typed in her name excitedly, and sure enough, Nonita appeared, looking all glossy and gorgeous in her picture. "That's my best friend from Mumbai," Anu said proudly.

"She's very pretty! Go on, send her a friend request."

Later, after having exhausted her curiosity, Anu sat back and dipped her biscuit in the tea.

"Are you excited about Mel starting pre-school?"

"Yes, and no. I'll miss her like mad, but it'll be nice to get a few hours to myself. Maybe I can finally get to grips with the house," Cathy chuckled, looking around at the mess.

"Say Cathy, would you like to come over for drinks next week on Saturday?"

"Just me?"

"Yeah, it's like a ladies' evening. And it'll give you a night out. Will Andy be okay with taking care of Mel?"

"He better be! I've let him have enough evenings out with the blokes. I'd love to, Anoo! Anyone I know coming?"

"I was thinking of calling Susan too, and a few other mums from school. It'll be a small gathering, a pre-Christmas drinks do."

"Sounds lovely! I'll be there, with bells on."

That afternoon, Anu took the bull by its horns and approached Julie in the playground.

"Hi Julie!"

"Oh, hi Anoo! Where have you been? Still caught up with all your sketching and painting?"

Julie appeared just as warm as before.

"No, all that's over and done with. I was wondering if you and the other ladies would like to come over to mine for drinks next Saturday?"

"Anything special happening?"

"No, just a pre-Christmas drinks thing, before everyone gets too busy with family events."

"Sounds nice. I'll check my diary and let you know. Have you spoken to Jem and Lou already?"

"Not yet, but I was planning to. Oh, here they are... "

Jemima and Louise walked in with Jill next to them. They approached them casually, not betraying the tiniest bit of surprise at seeing Anu standing next to Julie.

"Hey girls, Anoo here would like us over for drinks at hers next Saturday."

Anu felt herself cornered into inviting Jill as well.

"Y...yes, if you're free. Just having a little get together at mine."

"Nice! Are you making Indian food again?" Louise asked, smiling at her. "I adore Anoo's cooking."

Jill wrinkled her nose. "Oh, I'm not a big fan of Indian food! Bloats me terribly."

"Well, actually I was just going to do some knick-knacks, not a full meal."

"Want us to bring anything?" Jemima asked.

"No, just yourselves. I've called a few of the neighbourhood ladies too. A small group of us, it should be nice..."

"Okay, why not?" Jemima nodded. "What time?"

"7 p.m. onwards?" Anu asked.

"Sounds good."

"Hang on!" Louise said. "Next Saturday? Oh, I'm out

with Bob. Some work do. Sorry Anoo, I'll have to give this one a miss."

"Never mind, Louise, there'll be other occasions." Anu smiled at her, hoping Jill would back out too.

"Actually, I think I've got something going on as well..." Jill said, right on cue.

"I suppose it'll be a smaller group then, hey Anoo?" Julie laughed, not unkindly.

"That's okay. We'll still have fun!"

Busy planning her evening, Anu nearly missed the flyer in Neha's bag, almost throwing it out with all the other scraps of paper Neha had collected in the course of a week.

Smoothening it out, she read:

'Fundraising Ball for Brownies.'

She remembered hearing the mothers discuss how much fun it had been the previous years and wondered if she could go, regardless of Neha not being a Brownie. Noticing the number at the bottom of the page, she rang it quickly before she lost her nerve.

"Hello?" A friendly voice chirped at the other end.

"Hi, this is Mrs Dhawan. Neha Dhawan's mother. She's in Year 4. I was wondering if it would be possible to buy a couple of tickets to the Ball?"

"Anoo, it's Natalie here! Rebecca's mum? Of course you can buy the tickets."

"Oh! Hi Natalie. Even if Neha's not in Brownies?"

"Goodness! That doesn't matter. Any idea where you want to be seated? Wait, there's still two places available at Julie's table. You're good friends with her, why don't I put you down there?"

"That'll be lovely. How do I pay you?"

"No rush on that, lovely. Pay me cash whenever you see me, okay? As long as it's before the 15th. You know that the ball is in January, right? Normally January is so gloomy after Christmas, so it'll be something to look forward to."

"Yes, you're right, it will. Thank you, Natalie, I'll bring in the money as soon as I can."

"No worries. Take care, Anoo."

Anu replaced the receiver, wondering if she should have run it past Julie first, but then decided to let it be. It would be nice to sit with someone they knew rather than at another anonymous table. Now, to convince Ravi that this impulse purchase had been worth it.

"Who will take care of Neha?"

"Helen has given me the number of this girl who babysits for her occasionally. She's reliable, a sensible sort apparently. Ravi, we haven't been out together in so long. This will be fun."

"It's black tie Anu. I don't even own a dress suit and bow tie."

"We can hire! That's what most men do, anyway."

"I can see you've done your research. So, are you hiring your outfit as well?"

"Actually, there's this dress I've seen... "

"Why doesn't that surprise me?" He grinned down at her. "Okay, why the heck not? Time to break out of the parent mould and have some fun."

"Aww, thanks Ravi! I'm going to pay for the tickets tomorrow then."

Excited, Neha made her way towards Natalie in the playground, clutching the money in her palm. Zoe and

Dawn were standing next to her and as they saw her approaching, they said something to Natalie and walked away.

She turned as Anu approached, her smile as friendly as always.

"My, you're prompt! Normally I'm the one chasing people."

"Yes, well, I thought I'd give it before you got busy with other things."

"Good call! Now, let me just find the papers." She rifled through her bag, pulling out a sheaf of papers. "Here we are! Okay, there's your name, so let me tick you off as having paid. And here's the seating arrangement... There, I've got you sitting with Julie, Jemima, Jill, Louise and all the husbands. Ten to a table."

"Thanks, Natalie."

"No problem! Look forward to seeing you at the ball. Are you going to wear a beautiful sari?"

"Umm, no. I was planning on wearing a dress."

"Sensible, I suppose, with all the dancing, but I love the Indian saris. Maybe another time you could wear one?"

"S... sure."

"Any plans for Christmas?"

"Not really. We were planning to go to Dubai to see Ravi's brother and family, but that got cancelled as my sister-in-law has to visit her parents in India. How about you?"

"Scotland, to see my folks. I am looking forward to it... "

As they chatted, Anu responded mechanically to Natalie's questions, barely keeping up her end of the conversation. So Julie had booked a table for all of them, without even asking Anu once if she'd be interested. Admittedly, Ravi and she had never been to one of these balls, still it would've been nice to have been asked.

"Have a lovely Christmas, Anoo. Maybe you'd like to come for one of our Friday coffee mornings next year? It's been a while since we saw you there."

"Sure, I'd like that." Anu smiled wanly, watching the children emerge from their classrooms.

Later she decided she would mention nothing to Ravi. Maybe her imagination was in overdrive, fabricating a deliberate exclusion. These were her friends, and they'd all agreed to come to her drinks evening. Why would they leave her out? It must have been an oversight.

On Saturday evening, Ravi and Neha left at 6 p.m. for their movie. Before leaving, Ravi gave her a quick kiss on the cheek, mouthing, "Have fun."

She had the Prosecco and white wine chilling in the fridge; the ice was already in the ice bucket in case people chose cocktails, and a few bottles of red wine stood on the sideboard alongside the wine glasses she'd lined up. For snacks, she had *samosas*[1] and *pakoras*[2] with mint chutney, some nibbles by way of cheese sticks and crisps, and bowls of peanuts dotted around the room. She recalled Cathy telling her that the mark of a good party was the amount of booze, not the amount of food, and tonight she was going to test that theory.

The living room had a cosy vibe to it, with the fragranced candles and tea lights she'd placed all around. There were cushions and throws for people to get comfortable on. She hoped it would be a nice, relaxed evening. One in which she could find out why she'd been feeling a change in her friends, and whether it was just in her mind.

Shortly before 7 p.m. she got a text from Jemima:

"Sorry, have had a bit of an emergency. Won't be able to make it tonight."

And just like that, she was down to three guests. Anu felt a slight twinge of shame looking at the extent she'd gone to in trying to create a perfect evening, but calmed herself down. It would still be okay, she assured herself under her breath.

"Hope everything's ok? Take care & don't worry about it." She texted Jemima back and waited for a response. There was none.

Just then the doorbell rang. Susan was at the door holding a pretty bouquet of lilies and a bottle of wine.

"How lovely you look, Susan! Do come in. You're my first guest. Sorry, a few people have dropped out so it will be quite an intimate gathering."

"That's all right, my dear. Even if it's just the two us, it will be fine." She placed her bottle next to the others on the sideboard. "The house looks very nice. I like all the candles and is that a new rug?"

As Anu handed Susan her drink, the doorbell rang again. This time it was Julie. Hiding her relief, Anu ushered her in.

"Glad you could make it, Julie. Oh, Lindt chocolates… my favourite! Thank you."

As she made the introductions, she wondered how this motley group of women would interact, but she needn't have worried as Susan was chatting away merrily with Julie.

When Cathy finally arrived fifteen minutes later, they were debating the merits of the reality show 'I'm a Celebrity…Get Me Out of Here!'

Anu gasped when she opened the door. Cathy was wearing a gunmetal grey dress with studs all over it, and a pair of vertiginous black heels. She'd swept her chestnut-brown hair up into a French chignon, and a bright red lipstick adorned her full lips.

"My goodness, you look like a model!"

"Don't be silly, luv!" She air-kissed Anu on both cheeks before making her way in.

"Sue, hi! Is this all of us?" She looked around the room, and when Anu nodded, she kicked off her heels. "Ooh, much better! They were killing me."

Before long, she was absorbed in conversation with the other women as Anu kept topping up their wine glasses, handing out the snacks intermittently. Slowly, they all relaxed, dropping their inhibitions and chatting more candidly about their lives.

"Andy is a sweetie, but his family! They are so annoying. I never get a break from them. Every weekend it's something or the other with all those nieces and nephews. It's put me right off having more kids."

Julie leaned in, fascinated. "How many do you have?"

"Just one little girl. She'll be starting pre-school in January."

"I think two is a good number. I have two boys and they get along so well. Any more than that and I think you're asking for trouble... "

"I have two grown-up children, but sadly, they don't really see eye-to-eye. Brought them both up the exact same way, but they are as different as chalk and cheese." Susan said.

"Oh, it's the whole nature vs nurture debate, isn't it? You can't change who they are personality-wise, even if they've grown up in the same environment." Cathy said.

"Gosh! You're clever." Julie looked at her. "And pretty. Anoo didn't tell me she had a supermodel living on her street."

Cathy laughed. "I just scrub up well, and it's been such

a long time since I went out anywhere I might have gone a bit overboard." She looked down at her dress, shrugging in a self-deprecating manner.

Anu was hoping to have a private word with Julie, but so far Julie had stuck to Cathy's side, so she went and sat next to Susan.

"What are you doing for Christmas, Susan?"

"Jan said she'd pick me up and take me to hers. I am looking forward to spending time out of my house for a change."

"That's nice of her."

"Well, she was very upset when I wasn't willing to sign the documents at first, but once I agreed to consider it, she suggested the Christmas plan."

"I see. Did you find out any more about the legalities of it all?"

"I did, and as long as I have Mark listed in my will, I should think it will all work out."

"As long as you're happy with it... " Anu said, trying to hide her doubts.

There was a sudden buzzing noise, and they all looked around for their phones.

"It's mine, it's mine!" Julie brandished hers, reading the text message that had popped up. "Oh, dear!" She bit her lip.

"Everything okay?"

"Lou's locked out of her house, and Jem's got the spare keys, but she's not answering her phone."

"I think there was some kind of emergency, which is why she didn't come today... "

But Julie wasn't listening. She had already dialled Jemima.

Both Cathy and Susan had fallen silent, watching them with interest.

The phone rang for a bit, then Jemima picked up.

"Jem! Lou's been trying to get in touch. What? Oh, you've given them to her. Good! She was panicking... Yeah, no, I'll see you soon. Bye, luv. Bye, bye."

"Crisis averted?" Susan asked Julie when she'd hung up.

"Yes, thankfully! Jem was soaking in the tub and didn't hear her phone the first few times. But luckily she picked up soon after."

"And the emergency?"

"What emergency?"

"Jemima said something had happened... "

"Not to my knowledge. She just wanted a soak in the bath for a bit. You know Jem, she can be so lazy."

Anu's heart lurched at the realisation that Jemima had lied to get out of the evening. What did that say about their once fast friendship?

Christmas was quiet. They'd placed a few presents under the tree for each other, and Anu had hung up a stocking for Neha with little books and oranges as stocking fillers. She'd bought Neha some toys, and Ravi the cologne he'd been coveting the last few months. But come Christmas morning, there was an enormous package with her name on it under the tree.

"What's this?"

"Open it. You won't find out until you do."

She unwrapped the package carefully, revealing a Professional Artists Oil Colour box that contained a variety of oil paints and accessories. There was a wooden palette, a painting knife, three charcoal sticks, brushes, white spirit, a colour mixing brochure and a variety of oil colours.

"Ravi!" She gasped. "This is too much."

"No, I don't think it is. I saw you trying to squeeze colour out of those tubes you have upstairs. How old are they anyway? So, this is absolutely spot on."

"My goodness, it's wonderful! I feel so guilty now for not doing enough painting."

"As you should! This is my little kick up your rear to get you started again. Why don't you finish that scary one first, and then maybe you can paint something more cheerful?"

She hugged him, nodding, too choked up to say any more.

After a lunch of turkey and trimmings that he'd insisted on cooking, they lazed in front of the television, watching Neha lick her ice cream as she assembled the Lego that Ravi had bought her.

"You never told me how that drinks evening went."

"It was okay."

"Did you find out what was going on with those ladies?"

"No, not really. Didn't get a chance to talk to Julie much. She was much too fascinated with Cathy that evening."

"She looked amazing, Anu. My mouth fell open when I saw her leaving as we arrived."

"Not you too!" Anu elbowed him in the ribs.

"Oww! Here have some more cheese."

He poured her a glass of port to go with the Brie.

"Cathy is the flavour of the month now. Julie's invited her to the Ball."

"I thought the table only sits ten?"

"She's not sitting at our table, but Andy and her will be at one nearby. Julie is making sure of it."

"Do I detect jealousy?"

"Of course not. You know how much I like Cathy. I'm just not sure anymore about what the politics of the situation are?"

"Politics of the situation? Aren't you reading too much into it? It'll be fun to have Cathy and Andy there. At least there'll be another bloke I know, not just the husbands of these ladies."

"That's true. I think you'll enjoy it, Ravi. When was the last time we danced the night away?"

"Not for a long, long time. But madame, that can be amended straight away."

With that, Ravi turned up the volume on the Christmas carols, hauled her out of the sofa despite her protestations and started twirling her around the room. Neha sat up, clapping her hands and squealing. He grabbed her as well, and they ended up dancing together. In that moment, Anu felt such unadulterated happiness that she thought her heart might burst with it.

CHAPTER ELEVEN

When they got to the Ball, it was already past 8 p.m. and Anu was slightly panicked at being late.

"It's a ball, Anu, trust me, they'll still be drinking and mingling. The dinner won't be served till 8:30 p.m., remember?"

"I know Ravi, but I've got this fear of being late…"

"Of being judged, you mean? As if these people don't have issues that delay them."

"What was wrong with Neha?"

"Nothing. She was just a little freaked to be left with someone she doesn't know."

"But Lauren seems like such a sweet girl? I'm glad she calmed Neha down."

"They'll be fine. If there's any trouble I'll go, okay? You can stay and enjoy yourself."

"If anything happens, we'll both leave. I don't want to stay without you."

"Okay, deal! Now, let's go have some fun."

. . .

Julie, Jemima, Louise and Jill were all chatting together at the table. Their husbands were standing at the bar. Ravi gave her hand a gentle squeeze.

"What did I tell you?"

Anu approached them, noting how absorbed they were in their conversation. Louise was the first one to look up.

"Oh look, Anoo's here. What a pretty dress that is!"

"Thank you," Anu mouthed, slipping in next to them.

Jemima didn't betray the slightest hint of embarrassment at having been caught out in the midst of a lie as she remarked, "Have you been to the hairdresser's? That's a pretty elaborate hairdo!"

Anu had gone the extra mile, not knowing just how much one needed to dress up for these parties. A ball sounded grand, so she'd had her hair done professionally. But looking around her, she wondered if she'd overdone it. The women at her table had a casual elegance about them, as if they'd pulled an old frock out of their wardrobes, thrown it on with a few diamonds and a slick of lipstick, brushed their hair and headed out. In comparison, her efforts seemed ludicrous.

She wondered whether asking Jemima about her excuse would be enough of a repartee, but decided not to. What was the point, anyway? So, she just smiled and shrugged, looking around to see if Cathy and Andy had arrived.

It didn't take long to spot Cathy, who was surrounded by a group of admiring men and women.

"Who is that woman?" Jill asked, looking in the same direction as her.

Cathy was wearing a fitted red dress, with a neckline that plunged down to her navel. Her long hair was swept to one side reminiscent of Veronica Lake, her earlobes and wrists glittered with a profusion of diamanté's that gave the entire ensemble an old Hollywood vibe.

"She's the one I told you about. Anoo's neighbour. Isn't she gorgeous?"

"Mmmm. Let's call her over before she gets swooped up by Zoe's lot."

Zoe had just walked in with a handsome older man.

"Oooh, look Jill! Look who's just walked in."

"She's looking very thin, isn't she?"

"Is that Balenciaga?"

"It would be, with Zoe! She doesn't do Karen Millen."

Anu leaned towards Jill and asked, "Didn't you used to be good friends with Zoe?"

Jill gave her a look that could curdle milk.

"We're still friends."

"Oh. I just thought… "

"Well, don't."

When the men came back to the table, they sat in the alternate fashion that the table placements indicated. Anu had Ravi on her right and Paul, Jemima's husband, on her left. Ravi was busy chatting with Louise, so Anu turned to Paul, not sure how to start a conversation. She'd only met Paul in passing, and knew him to be a quiet, gentlemanly sort. Thin and greying, he was Jemima's perfect foil, never saying much to her outlandish ideas, her strange obsessions, and her extravagant habits. This she knew because of all that Jemima had told her over the years. There was a solid kind of love there, which Anu wondered if Jemima truly appreciated. At any rate, he was always happy to leave the ladies to their karaoke or movie evenings, saying a quick 'hello' before melting into the background.

"This is nice, isn't it?" She said, hoping it would be enough of an opening.

"Yes." He nodded, biting into the carpaccio.

"Although," he took a sip of his water, "after a while, they all blend into one. I couldn't tell one ball apart from another."

"It's my first one, so I am quite excited! Ravi has loads of work things he goes to in London, but I don't really get the opportunity."

"Then I'm glad you're enjoying it." He smiled at her kindly. "Jemima tells me you're an artist?"

"I used to be. Not really much of one now. I've got this one piece that I've been working on for such a long time that I think Ravi's given up hope that I'll ever complete it."

"Tell me, do you have some sort of idea in your mind, or is it all very organic the way you paint?"

"I think it's a bit of both, really. I mean, a lot of it is very emotional with me. Normally I start a painting as a response to something that's going on in my life, then I keep layering those emotions on in different ways. So, it can begin as one thing and end up as something else entirely!"

"And why is this latest one taking you so long?"

"A lot of it is just my being confused internally... " She paused as the waiter took away their appetiser plates and refilled her wine glass. "When I can't make sense of my emotions, I tend to stall."

Later, as the desserts were being served, Ravi leaned her way conspiratorially. "You're getting along well with what's-his-name?"

"Paul is his name Ravi, don't be rude. He's really nice, much more than Jemima's ever led me to believe."

"Well, this is one smart lady on my right. Did you know she's the head of... "

Just then Andy clapped his hands on Ravi's shoulders.

"Hello mate! Been wanting to come over and see you, but they keep feeding us. How are you, Anoo?"

She smiled up at Andy, wondering where Cathy had gotten to.

"Must say, I wasn't keen on coming, but Cath insisted. I'm glad we did, though. Friendly folk here. I'm making loads of connections for my business too."

Ravi and he fell into a conversation as Anu scanned the room. She spotted lots of familiar faces. At one point Natalie, dressed in electric blue, waved to her from the other side of the room. Zoe, shimmering in her gold ensemble, table-hopped with a glass of wine in her hand, her escort moodily following her.

Mums she only saw in passing in school looked glamorous in their sparkly dresses and heels, their husbands bonding together over their beers.

Paul had left the table, so she looked to her left at Jemima, who had taken a bite of her dessert and pushed the plate away.

"Don't you like it?"

Anu had polished off her own Tiramisu, loving every bit.

"It's okay. I'm really quite full. I see that you liked yours?" She grinned at Anu, a glimpse of the earlier Jemima emerging.

"You know what a sweet tooth I have..."

"Staying for the dancing?"

"Yes, but only till 1 a.m. Then we have to go home to relieve the babysitter."

"How are you getting home?"

"Oh, we'll get a cab. Ravi will call for one."

"Anoo, don't be silly. You'll never get a cab on a Saturday evening. All these people have probably pre-booked theirs."

"I didn't realise... "

"Don't worry, I'll get Paul to drop you home."

"No, no. We'll figure something out. Please don't bother Paul."

"It's no bother. You know he doesn't drink, so he'll be happy to drive you home."

When they were on the dance floor, Anu told Ravi of Jemima's offer. The music was so loud she had to lean towards him, shouting it into his ear.

"That's cool!" He gave her a thumbs-up, happy to boogie away.

She danced self-consciously, looking at all the surrounding couples who seemed to be having a grand time. She should have been enjoying herself similarly, but a familiar thought nagged at her. She didn't belong, she would never belong.

A lady in a short black dress shimmied past her, another mother from the school whose name Anu did not know. She would never have recognised her if it wasn't for her distinctive pageboy haircut. Normally always in sensible trousers and shoes, this transformation was startling. Coy at times, flirtatious at others, the woman danced with all the school dads in her vicinity, spinning and twirling, crooking her index finger in a 'come hither' way to her next partner. Anu wondered who her husband was, but in a sea of penguin-like men, it was impossible to distinguish him. So many of the mothers looked and behaved so differently, as though they had shed their normal personas to emerge Cinderella-like, transformed for this one night alone. She wondered what they thought of her. Did she still come across as dowdy or was her glammed-up self matching up to theirs?

Two arms encircled her from the back, and Anu nearly jumped out of her skin. She turned around to look into Cathy's laughing face.

"Little Anoo! You look so scared. Nobody's going to bite here. They are all wonderful... just wonderful... "

Anu laughed at an obviously tipsy Cathy, hooking her arm with hers and thinking to herself, this is wonderful, stop all your silly worrying!

❖

Once the babysitter had been paid and dispatched, and Neha looked in on, Anu left the door to their ensuite bathroom open as she wiped the makeup off her face

"Did you enjoy yourself tonight, Ravi?"

"Yes, it was fine."

"Just fine?"

"No, it was nice. But more importantly, did you have fun?"

"Oh, I loved it!" Anu swiped the eyeliner off an eye, then looked out at Ravi sprawled on the bed, his arms behind his head, almost dozing. "But there was a moment there when I felt like we were... I was... a bit out of place."

"When was this?"

"On the dance floor. I don't know, it was a strange feeling. I get it sometimes."

"I noticed that your friends didn't dance at all."

"Yeah, that was a bit odd. They seemed happy to sit and chat."

She got into bed with him, smelling of minty toothpaste and lingering perfume, her hair unpinned and falling in waves on her shoulder.

Ravi nuzzled her shoulder.

"Anu..."

"Mmmm?"

"Don't mind what I'm about to say."

Her eyes flew open, and she turned to him inquiringly.

"You do know that they were all headed to Jemima's place afterwards?"

"What?"

"Yeah, I heard the other husbands discussing it. They were going over for a nightcap. One of them - Charles, is it? I think he saw I'd overheard, and he just gave me a sheepish look and changed the topic."

"Who was going?"

"Everyone at that table but us."

"I see."

"I didn't want you to find out later from someone else."

Her eyes filled with tears.

"And here I thought Jemima was being so kind, getting Paul to drop us off."

"Anu, listen! Look at me. Shhh, no tears please. These aren't your friends, not really. I think the sooner you come to terms with this, the better it will be."

"But what have I done, Ravi? Why have I suddenly been cut out like this?"

"Does it matter? From what I saw today, and from what I've heard from you over the last few months, these are shallow women. You were an amusement for a while, and now they're bored with you. They've moved on to newer and shinier toys. Let it go, Anu. It's their loss much more than it is yours."

Loss was a word Anu had lived with all her life. From losing her father as a toddler to never having the stable influence of a mother, from living in a hostel to moving in with her elderly grandparents, she had never once felt that anything in her life was solid or concrete. Not until Ravi and Neha had she ever been able to call someone her own. In her futile search for belonging and sisterhood, she had invested far too much in the wrong people. Why couldn't she be like the others - able to take or leave relationships? Able to accept people at face value and not delve too deep into their motivations? Was her intensity, her commitment, a turnoff? Was she herself so pitiable, so contemptible, that she could only repel those that she wished to belong with?

The edges of her canvas seemed to ooze with the darkness of her despair. The black paint that she applied layer after layer enhanced the crimsons and the browns she had started out with. With each additional brushstroke, she painted on her loneliness, her anger and the sharpness of the rejection inflicted upon her. It was easy for Ravi to say "let it go", for Nonita to tell her not to change, for Simone to accuse her of being vacuous. But what did they understand of her need to belong? This need that sprung up from some deep, hidden place that propelled her to search for unconditional acceptance. If only love was enough - because love she had, from her husband and her daughter, who were her world. Yet this need, this desire, was something entirely different. Perhaps it was wanting to set down roots in a land and amongst people who were not her own, or perhaps it was a symptom of her acute and inescapable loneliness.

Emptying her emotions on the canvas should have been cathartic. Instead, she felt bereft.

Looking at the painting in front of her, she realised that it had morphed to something beyond the original horror show that Ravi and Neha had recoiled from. There was something disturbing about it now, as though every curve and every sharp corner was designed to weep as well as wound. It was not complete, but in its incompleteness, it screamed a silent and plaintive cry - a plea for understanding. A plea that seemed to come from a void and fall on deliberately deaf ears. No words could capture the emotions that swirled upon that canvas. No words were needed.

Suddenly exhausted, Anu stepped away from her painting, unable to look at it any more. She was done. If it was to be unfinished, then so be it. Turning her back on it, Anu decided that it was time to turn her back on this chapter of her life too.

Determined to put on a brave face, Anu smiled at the group of mothers gathered at the gate as she ushered Neha in on Monday morning. What good would it do to show her hurt? So she pretended to be preoccupied, waving briefly at Julie as she walked back to her car.

Getting in, she decided that she was through with looking for approval or acceptance. Yes, it would have been nice to have had a group of good and loyal friends, but maybe it just wasn't meant to be. Maybe people like her didn't get things like that. Maybe they didn't deserve it.

At home she cleaned the house from top to bottom, emptying her mind as she did. The music was on, loud, too loud, so that nothing but the drum beat would fill her as she scrubbed the floors.

Later, after she had cooked and showered, she went upstairs to look at the painting. Ravi had seen it over the weekend but said nothing. Instead, he'd pulled her close and held her against his chest for a long time. Now, she examined it anew.

There was a raw energy about it that was compelling. It was undoubtedly dark, one of her darkest works ever. From the way she had layered the paint, creating grooves with her nails, it seemed like the rivers in Hades, her own personal hell swirling in front of her. The black converged upon the crimson and mahogany in the centre, as though at the very heart of this darkness lay an exposed and bleeding heart.

Was it good? In the cold light of day, it seemed as if it was her best work. But was she being objective enough? Replacing the muslin cover over it, she mulled over the possibilities. Was it worth approaching a gallery? How did one go about it, anyway? In India it had been easy. Word-of-mouth had ensured her first foray into the art world. Here, she knew no one, and she herself was an unknown quantity. Who would take a chance on her?

Still lost in her own thoughts, Anu didn't notice Natalie's car next to her own when she went to pick Neha up. She was a few minutes early, and she'd brought her book to read, but when Natalie knocked on her car window, she reluctantly rolled it down, hiding her irritation.

"Anoo, did you enjoy the ball? We raised a lot of money, and I wanted to thank you and your husband for bidding for the weekend away, even though you didn't win."

"Oh, that's no problem. We enjoyed ourselves very much, thank you."

"Great! Well, I'll add you on to our email list for next year." She smiled down at her kindly. "Shall we walk together?"

Anu locked her car and fell into step with her. Fortunately, with Natalie, she'd never needed to worry about small talk, as Natalie had a comfortable way of filling silences with random observations and harmless chatter that soon put the other person at ease.

"That was a lovely black dress you had on that night. Very chic!"

"I liked your blue dress too."

"We're all like peacocks, aren't we? Showing off our gaudy feathers. Although your table I recall was mostly monochrome. Was it planned?"

Anu let out a surprised laugh.

"No, not at all. I didn't have a clue what the others were wearing."

"Well, you all looked very coordinated indeed. Oh look, there's Zoe!"

Anu's heart sank as she saw Zoe walk over to them. This was one thing she could have done without at the start of her week.

"Hi Nat, hi Anoo." Zoe said tonelessly. Anu noticed how gaunt she was looking. Divested of her designer togs, she looked skeletal in her jeans and jumper.

Anu murmured a polite 'hello' before moving away from them. They barely noticed her leave, falling into a deep discussion. In the distance she saw Jemima walk in with Louise, but pretended to fiddle with her bag strap so she could avoid their eyes.

Grabbing Neha, she fairly scooted out of the school gates, almost making it to the car before she heard Natalie's voice behind her.

"Hey Anoo, hold up! Gosh, you were going so fast there... "

Neha and Rebecca immediately started giggling and examining each other's nails, while Natalie gently took Anu's elbow and steered her over to the other side of the car.

"I'm sorry about earlier, I realised how rude we must have come across to you."

"It's okay. No, really, I didn't mind."

"It's just that... " Natalie seemed to be weighing up in her mind whether or not to proceed. Then, as if reaching some internal decision, she gave a brief nod before saying,

"Zoe's going through a really tough time right now. The divorce caught her completely by surprise."

Anu wasn't sure what to say to this, so kept quiet.

"She's been pretending she's fine, but she's not. Not really."

"I'm sorry to hear that." Anu was sorry, but just barely, remembering the several times that Zoe had treated her like she was a bit of dirt on her shoe.

"I was thinking of doing a little lunch to cheer her up. Would you like to join us?"

"That's really nice of you, Natalie, but I'm very caught up in stuff right now, so I'll have to take a rain check on it."

"Sure! I just thought I'd mention it."

Driving away, Anu half-listened to Neha's story but wondered alongside if she'd responded correctly to Natalie. Her resolve to separate herself from the mothers had been tested today, but instinctively she had known that the only answer she could give was in the negative. She had no intentions of getting burnt again.

In the days that followed, Anu occupied herself by clearing out the wardrobes, mending the things she had put off for a while, and running the errands she had procrastinated on. There was a simple satisfaction to be derived from finally completing long overdue tasks.

On Thursday she decided to tackle the emails that had clogged up her inbox. 1042 unread! Who were all these emails from? Then she looked through them and realised they were mostly notifications from Facebook. She had completely forgotten about being signed up to the site by Cathy.

Determined, she deleted all the emails and then signed in to Facebook, thankful that she had picked an easy password she could recall. She intended to get rid of the notifications and sign herself out. But as she went through all the friend requests she had received, she found herself being pulled into this world of people, their activities and their adventures quite against her will.

Slowly, she started accepting the requests of the people she knew - Julie, Natalie, Helen, Jemima, Louise - the list of school mums was as long as her arm. It was ironic that some of these women had barely exchanged two words with her, but here they were, wanting to be her friend online.

With the tiniest bit of trepidation she went into Jemima's Facebook, but noticed that all she had were pictures of beaches with funny captions. Julie's proved more revelatory.

From holidays, to lunches and dinners, to the many karaoke evenings she'd organised, Julie was a compulsive over-sharer. Anu even got a glimpse of herself in one picture. But it was the pictures of the evening after the ball that caught and held her attention.

They were all there - Julie, Jemima, Louise, Jill, their husbands, and the new entrants into their charmed circle - Andy and Cathy. Anu bit her lip as she scrolled through the pictures, noticing how relaxed everyone looked. The men had their bow-ties undone; the women had kicked off their heels. Champagne flutes in hand, they posed together, laughing at something beyond the camera.

Anu shut the laptop, feeling slightly sick. Was this peek into their lives worth the heartache?

· · ·

That evening when Ravi was lounging on the sofa, she went and sat next to him.

"Ravi, have you heard of Facebook?"

"Uh-huh. That thing where everyone is putting their pictures up?"

"Yes, it's like this site to connect you to your friends."

"Wouldn't you be 'connected' to your friends, anyway? What do you need a site for?"

"I don't know, don't ask me stuff like that. Anyway, Cathy signed me up for it, and now all these people from way-back-when have contacted me to be friends with them."

"Were you friends with them way-back-when?"

"No, not really."

"Then why bother?"

"Well, it seems to be the done thing."

"Anu, do you see me doing it? It's only the done thing if you get sucked into it. I don't see the point of things like this. Trust me, all it will be is a place where people show off their so-called fabulous lives. I've seen some women at the office sifting through photos to put the best ones on. No one wants to show reality, do they?"

"Speaking of reality, guess what I saw today." Anu told him about the pictures from Jemima's after-party.

"Anu, seriously, come off this thing. It will drive you bananas. It's bad enough the way they behaved without it being flaunted for the world to see, and for your nose to be rubbed in it. Just come off it, it's toxic I'm telling you."

On some level, Ravi's cautionary tone resonated with her, but on another, she couldn't wait to see what else they were doing, and how long Cathy would last in their midst.

The sting of the betrayal was still sharp, and perhaps she was masochistic, but for now, she had no intention of signing off Facebook.

❖

"You've forgotten all about me again, haven't you?"

Anu had just started work on a new painting when the phone rang. She'd almost left it to go into voicemail, then grabbed it just in case it was the school calling.

"Annie," she breathed, her hackles rising at the accusatory tone her cousin had adopted.

"You were meant to stay in touch!"

"I know. I'm sorry, it's been a bit mad here."

"And you haven't accepted my friend request on Facebook."

"Annie, I'm barely on it, I don't even know how it works."

"Well, perhaps it's wise you're not really on it. You can't imagine the people getting in touch and wanting to be friends."

"Oh?"

"Like those real loser types, you know, the chubby, dorky one that I never gave the time of the day to. Now, he wants to be a friend! Just to nose around my life."

"Ummm, yeah."

"Anyway, I thought I'd let you know that Richard and I will be featured in a BBC program set in Bath."

"Really? That's great! When will it be telecast?"

"Soon. I'll tell you when they tell me. Be sure to watch it."

"Of course, we will. How are you both, anyway?"

"Fine, good. You? What are you up to that keeps you so busy?"

"I've taken up painting again."

"Oh, that's nice. It's always good to have hobbies."

Annie had never thought much of Anu's paintings,

always dismissing them as a little joke. Something that had kept Anu occupied before she got married.

"I'm thinking I should contact a gallery, maybe see if they'd be willing to display my work."

"Well... " Annie's drawl was laced with sarcasm. "Good luck with that, Picasso."

Bristling, Anu snapped at her.

"You know Annie, it's one thing to never have a pleasant thing to say to my face, it's quite another to be so obviously patronising about my work too!"

"Goodness Anu, calm down! I was just wishing you luck. And when have I been nasty to you?" Her voice had risen in pitch too, but this time Anu refused to back down.

"Puh-lease! How about all our lives? Remember the time you pointed out at your wedding that mine was nowhere near as nice or grand? Or, how about saying I have a resting bitch face? Annie, all you've ever done is wipe your feet on me all your life, and then you wonder why I don't stay in touch with you? Are you surprised?!"

There was silence on the other end of the line, but Anu was used to the long silences that Annie punctuated her conversations with. It was a psychological tactic she had used for years, making the other party uncomfortable enough to jump in and try to fill the gaps, and perhaps say too much. Anu stayed quiet too.

After a few minutes Annie said, "I had no idea you felt this way."

"Well, now you know."

"Yes, so I do. Very well. I won't bother you again, seeing as I'm such an awful person. Bye Anu."

She hung up, leaving Anu feeling strangely guilty.

. . .

That afternoon, as Neha and Anu trooped over to Susan's, she wondered whether Cathy had been staying in touch with her or if all her time was being taken up by her new friends.

"And what's this you're carrying, my little one?" Susan beamed at Neha.

"We made chocolate cupcakes." Neha had a telltale smear of chocolate on the side of her face, from the icing she'd licked off the spoon.

"Then I need to put the kettle on, don't I?"

Anu set the cupcakes down, allowing Neha to change the television channel to cartoons while she helped Susan with the tea.

"I'm glad you came today, Anu. I was feeling quite sad."

"Hasn't Cathy been to see you?"

"Oh, she has. She's brought Mel in a few times too. But it's not that. I just heard that my sister passed away."

"I'm sorry, Susan! Here, you sit down. Let me make the tea."

"No, no. I'm all right. It's just that she was the last of my family, and it's the end of an era I suppose."

"Was she ill?"

"Healthy as a horse, but her mind had gone completely."

"That's so sad."

"Yes. I often think I'd rather my body go than my mind."

"Please don't think like that. Hopefully, both your mind and body will stay healthy."

"Hopefully. Anyway, her funeral is in Birmingham, and I'm thinking of taking the train there."

"Couldn't Jan take you?"

"I asked her, but she says she's too busy."

"Do you need a lift to the train station?"

Susan looked at her gratefully.

"I was afraid to ask, but if it's not too much trouble… "

"Of course it isn't! Please Susan, I know I'm not always around, but if ever you need anything, you must let me know!"

"Very well, my dear. But now you have to tell me why you've been looking so downcast lately?"

Anu looked around the room with its patterned curtains and flowered upholstery. She looked at her daughter lying on her stomach, her face balanced on her hands as she watched television. Then she looked outside the window, at the grey and drizzly day. When she spoke, her voice held a tremor.

"Sometimes, I feel like I'm standing outside, looking in. As though all of this, my life, is happening to someone else. I feel detached, disconnected from everyone and everything. I feel like I am damaged, and that quite like pack animals that abandon a sick member, people abandon me. Because they sense that I am not right, that there is a fundamental flaw in my make-up, and they don't want to have anything to do with me."

Susan looked at her intently as she spoke, then she placed a wrinkled hand over hers.

"Anoo, all I see before me is a young and beautiful woman. A very talented one, too. Someone who is loved and loves with equal intensity. I do not know why you feel the way you do, but have you considered getting help? Some kind of medical intervention? You know, these days there is no stigma attached to mental health."

CHAPTER TWELVE

"Do you think I need to get checked out at the GP?" Anu asked, loitering in the door to their ensuite while Ravi brushed his teeth.

"Why?"

"Well, I have been feeling low, and you know how sometimes it gets really bad. Maybe they can diagnose what's wrong with me?"

"Anu, nothing is wrong with you. We all go through cycles of feeling low, that's life! Remember how bad it had hit you after Neha's birth, but you climbed out of that."

"Ravi, it's not just that. It's a general feeling of being different, of standing apart from everyone else. Like I don't belong here or anywhere else either."

"Are you sure it's not just these women that are affecting you in this way?"

"No, it's not just them. It's everything. I just feel sad all the time. Sad, lonely and disconnected."

"Come here." Ravi hugged her, smoothening her hair down and planting a kiss on the top of her head. "I didn't realise it was that bad. Okay, go on and book an appointment with the GP. Do you want me to come along?"

She shook her head. This was something she needed to tackle on her own.

"Okay, no problem. But promise me you'll discuss everything with me from now on. Don't look at me like that, I want to know. You and Neha are my world, and when I married you I promised to look after you in sickness and in health."

She tightened her arms around Ravi, sending a quiet 'thank you' to him.

The waiting room at the Doctor's Surgery was half-full with people of all kinds waiting for their names to be called out. There was an elderly couple in the corner who looked up as she walked in, then looked back down almost immediately. The woman with the toddler was trying to read to him in an undertone, but he kept twisting out of her grip and messing up the magazines in their corner. A large Gucci bag sat in the chair next to a heavyset woman with a shock of red hair and sunglasses, who scrolled through her phone rapidly. Anu went and sat in the middle, knowing she was early for her appointment, but willing to wait extra just for a guaranteed parking spot.

Flicking through a magazine, she noticed movement from the corner of her eye. Then a sigh and a familiar whiff as someone lowered themselves into the chair next to her. She looked up in surprise at Jemima.

"Hey you," she whispered, looking a bit ragged.

"Hi," Anu responded, not sure whether it was appropriate to ask why she was there.

"Changing my prescription." Jemima filled in, as if

knowing exactly what Anu had been thinking, waiting for Anu's response.

"Just here to see the GP about my allergies." Anu lied, not wanting to confide in Jemima anymore. The trust had evaporated along with their once strong friendship.

Jemima looked at her searchingly.

"Everything okay with you, Anoo? We haven't really seen you around much lately."

And whose fault is that, Anu wanted to ask. Instead, she pasted a polite smile on her face and nodded to show that all was fine.

"Which doctor are you seeing?"

"Dr Donaldson."

"Yes, she's really nice. I've had to ask for a different one this time. The old GP, what's-his-name, refused to change my prescription. Doesn't believe I need a stronger dose! Can you imagine? As if I don't know my own body."

"Umm, who are you seeing then?"

"Dr Joshi, the handsome Indian man. He's rather dishy, isn't he?"

"I don't know, I've never seen him."

"Well, anyway, I think he'll be willing to up the dose. I mean, what does it matter to them if it's Prozac or Citalopram?"

All this was said in a hushed whisper, and as Anu leaned forward to catch the end of the sentence, her name was called out. She stood up, saying a hasty goodbye to Jemima, and made her way up the stairs.

Dr Donaldson was a neatly dressed lady around her own age. She looked up from her screen and smiled at Anu as she walked in.

"Nice to see you again, Mrs Dhawan. The last time I saw

you it was for your Urticaria, it shows here in the records. Has that settled down?"

"Yes, thank you. It's something different this time."

As she spelled out her feelings, her low phases and the general lassitude she had been experiencing, she wondered if she was being silly. If someone like Jemima who seemed to have it all was on antidepressants, then maybe it was more of a general malaise than she had imagined.

Dr Donaldson listened to her carefully, taking notes alongside. When Anu had finished, she tapped the pen on her notepad a few times before looking up.

"The first thing I would recommend is a blood test. You may just be deficient in Vitamin D. If that is the case, then a regular dose should help ease the symptoms. You are from India, right?"

Anu nodded her yes.

"Well," the doctor continued, "your body is used to much more sunshine than you get here. The extra melanin in your skin means that you require six times more sun than white-skinned people to get the required Vitamin D. Let's get the results of that blood test, and we can take it from there."

"So, you don't think I need antidepressants?"

Dr Donaldson leaned back in her chair.

"I'm not saying that you don't, but I'm not someone who likes to start there. Let's explore all the other options first. Diet, exercise, rest and other factors can affect a person's mental well-being quite a bit. If we address those first and find that it doesn't work, then we can move on to medication."

"I see. So, it really has to be quite severe before you resort to these pills?"

The doctor looked at Anu quizzically.

"Yes, I'd like to think so."

❖

Parking her car in the drive, Anu didn't notice Cathy come up behind her.

"Hi Anoo!" She waved from her own drive.

Anu waved back politely, not wanting to engage in any conversation. But Cathy was in the mood for a chat and crossed the road to speak with her.

"Time for a quick cuppa?"

Anu sighed internally and said, "Come on in."

Her feelings towards Cathy were mixed at this point. She knew it was pointless to blame her as Cathy was just being herself. She was young, beautiful, and had a vibrant personality. That Anu's friends had found her more interesting than Anu was not her fault.

"What's this?" Cathy walked right up to the easel in the middle of the room.

Anu had forgotten she'd brought her half-finished work downstairs in search of better light and left it there before rushing off to the General Practitioners surgery.

"That's just the latest painting I'm working on."

"It's beautiful," Cathy remarked, scrutinising it. "I love the way you've used the green and the grey together."

"I'm not done yet, it's only halfway there."

"What does it mean?"

Anu laughed. This was the first time anyone had asked her this question.

"I don't know. It could mean different things to different people." She shrugged. "It's open to interpretation."

"To me it looks like the moss or lichen that grows on that wall in the park, you know the one I mean? It's like nature is climbing upon history. Am I being fanciful?"

Anu looked at her carefully before responding.

"That's an interesting viewpoint. I'm not sure that was what I was referencing, but sure, if you see that, then that's what it is."

"You're so clever, Anoo."

"Far from it!" Anu set the mug of tea in front of her. "How are you, anyway?"

"I'm fine! Missed you at Jemima's party the other night. Why didn't you come?"

"Which one?"

"After the ball?"

"Oh, that! I wasn't invited."

Cathy looked shocked.

"What?! I thought for sure you'd both be there. That's the only reason Andy agreed to go."

Somewhat soothed, Anu smiled at her.

"Maybe because we had to release the babysitter at 1 a.m. Jemima knew that, so she must have thought to spare us the dilemma."

Even as she said it, Anu knew it sounded lame, but it was the best she could come up with.

"Aww, we really did miss you there! But listen, I'm finally getting around to organising that dinner party. I wanted to give you an early heads-up. Make sure you and Ravi are free on the 14th of March, okay?"

Anu nodded gamely, warming once more towards her entirely unpretentious neighbour.

"Annie, I'm sorry about the other day." Anu voiced her contrition over voicemail. Annie was refusing to answer her calls, and now she felt worse than ever over what had transpired between them. Maybe she should have just let it go. Sometimes, as Ravi had pointed out, people behaved in the ways they did more out of habit than malice. Annie had always cast herself in the role of someone more worldly wise than Anu, and the fact that Anu had found her feet in her own way, quite without Annie's help, must have rankled at some deep subconscious level.

"She's refusing to answer my calls, Ravi," Anu sighed while plaiting Neha's hair before bedtime.

"Then leave it. She's probably still upset over the conversation. Let her calm down, I'm sure she'll come around."

"Libby isn't talking to me either, Mummy." Neha said out of the blue.

"Why is that baby? Did you two have a fight?"

"She said I was bullying her."

"What?!"

Neha's lower lip trembled. "Only because I wanted to sit with Rebecca for lunch and Libby was sitting there. I asked her to move, and she started saying that I was bullying her."

"But I thought Libby and Daisy were good friends now. Why is she getting upset about Rebecca?"

"I don't know, Mummy. But I didn't bully her."

The tears finally came, and Anu pulled her into an embrace.

"I believe you, darling." Her eyes met Ravi's questioningly. He came over and gently turned Neha to face him. Kneeling down, he asked her, "Neha, be honest. Have you ever said or done anything to Libby that she might think was bullying?"

"No Daddy, I promise." A fresh flood of tears.

"Okay honey, don't worry about it. We'll have a chat with the teacher and see how this can be sorted out."

. . .

Later, Anu asked Ravi, "Did you honestly believe that Neha could be capable of bullying? Especially since she was subjected to it at the start?"

"Anu, we always look at our own as completely blameless, but we are all capable of being mean and unkind. Not that..." he raised his hand to ward off her objections, "... I'm saying that Neha did anything. But it was important to ask."

"Will you go with me to see the teacher?"

"Yes, this time I will."

"I'm just sad that Libby and Neha have fallen out as well. I wish the parents' dynamics didn't affect the children, but they do, don't they?"

"It depends. Some parents can be mature enough to let children sort their own disagreements, while others... "

"Speaking of Jemima, I ran into her at the GP's. She behaved as though nothing was wrong, as if all of it is in my mind. But can you believe that she's on antidepressants? I mean, what does she have to be depressed over?"

"Anu," Ravi looked at her. "Don't judge. You have no idea what may be happening in her life. Look at that Zoe woman. Seemingly perfect life gone like this!" He clicked his fingers. "And look at yourself. Someone on the outside could say the same about you. Yet, here you are."

Anu dropped her eyes, ashamed at her own cattiness. No matter what her equation with Jemima was, it was unkind of her to pass any judgement on her. So she nestled into Ravi, once again thanking her lucky stars that she had a husband she could count on to be kind and set her right when she needed it.

❖

On Monday morning, miraculously, Anu and Neha were the first ones in the school playground.

"Only another two years here, baby. Can you believe how quickly it's gone?"

Neha nodded. It always surprised Anu to see how much she had grown in confidence. No longer the slow moving, shy child from her initial years in the school, she had developed into a young girl with a quirky sense of humour, a quick intelligence and a warm-hearted approach to life that ensured her plenty of friends. No longer bullied, she was still sensitive to children who were left on the fringes, always watching out for them, relating stories of the games she'd invented to get them involved. Anu was proud of her, but worried too. Was it too much to expect her to have the same easy-going charm that Ravi possessed? Had her own neurosis completely skipped her child, or was it lying in wait for the right moment to ambush her?

Slowly, as the playground filled with other mothers and children, Anu moved to one side, leaning against a wall. She spotted the usual groups of women chatting with each other. A few smiled at her as they walked by, but most just ignored her. She marvelled at how, even after all these years of picking and dropping Neha off at school, she had developed no comfort here. Was it her own complexes, or did they still view her as an interloper - someone who should have stayed amongst her own kind?

Neha had run off to play with her friends before the bell rang to indicate that school had begun. Anu spotted a few other Indian faces amongst the new mothers. But how comfortable they looked in their surroundings! They seemed completely at ease amongst the other young mothers whose children had just joined school the previous year, completely decimating her earlier belief that as an Indian she'd been made to believe that she wasn't one of them. So, had it been her own insecurities that had set her apart?

"You are a million miles away!" A voice said at her side.

She turned to look at Helen, who was holding a sheet of paper and pen, looking at her expectantly.

"I'm sorry, I was! Did you say something then?"

"I was asking if you'd be interested in sponsoring the marathon I'm running?" She handed the sheet of paper over to Anu to look at.

"Breast cancer research? Yes, of course!" Anu scribbled her name and £20 next to it. "I'll have to give you the money in the afternoon as I'm not carrying my wallet."

"No rush on it, Anoo."

"I didn't know you were a runner, Helen?"

"I'm not," she laughed self-consciously. "But I'm going to do this even if it kills me." Then she laughed again, realising how that sounded. "Oh dear, that came out all wrong."

The bell rang just then, and Anu rushed to give Neha a kiss before seeing her off to her classroom.

On her way out, she saw Helen's lycra-clad legs between the other mothers. Overtaking them, she caught up with her.

"I forgot to ask - are you running this for someone special?"

Helen glanced at her sideways. "So you don't know?"

"Know what?"

"Dawn Davies has it."

"Gina's mother?" Anu gasped.

"Yeah. She found out a while ago, but has kept it quiet. The treatment seems to be working, so it's not all bad news."

"I'm so sorry! I wish I'd known."

"Not much you could have done, anyway. But you

should come in for the occasional Friday coffee morning. It'll keep you in the loop."

"Isn't she... Dawn... Zoe's very good friend?"

"Yes, and Blondie is taking it really badly, what with the divorce and all. She's really cut up about it. I hear she's been an enormous support to Dawn. Wouldn't have thought she had it in her."

"And Gina?"

"Oh, you know what kids that age are like. I don't think it's even registered. But that is probably for the best."

"Thank you for filling me in Helen. I'll bring the money this afternoon."

"No problem! I better get on with my training. Nice seeing you, Anoo."

As she waved Helen off, Anu wondered how she'd missed all the signs. She hadn't seen Dawn in the school playground for a while, but as she was never in that circle, she'd barely spared it a thought. Her own misery and self-loathing had preoccupied her to such a degree that she'd been completely oblivious to someone else's pain and suffering.

Neha's Year 4 teacher was a thin, spare woman by the name of Miss Brown. Not particularly friendly, Anu had always found her quite intimidating to approach, but Neha loved her. Whatever lack of charm she displayed towards the parents, she more than made up for with the children.

Setting up a meeting with her had been difficult, caught up as she was with multiple other projects at school. But having finally sorted out a time that suited all three of them,

Anu had reminded Ravi several times to not miss the appointment.

As they were ushered into the classroom, Anu couldn't help but notice the difference between the younger children's classrooms and this. Here, the pictures on the wall were far more sophisticated; a large map was pinned to the board behind them and the tables and chairs were much higher too. In one corner there was an aquarium with tropical fish swimming within.

Noticing her gaze, Miss Brown pointed out their latest acquisition - a crimson spotted rainbow fish named Hopper.

"That's a strange name for a fish," Ravi remarked.

"Ah, but children are imaginative creatures, and in their world a fish can be called anything." She didn't smile as she said this, but Anu thought she spied a twinkle in the bespectacled eyes.

"So, what can I do for you, Mr and Mrs Dhawan?"

Anu let Ravi explain the situation to her. He finished by saying, "As you can see, this concerns us enormously. Neha had a tough time at school initially, and my wife had to intervene a few times. The school was great at taking care of the situation. However, this time the allegation has been made against her. Now, Neha insists that she has done nothing that might be construed as bullying. But we would like your input here, and before any of this gets out of hand, we'd like to nip things in the bud."

Miss Brown nodded thoughtfully.

"Neha isn't the sort of child I would associate with behaviour like this. In fact, it's quite the opposite. I'm surprised this allegation has come from Libby. Haven't they been fast friends all these years?" She looked at Anu.

"Yes, but lately they've started drifting apart. Neha is getting closer to Rebecca Shaw."

"Could that be the underlying reason? Maybe Libby isn't happy about this?"

"Libby was the one to break away, so I can't imagine that Neha's friendship with anyone else would bother her."

Ravi leaned forward.

"Have you had any complaints from this child or her parents regarding Neha's behaviour?"

"No, I haven't. Which is why I'm perplexed by our conversation? I can see that you're concerned about your child being labelled unfairly, but honestly, I don't see any cause for alarm. This might just have been a minor spat between the girls. Anyhow, I will monitor the both of them, and if I need to step in, I will."

As they both thanked her at the door, she suddenly looked at Anu and said, "Neha is a bright and talented girl and a credit to you both. I wouldn't worry too much if I were you."

"Is it going to be awkward at the party tonight?" Anu asked as she draped the sari around her.

"Why would it be? You carry on being normal with everyone. If anything comes up in conversation, we'll tackle it together."

Ravi sprayed his cologne, then turned around to survey her.

"I wish you'd wear saris more often, Anu, they really suit you."

She glanced at herself in the mirror. The sari she'd chosen was a simple one, a parrot green shot with black thread and a black border that had pink and green embroidery on it. This had been a part of her trousseau, a sari picked out by her grandmother. She'd barely had occasion to wear it and was glad she'd pulled it out from the back of her wardrobe today.

"I'd love to Ravi, but where exactly would I go in them? To the school or the grocery store?"

"I see your point. Still, you look like a million bucks today!"

"I'm wearing it like armour, hoping that *Nani*'s blessings are with me."

"What do you need armour for?"

"All the ladies will be there, Ravi. I just want to get through the evening without embarrassing myself."

"Now, look here Anu! Cathy and Andy have been our friends for much longer than they've known these people. We are going as their guests. Don't let these women bother you, okay?"

Anu nodded and swallowed. She'd never been good at hiding her feelings. Would she be able to hide her hurt and confusion from the perpetrators?

They were among the first to arrive. Cathy was dressed down in a pair of jeans and a black top with a colourful brooch pinned on, that somehow pulled the whole look together. On anyone else it would have looked old-fashioned or boring, but Cathy's sense of style set her apart.

"Am I overdressed?" Anu asked.

"Don't be ridiculous! You look gorgeous." She kissed her on the cheek and led her in.

Ravi handed the wine and flowers over to Andy, immediately falling into a cheerful conversation with him.

Anu was relieved to see the house looking tidy.

"Where's Mel?"

"Mum's got her for the weekend, so we can have as late a night as we want. And Neha?"

"Lauren's over, and happy to stay late if we need her to. Poor girl's trying to make as much money as possible for her trip to Europe this Summer."

Andy came over and gave her a peck on the cheek, handing her a gin and tonic straight away.

"You taste it, Anoo. Cath says I make it too strong. I say there's no such thing!"

Anu took a cautious sip and blanched. "Umm, Andy?"

"Nah!" He'd already turned away.

"He can be such a sod. Wait, I'll add some more tonic to it." Cathy laughed and topped up her glass.

Soon the doorbell started to ring constantly as more guests arrived. There were friends from Cathy's University days, some preschool mothers and then Susan who arrived with an armful of lilies. There was no sign of Louise or Jemima, and she wondered if they'd stand Cathy up the same way they'd done her.

"What are you thinking, Anoo?" Susan came and stood next to her.

"Oh, nothing." She leaned down to give her a hug.

"Look at the silk on this! You are lucky to have such beautiful saris. Which part of India is this one from?"

Even as Anu explained where *Kanjeevaram*[1] saris came from, she heard Julie's laugh from across the room. Slowly, and with a careful deliberateness, she turned her back to the newest entrants, the trio of Julie, Jemima and Louise.

As she chatted with Susan, her senses were on high alert. She wondered if they'd acknowledge her, or whether she ought to approach them. Then the decision was taken out of her hands as she heard Louise yelp next to her. "Oh, damn!"

She spun around to see that Louise had dropped her glass of red wine just behind Anu. The wine had splattered everywhere, drops splashing on to her sari as well.

Louise caught her eye and grimaced. "I'm sorry, Anoo, that was an accident."

"Move aside, move aside." Andy came out brandishing a dustpan, and Cathy followed with a mop.

Anu contorted herself to look at the damage inflicted on her sari.

"It's not too bad," Ravi whispered. "We'll have it dry-cleaned."

"I'll pay for it," Louise slurred next to them.

Julie came up to join her. "Someone's had a little too much wine... "

"Already?" Ravi asked, raising an eyebrow.

"Yeah, we met up earlier at mine, and may have lost track of how much we drank..."

Jemima joined them. "I'm the only one who stayed sober." She grinned. "...ish."

"You had to drive us here!"

"Well, we're taking a taxi back. Anoo, I've parked in front of yours. Is it okay to leave the car there for the night?"

Anu nodded, not sure how to respond to this show of normality and friendliness. She admired their ability to ignore the elephant in the room. How easy it was for them to not even dignify her discomfort by addressing it. And what could she say to them? Why did you drop me so suddenly? What did I do to upset you? How could we have spent all that time in each other's company only for you to turn your backs on me so completely?

"The problem is, Anu, that you're much too sentimental, you take far too much to heart. I watched them today and I don't think it's even occurred to them they've done anything wrong." Ravi said, unbuttoning his shirt.

"But at some level they must realise that they have! We

spent years together - lunching, dining, holidaying, and suddenly I'm persona non grata. Surely there must be a reason?"

"Why don't you ask them?"

"How? They'll just deny anything is wrong. You saw how they behaved so naturally. It's enough to make the other person question their own sanity!"

"Don't waste any more time over them. Did you enjoy the party otherwise?"

"They did a good job, Cathy and Andy. I think they will be the new golden couple in the village."

"I didn't realise we were giving out titles?"

"What I mean, Ravi, is that they've got everything going for them. They're young, good looking, white... "

"Don't start with that again, Anu!"

Anu fell back on the bed, her sari half-undone. She was tired. Tired of the hypocrisy, of the double standards, of the undercurrents of her life here. But what could she do about it? Whom could she talk to without being judged as para-noid or hyper-sensitive?

When she'd approached Natalie with the suggestion of visiting Dawn, Anu had expected the response to be in the negative. So, as she accompanied Natalie in her car to Dawn's house, she still felt slightly shocked that her over-tures had been acknowledged and accepted.

Anu had made a chicken curry for Dawn, checking with Natalie first if that would be acceptable.

"It's nice of you to want to do something, Anoo. Not everyone has been that kind." Natalie smiled at her sadly.

"But I thought they were running a marathon for her?"

"That's Helen. Some mothers haven't even rung her or sent a card. Shameful! The chemo's been really hard on her. Don't be shocked when you see Dawn, she's lost a lot of weight."

As they parked outside her house in Grisham Place, Anu recalled the last time she had come here years ago to collect Neha after Gina's birthday party. How different things had been then. She had been an outsider looking in, fearful of being invited in and yet desperate to be. Today she was walking in, dish in hand, fearful of what she'd find behind the doors.

Dawn sat on an armchair with a silk scarf on her head, grey and wan from the treatment. Her toothy smile was missing and she just about had enough energy to acknowledge Anu with a slight tilt of her head.

"I've brought you some curry!" Anu announced with a forced bonhomie.

Zoe came forward and took the dish from her hands, her eyes signalling that they should move towards the kitchen.

"Be back in a sec, hon! Just getting these two some tea."

"I thought she was getting better?" Anu asked in an undertone.

"We've had a setback. The tumour's metastasised."

"Oh."

Zoe looked tired. Somehow, she seemed smaller, as though life and circumstances had shrunk her. This was the same woman who'd been such an ogre to her all those years ago. Today, Anu just felt pity for her.

"She's still getting the chemo, but we don't know if it's going to be effective."

"I'm sorry, I thought she was improving."

Zoe's eyes filled with tears, and she looked away. Natalie went up to her and hugged her from the side.

"It's okay, Zo. We'll get through it."

For a moment they forgot she was there. Anu watched them at their most vulnerable and realised that people, ultimately, were not that different from one another. Pain and tragedy spared no one, and no amount of money or clout could protect you from the Grim Reaper.

"Has Jill rung?" Natalie asked.

"Nope." Zoe wiped her eyes while dipping the tea bags in the mugs. "Cow."

"I can't believe it! At a time like this... "

"She's a fucking coward, Nat! I know what she did and now, she's afraid to face me. So she's ignoring Dawn too."

"What did she do?" Anu asked softly.

They both looked at her in surprise, as though they'd just spotted her. Then they exchanged glances, as though wondering whether to say anything. Zoe gave Natalie a brief nod.

Natalie said, "Jill was the one who told the entire world about Zoe's... uhh... situation."

"Sometimes the people you trust are the first ones to let you down." Zoe's eyes blazed as she looked at Anu.

Anu dipped her head in confusion. Jill had made it sound as though she was still friends with Zoe & Co. when clearly this had been the reason she had defected. Could she have been the one to stir up trouble for Anu too? Was she the reason that Anu had been ousted from her friends' group?

"Let's go sit with Dawn now. Come on." Natalie passed Anu her mug of tea, gently guiding a trembling Zoe out of the kitchen.

An unspoken sadness lingered in the air. Anu remembered how desperately she had wanted to belong to this hallowed circle of women, and now that she was here, she saw how sad and complicated their lives really were. None of Dawn's obvious wealth, her stunning high-ceilinged Edwardian home, her devoted husband or her beautiful children had protected her from life's vagaries.

Anu tried to make small chat about their children, the various art projects she'd helped with, the end-of-year production, but Dawn just sat listlessly, her pallor enhanced by the sudden beam of sunlight that shone through the French windows.

Finally Natalie said, "I think we should get going, Anoo. Dawn, I'll bring Gina home this afternoon, I'll see you then. Do you want to say bye to Anoo?"

Dawn blinked slowly and half-raised her hand, only to let it fall back into her lap limply.

Zoe came to the door.

"She was happy to see you Anoo, even if she didn't show it."

"I'm glad. Please let me know if there's anything else I can do?"

Zoe's gaze softened as she looked at her.

"Thank you," she said, before shutting the door.

Back in the car, both Natalie and Anu stayed silent. Then Natalie said, "She's not going to make it, Anoo."

"Why do you say that?"

"It's too far gone. But Jeremy, her husband, is refusing to give up. He's insisting on the best treatment, on attacking it from every angle."

"But isn't that how it should be?" Anu turned to look at Natalie's profile. "They've got young children. She has to fight this and win."

"Anoo, you saw her. She has no fight left in her anymore." A tear trickled down Natalie's cheek.

"All of you are very close, aren't you?" She asked, handing Natalie a tissue from her bag.

"Yes," she sniffed, "we've known each other since our children first met in the nursery. Our families are interwoven with each other. But look at us now! Everything is falling apart... "

"I'm so sorry," Anu said, meaning it with every fibre of her being.

Natalie carried on, not registering Anu's sympathy.

"First Zoe's marriage fell apart, then Jill did the dirty on her. Now Dawn's sick and probably dying. How can I even tell them?"

"Tell them what?"

"We're moving back to Scotland in a year's time."

Still trying to digest everything, Anu made a quick pasta meal for Neha. As she was dishing it up, the phone rang.

"It's me, Anu," Ravi said. "I'll be home late. The meeting overran and now they want to have dinner here in the city."

"Oh."

"Hey, you okay? I'm sorry, this wasn't planned. Just one of those things."

"No, it's okay. I'll speak to you later."

"Bye then."

He hung up. She served herself a small portion of the pasta and sat next to Neha. Today was a day she could have used a sounding board, but it wasn't to be. The phone rang again.

"Hello?"

"It's only me. Eat, okay? Don't wait up."

"I'm eating now, Ravi."

"Good. I'll see you later."

"Bye."

She'd just finished when the phone rang again.

"Hello?"

"Me again."

"What now, Ravi?"

"Just calling to say - I love you!"

"Ravi, go! You're at work. All the mushy stuff can wait."

"Okay, bye."

She hung up, shaking her head. He'd cheered her up inadvertently and as she took the dishes into the kitchen, she heard the phone ring once more.

"I'll get it Neha. You go upstairs and brush your teeth."

She answered, ready to mock-scold her husband.

"Ravi..."

"Anu *didi*[2]?"

"Yes?" She recognised her half-sister's voice over the phone, rapidly calculating the time difference between the UK and India.

"Kriti here, *didi*. Just calling to tell you that Mama's no more."

PART 4

CHAPTER THIRTEEN

Varsha *bua*[1] had been surprisingly accommodating. She had prepared the room in time for Anu's arrival, not asking too many questions when she'd walked in past midnight.

Anu was exhausted from the last-minute packing and a flight that had seen her wedged next to a window for the better part of nine hours. She hadn't even examined the emotional toll that the news had taken on her, unable to think beyond the next step. From the moment she'd heard of Mama's death, she had gone into an automaton-like mode, getting tickets organised, sorting out Neha's after-school care, and preparing herself for her journey to India. Everything else she had pushed to the back of her mind.

"Do you want some chai, Anu?" Varsha *bua* asked after Anu had showered and changed into her pyjamas.

"No, thank you, *bua*. I should try to get some sleep. Tomorrow will be busy."

"So the prayer meet is in Delhi, not Nainital?"

"From what Kriti told me, they did the cremation within 24 hours, before anyone from the family could get there."

Varsha *bua* nodded. "It is normally like that here, *beta*[2]. We don't hang around."

"But," Anu bit her lip, not sure why she was confiding in Ravi's aunt, "Kriti said that something was suspicious about Mama's death."

"In what way?"

"The maid said she'd had some black stuff oozing out of her mouth when she found her in the morning..." Anu choked on the last few words.

"Was that man back with her?"

"Abhishek? Yes, I believe they'd made up. But he'd only visited the night before, not stayed over."

"Do you think he gave her something?"

"I don't know what to think *bua*."

Varsha *bua* looked at her with uncharacteristic sympathy.

"Get some rest, child. Tomorrow things will be a lot clearer."

But Anu got very little rest that night. She tossed and turned, dropping off for a few minutes and then startling herself awake, her heart thudding uncomfortably. In one hazy dream she found herself walking on the hillside behind Mama's cottage, her foot slipping just as she reached the edge. Her leg jerked back in her sleep and she woke herself up once again. Finally she sat up in bed, realising that sleep was planning to elude her completely that night.

She had tried examining her feelings about Mama's death in the last few days, but had drawn a blank. Was it shock, or was she truly numb to the loss? Her mind had circled the various scenarios that the maid's words had presented. Would Abhishek have given something to her mother, and why? And how could they prove it? Anu had seen how weak and ill her mother had been the last time she'd visited her. Maybe it was old age that had taken her. But then, why not wait for someone to arrive from Delhi? Why the great hurry to cremate her?

Anu expected she'd hear more from her half-brothers and sisters the next day. Aside from Kriti, no one else had really kept in touch with her. Her elder brothers, Nitin and Nirav, had never really bothered with her much even in their childhood. Kriti and Kaveri, her younger sisters, had bonded with each other and kept a polite distance from Anu. Yet, they could not deny that all of them shared their mother's blood. And her abandonment of them.

At 6 a.m. she hauled herself out of bed and proceeded to the bathroom to turn the geyser on for ten minutes so she'd have hot water for her shower. It wasn't exactly cold in May, but early mornings still had a slight nip in the air. As she washed her face, she looked at herself in the mirror and felt a chill go through her. Just for a moment there, something about her face had been so like her mother's.

Dressed in a lavender salwar kameez, she finally emerged at 7 a.m. to find Varsha *bua* doing her prayers in the small *puja* [3] room she had on the side of the living room. The maid did not arrive till 8:30 a.m. so Anu went into the kitchen to make some chai for them.

Rooting around, she found the aluminium *pateela* [4] that was used for boiling tea in. She boiled the water over the stove, adding the loose tea leaves, a piece of ginger and a good portion of milk, allowing the mix to bubble until the right colour and consistency had been achieved. As she sieved the liquid into two mugs, she heard Varsha *bua* enter the kitchen behind her.

"I was going to make the tea Anu, you shouldn't have taken the trouble."

"It's no trouble, *bua*. Would you like some sugar in it? I don't take sugar anymore."

They both sat on the adjoining sofas, looking out into the small garden.

"You know, Anu, I can still remember when my mother died. I was eleven. Amma*ji* had gone to visit her sister in Ambala, and she had a cardiac arrest there. For many years after, I still believed that she was staying at her sister's, just pretending to be dead because she didn't want to come home. I was so angry with her. It took me a long time to come to terms with the reality of her passing so suddenly."

This was the most that Varsha *bua* had ever told her about her past. Anu stayed silent out of respect for this confession, unwilling to break this sudden mood between them.

"Whatever your Mama did or didn't do, remember she was only human. Forgive her if you can. It will make your path ahead easier."

Anu blew on the tea and took a cautious sip. Her eyes filled with tears that she tried hard to blink back.

"Anu *beta*, you have always been very reserved with me, and I cannot blame you. I think I judged you harshly in the beginning without knowing what lay behind your diffidence. Over the years, Ravi has told me a few things. But last night, before your arrival, he called and explained it all to me." She placed a hand on Anu's shoulder. "I lost my mother young, but you never had one even while she lived. And now, you have lost her once again. I cannot imagine what you are going through, but *beta*, please believe me when I say, you will survive this."

The taxi took them through the leafy boulevards of

Central Delhi towards the Arya Samaj *Mandir* [5]where the prayer meet was to be held. Anu and Varsha *bua* sat at the back, each lost in their own thoughts.

The cool morning had given way to warmer weather as the sun rose in the sky. Delhi had started waking up, and as they fought the rush hour traffic at 10 a.m. Anu watched the passing scenes with a disembodied interest.

Over-crowded bus stops awaited over-crowded buses. People were clinging on for dear life out of doorways on the heaving buses, whilst others fought for a foothold as the bus moved away, leaving hordes of frustrated passengers behind. A woman stopped to fix a broken *chappal*,[6] while two friends cycling side-by-side conducted a leisurely conversation as motorists honked angrily behind them. Vegetable hawkers pushed their trolleys with weary resignation, labourers squatted in front of an unfinished building waiting for the *thekedar* [7]to arrive. Some men walked with purpose towards their destination while others loitered aimlessly. Car horns sounded between the hubbub of conversation and music blared out of an auto-rickshaw. Peddlers called out, inviting people to sample their wares. Maids rushed from one house to another to complete their morning chores.

The hum and throb of daily living surrounded them as they journeyed on to honour the dead. Anu had once belonged to this city, her life in sync with its rhythm. Now it seemed like a distant entity, at once attracting and repelling her with its chaos, its noise, its overpowering identity.

The driver turned left through a gateway, signalling that they had arrived. As she disembarked, she wondered where her mother had gone to. Had she finally found the peace that had eluded her her entire lifetime?

. . .

Nirav stood outside the hall, speaking to someone on his mobile phone. Dressed in a white *kurta-pyjama*[8], he waved absently to her as she entered. Inside, the hall was cool and dark. Clusters of people stood around talking to each other. Right next to a small dais, a marigold garland adorned a large photograph of Mama. Anu went up to it, curious to see which picture they had selected. Mama must have been in her thirties, still strikingly beautiful, perhaps married to the girls' father then. Dressed in a pink sari, she smiled out of the frame, the smile not reaching her eyes. Had she already been planning her escape then - from the arms of one lover to another, far, far away from the responsibilities that homes and children entailed?

"Isn't she beautiful?" Kaveri said.

Anu turned around and hugged her younger sister. "You look so much like her, Kav."

"How are you, *didi*[9]? You look exhausted."

"I am. Thank you for organising all this."

"*Bhaiyyas*[10] did it. We've organised the family lunch afterwards. You are coming?"

"Yes, of course I am. Isn't the will going to be read afterwards?"

"We already know that the Nainital house is going to the boys. The jewellery and saris have to be split between us. Mama told us all the time."

"When did you see her last?"

"She came down to Delhi briefly last year, but wouldn't come to any of our homes. We had to pay obeisance to her at The Imperial Hotel. You know what she was like... "

"Was she back with him?"

"Abhishek? Who knows? She didn't mention him then. But just be warned that he is here."

"Oh."

Just then Kriti came up and hugged Anu.

"Glad you could make it, *didi*. We were worried that with Neha being so young, you wouldn't be able to come."

Nitin and Nirav came over to her as well. Talking in an undertone, they told them to take their places at the front as extended family, Mama's friends and acquaintances from over the years started filling the hall.

"Who would have thought she was this popular?" Nitin remarked, scanning the room with one raised eyebrow.

"How many jilted lovers here, do you think?" Nirav grinned at them.

It was ironic how for the first time in a long time, she felt like she was bonding with her siblings. It had taken a death for them to band in this way. Anu felt her grief dilute itself with tentative hope.

The Arya Samaj was an institution that was formed in 1875 by Maharishi Dayanand Saraswati. Its purpose was to move the Hindu Dharma away from superstition, idolatry and all forms of social oppression, and take it back to a more simple, logical and contemporary thinking on God and spirituality based upon the teachings of the Vedas. Anu's maternal grandparents had been Arya Samajis, and although Mama had displayed no spiritual leanings, it was only fitting that her prayer-meet be conducted here.

The priest was a man of around forty dressed in a simple green *khadi kurta*[11] and white pyjama, a red pen sticking out of his *kurta* pocket. As he spoke about death, karma, samsara and reincarnation, Anu drifted into a dreamlike state, where his words washed over her, but her mind wandered through the annals of her past, memories of her mother pressing upon her. Mama laughing, Mama angry, Mama remote and unreachable. Moments that were vivid and faded strung themselves together until she halted at that last image of her mother at the train station, seeing her off. Could either of them have known then that that would be the last time they saw each other? Would it have mattered?

Quite without knowing how, the tears came unbidden. She felt Kriti squeeze her hand and looked over to see her own sorrow reflected in her sister's face. She squeezed her hand back in acknowledgement.

Varsha *bua* called for a taxi, heading back home.

"This is a family lunch Anu. No place for me there. I'll see you later."

Anu got into a car with Nitin, her eldest sibling, the one she knew the least.

"*Bhaiyya*, what do you make of the maid's story?" she asked tentatively, not sure how he'd respond.

"Rubbish! You don't want to get into all this conspiracy nonsense now, Anu. Mama's dead and that's all there is to it."

She stared out of the window as he drove her to the restaurant, his own wife and kids having gone home too. Maybe he was right. What was the point in lending credence to a story none of them had any way of proving?

"We chose a Chinese restaurant because it was her favourite food." Kriti announced, leading them to the table that said 'Reserved.'

"Remember all the birthdays where she insisted we started every meal with chicken sweet corn soup?" Nirav asked.

"Only because she loved it!" Kaveri supplied, pulling out her chair.

"That was the only time all of us met up, on Mama's birthdays." Anu noted, softly.

"Yes, she never really gave us a chance to get to know one another."

Nitin and Nirav's father had remarried, as had Kriti and Kaveri's. Aside from the girls' father, who had attended the prayer meet, none of the other parents had come. Anu looked at the extra chair at the table.

"Are we expecting someone else?"

"Mama's lawyer. We thought it would be better to meet in informal surroundings. He was insistent we meet today."

"Did he say why?"

"No, but we can ask him now. There he is."

A bald, rotund man walked in, wiping the sweat off his forehead with a large, white handkerchief.

"Mr Madan," Nirav called out to him. "Here, here. We've saved this seat for you. You will join us for lunch, right? No, no, we insist! Please sit here."

Mr Madan squirmed uncomfortably in his seat. His voice was high-pitched, an unexpected contrast to his person.

"Thank you, but I cannot stay. All I've come to tell you is that your mother, Mrs Chauhan, had changed her will last year."

"Changed her will? What do you mean?"

"She came to see me in October when she was here. It's quite simple," he cleared his throat noisily. "She left every-thing - the house, her personal effects, her jewellery and clothes to Abhishek Gulati, her partner of the last few years."

There was pin-drop silence at the table. Anu looked around at the shocked faces of her siblings.

"Uh, Mr Madan, did she say why?"

"No, I'm sorry, but she didn't. She was very insistent that I tell all of you together, which is why it was important to meet you today."

"So, nothing? She's left us nothing?"

"Anything she may have given you in her lifetime is yours to keep, of course. But, nothing else, I'm afraid."

Nirav started laughing.

"Oh Mama, you just had to find one other way to show us how little we meant to you!"

"I must get going now." Mr Madan stood up. "I'll leave you a copy of the will to look at. The original will stay with me."

Numbly, they watched him leave.

"Chicken sweet corn soup, anyone?" Kriti asked.

"He has to have been behind it. That scoundrel, Abhishek!" Nitin exploded. "He must have brainwashed her, gotten her to change the will and then poisoned her before we got wind of it."

"But *bhaiyya*, you'd said that the poisoning theory was nonsense!" Kaveri pointed out.

"Because there was no motive! Now, there is a motive, don't you see?"

Anu watched them discuss things angrily, their voices rising in a babble. Once again she felt herself excluded. She had wanted nothing from her mother except love, and that she'd never had. What did it matter if she had written them out of their inheritance too?

Lunch had been a silent affair, with the food ordered hurriedly and consumed half-heartedly. A pall of gloom hung over them as they explored the various options ahead.

"We could challenge the will." Nitin said.

"How? It's clear that's why she came down last year, so it's not like she was being influenced by anyone. He didn't come down with her." Nirav countered.

"I suggest we meet with Abhishek," Kaveri reasoned. "Let's get to hear his side of things. Suss out just how much he knows."

"I'll call him to the club tomorrow. Let's get the bastard drunk!"

Anu looked at all of them. The anger and vitriol she understood, but why had no one spoken of their memories of Mama? Could it be that they had none to share?

Abhishek was only a few years older than Nitin and had been a very handsome man when Mama had first started dating him. Now, he looked seedy, his days-old stubble adding to the general dishevelment of his appearance. He'd flung an old jacket on top of his checked shirt and jeans in a nod to the club's dress policies. When Anu arrived, he was already a few whiskeys down.

Nitin had ordered platefuls of kebabs, and Abhishek was biting into a *tangdi kebab*[12] when she arrived, the orange juices running down his chin. She caught Kaveri's delicate shudder as she folded her hands together in a *namaste* to greet her mother's lover.

"Anu! So nice to see you," he boomed. "Missed you the last time you came to Nainital."

She nodded, keeping her smile neutral. Had they already pumped him for information or was this still the softening-up stage?

Accepting her gin and tonic, Anu leaned back on the sofa, waiting to see how this developed. Ravi's words from last night still rung in her ears. "Anu, you need nothing.

Don't get involved. You've done what you had to do, now just come back. We miss you."

"So, Benares, hey? You are really planning to take her ashes there?"

"That's the Hindu *vidhi*.[13]"

"But Mala couldn't care less, you know that! You could scatter her ashes under some anonymous tree and she'd be just as happy with that." Abhishek chuckled.

"You knew Mama the most out of all of us, didn't you, Abhishek?" Kaveri probed gently.

He grinned at her, revealing browned teeth. "I knew her all right - in more ways than one."

"When, ummm, did she decide to change her will?" Kaveri asked, ignoring his tasteless remark.

He took the napkin, wiped his hands carefully, then took a big glug of the whiskey, letting out a noisy belch, delighted to see the women flinch.

"Ah! So it's down to business now, I see." He surveyed the room. "I wondered how long it would take."

"Such selfish brats all of you are, just as she'd said." He sneered at them . "Look at you, gathered like vultures, wanting to pick her apart. Who was there with her in her last days? Who? Me, that's who! Who took care of her? Me! And now you're questioning why she left everything to me."

"Abhishek, we just want to know when she decided this?" Kaveri asked politely. Anu could see Nitin clenching his fist, his face turning white in anger.

"When? What does it matter when? It was all done legally. That *motu*[14] showed you the will, didn't he?" Abhishek looked around at them.

Nirav spoke slowly, biting out each word.

"So, you've got your claws into the property. At least let the girls have Mama's jewellery and saris."

"There is no jewellery left. She sold it all to pay for the upkeep of the house, and all her medical bills."

"More like you sold it, Abhishek." Kriti lashed out.

He leaned back once more, using a toothpick to clean his teeth.

"I didn't expect these two to be nice to me," he said, glancing at the men, "but I expected better from you."

Sighing, he dropped the toothpick on the table.

"I've brought some saris that your mother had set aside for you three. You can sort them out between yourselves."

He kicked a duffle bag over in Kriti's direction.

Then he stood up and looked at Nitin and Nirav, who glared back at him.

"You both are well off enough. What did you need that villa for, anyway? Mala's memories linger there. Let me live in peace and quiet with those."

"You liar! Murderer!" Nitin's control snapped as he jumped up, reached over and grabbed Abhishek's collar. "You gave her something, didn't you? The maid was right. You poisoned her!"

Abhishek threw his hand off, staggering back.

"Don't touch me, you *chutiya*[15]! Never try to get in touch with me again. I have lawyers too, and I'll wrangle you in so many cases you'll spend a lifetime fighting them!"

Then he adjusted his jacket, gave them one last smirk and walked out.

"It was ugly, Ravi!" Anu sobbed into the phone. "And the worst part is that we got no answers at all. Nothing to tell us why Mama did what she did, and if she was really murdered. He certainly seems capable of it."

"Anu, shhh, calm down. Surely the doctor wouldn't have provided a death certificate if it was murder?"

"Ravi, he could have bribed him for all we know!"

"Anu, listen, these are all theories. You have nothing but the maid's words to go on. No matter what you say or do at this juncture, your mother is not going to return. Let it go. Leave that entire sorry mess behind and come home."

"Y...yes, I'm packing right now."

"How are your brothers and sisters doing?"

"Everyone is in shock. Nitin is so furious with Mama that he keeps regurgitating everything from the past. The girls have just withdrawn once more. But we went through all the saris Abhishek had brought down from Nainital."

"Did you take any?"

"Just one. The one she got married to my father in."

As the plane took off from Delhi, Anu looked outside the window, watching the city lights recede. Unlike her brothers and sisters, she felt no anger towards Mama. She couldn't pretend to understand her motives, but for what it was worth, this entire episode had brought her a little closer to her half-siblings. All of them had come to see her off at the airport, promising to stay in touch, to meet and call more often. She took consolation from the fact that what Mama couldn't do in her life - bond them as a family - she had accomplished in her death.

Varsha *bua* had been a tower of strength, quietly helping Anu pack, buying the few extra things that Anu hadn't had the time to shop for, and trying to remain discreet with her opinions. This new side of hers warmed Anu towards her. There was a sense of new bridges being built with the people she'd always assumed to be on a different shore from her.

As she closed her eyes to drop off to sleep, she recalled her mother's face from the picture. How beautiful she had been, and how troubled too. She just hoped that Abhishek had given her some kind of happiness in her later years. And if he had, then he deserved whatever she'd bequeathed him.

CHAPTER FOURTEEN

Neha clung to her the entire evening of her return.

"Is she okay?" Anu mouthed to Ravi.

"She missed you, and there's been some drama at school. But let's spare Mummy today, Neha. She's tired, let her get some rest."

"Who are all the cards from?" Anu looked at the condolence cards on the mantelpiece.

"Susan, Cathy and Andy, and I think there's one here from Nonita too. She's called a few times, asking for you to ring her back. Said she couldn't get through to you in Delhi."

"Oh yes, Varsha *bua* mentioned her call, but it was just so hectic and draining, I didn't have the time to call her back."

"Mummy, did they burn *Nani*[1]?" Neha looked up at her, eyes as big as saucers.

"Baby, they cremated her as per the Hindu rites."

"Why didn't they bury her? Then we could visit her grave when we go to Delhi."

"Oh, darling!" Anu held Neha close to her. "We'll

remember her here, and here." She pointed to her head and her heart.

Before falling asleep, she cuddled up to Ravi.

"I think I'm still finding it hard to process that Mama's gone. I keep thinking I'll hear her voice again, that she'll call suddenly and be annoyed with me over something."

"That's perfectly normal, Anu. It'll take a while for you to accept her death. It's not like she was ever a constant in your life. Slowly, when you return to your routine, your mind will learn to accept that she's gone."

"My emotions are all a jumble right now. I'm not angry like the others, but I'm not exactly sad either. It's like I'm detached from it all."

"Shhh, Anu, you're tired. Just sleep. Time will heal everything."

Time was in short supply as school started winding down for the summer holidays. Her first morning back, Helen accosted her.

"Summer fête on the 22nd of June, the school picnic a week after, and then we're all going to the pub in the evening. Where have you been, anyway?"

"India. My mum passed away suddenly."

Helen clapped her hand to her mouth. "Anoo, I had no idea! I'm so sorry. I didn't mean to dump all this on you."

"It's okay. Probably best to get right back into the swing of things." She gave her a half-smile. "How's the training for the marathon going?"

"It's shite. Absolute shite! I'm not built for running. Look at this body." Helen grimaced, looking down at herself.

Anu couldn't help but giggle. Helen had a self-deprecating humour that she so admired.

"So, listen, are you up for coming to this Friday's coffee morning? Zoe might be discussing arrangements."

"For the school functions?"

"And what happens if Dawn doesn't make it."

"Oh! No, ummm, I think I'll skip it. I don't think I could be around any more sadness right now."

"Of course, I understand. I'll make your excuses."

At home, Anu made Neha a little snack while she sipped on her cup of tea. She knew she had many people to call and thank, but simply couldn't muster up the enthusiasm. Instead, she opened up her laptop on the kitchen counter and scrolled through Facebook.

More friend requests, lots of pictures of cats, and then, several of Julie on holiday with her family over the Easter break. Under each photo, a comment from Jemima or Louise. Lots of banter, a few pictures of their own. Anu shut the laptop.

"Neha baby, what's been happening at school when Mummy was away?"

"Nothing."

"Look at me, darling. I'm switching off the telly for a bit. No, stop pouting! What was the drama Daddy was talking about?"

Neha looked up at her mutinously, annoyed that her afternoon television binge had been cut short so abruptly.

"Come on, Neha. The quicker you tell me, the quicker you can go back to watching."

"It was nothing. Just that Daisy drew a picture of Miss Brown and Mr Roberts, and then I wrote 'kiss kiss' between them. Libby took the picture to Mr Roberts, and he got very angry."

"Is Mr Roberts the Year 6 teacher?"

"Yes. Then he called us all over, and Daisy said it was all my idea, and he punished me by saying I'd have to sit and do lines all week during lunch."

"Why didn't you say Daisy was just as much to blame?"

"Because Libby took her side and said it was all me."

"And was it?"

Neha's lower lip trembled.

"NO Mummy! I told you!!"

"Okay, okay. What did Daddy say?"

"He said to ignore it."

"Hmmm."

On Thursday, the doorbell rang mid-morning. Anu had just come home from her run and wondered who it could be at that hour.

She opened the door to Julie and Jemima standing outside.

"Hey Anoo! We've brought you this."

Julie handed over a beautiful deep purple orchid to her.

"Just wanted to say how sorry we were to hear about your mum." Jemima leaned forward and touched her arm.

Startled by their visit, it took a moment before Anu regained her wits enough to invite them in. But they refused politely.

"Oh no, you must have so much to sort out. We just wanted to drop by and give our sympathies in person. Lou would've come too, but she's tied up in some meeting."

"Thank you," Anu looked down at the orchid. "This is very kind of you."

Then she looked at Jemima in the face. "I really need to talk to you about something. When is a good time?"

Jemima shrugged. "Any time really."

"Then how about now?"

"Jules, do you mind?" Jemima said to Julie.

"No, it's okay. Shall I wait in the car?"

"Come in Julie, this won't take long." Anu said, taking a deep breath.

Having made cups of tea for all of them, she sat across from Jemima while Julie flicked through the pages of a magazine.

"It's about the girls - Libby, Daisy and Neha - to be precise."

"What about them?" Jemima looked bored.

"I know that Neha and Libby haven't been the best of friends lately, but it's gotten a bit out of hand now. Things are being pinned on Neha that aren't really her fault."

"Things?"

"Like a drawing that Daisy made that Neha got blamed for."

"Oh, that. I heard all about it. What a storm in a teacup! Honestly, Mr Roberts should be pleased he's been paired up with someone, even if it's that ugly prune!"

"Yes, but Libby ganged up with Daisy against Neha. And Neha had to take the punishment for them all."

"Is that it? Look Anu, I know you've just had a loss so you're bound to be overwrought, but this is just kids, playing, messing about. Why get so serious about these things, hey?"

Julie got up suddenly.

"I just remembered, I have an Ocado delivery. We've got to get back! Thanks for the tea Anoo. So sorry for your loss once again."

With that, they left their nearly-full mugs of tea and rushed out, leaving Anu with no clear answers once again.

❖

At Sainsbury, as she looked at the sell-by date on a yellow-stickered item, a voice next to her said, "Hello Anoo."

She looked up to see Simone standing there, her trolley filled with sale items.

"Bargain-hunting?" She asked sheepishly.

"Actually, no. I'd run out of bread so thought I'd nip down here to buy some." Anu couldn't help the trace of coldness in her voice. She still hadn't forgiven their last fracas, no matter how many times and in how many ways Simone had been proven right.

"Right! Well, I like to come in here just before closing so I can pick up as many discounted things as I can. Hashtag 'no shame'." She gave Anu a wry smile.

"Well, it was nice running into you, Simone. Take care." Anu started to move off.

"Wait! Hang on. I just wanted to apologise for the last time. I know I was harsh on you, but I had a lot on my mind. Also, I heard of your mother's passing, and... I'm sorry." She leaned in to give Anu an awkward hug.

Unsure what to say or do, Anu stayed rooted to the spot. Then she stammered out a 'thank you'.

"If you need a chat, I'm around. We can go down to the pub, if you like. I could tell you all about Kayla's sudden fondness for rolling up her skirt at secondary school."

Anu's gaze narrowed.

"Are you sure, Simone? I don't think I could handle any more accusations of being shallow and superficial."

"I'm sure, and I have apologised. Look, I'd heard that

my ex was being released from prison, and I did not have the bandwidth for you at the time."

"Oh." Anu looked at Simone properly. She looked healthy and happy. "You're not back with him, are you?"

"Heaven forbid! He's moved to Wales, and I couldn't be more chuffed. Good riddance to bad rubbish."

"Simone, I'm truly sorry if I made you feel like I'd dropped you. That was never my intention. I got very caught up with those ladies, but... never mind. I'll save the complaints for another time. Yes, I'd very much like to meet up for drinks. Text me a few dates, and I'll get back to you."

"Absolutely, Anoo. And listen, I'll just say the same thing about those ladies - good riddance to bad rubbish!"

"Haha! Well, we have plenty to catch up on..."

"And we've wasted too much time being annoyed with each other."

"True!"

"Happy shopping, Anoo! I'm going to take all my bargains to the till now."

Simone gave her a little wave before joining the checkout queue. Anu smiled to herself as she moved down the aisle with her trolley. Maybe she'd check out the discounted deals too.

At home, she chatted with Ravi while putting all the meats in the freezer.

"Gosh, Anu! Are we having a party? What's all this food for?"

"I've bought all the discounted items, and I'm freezing them for the future."

"And who gave you this idea?"

"I ran into Simone..."

"Say no more! It's Chanel bags one day and discounted

sausages the next. Really Anu, you need to stop being so influenced by people around you."

"Ravi, I don't see it as being influenced. I'm imbibing the best from everyone." She winked at him, cheekily. "And I'm saving you money, so don't complain! Not until the next Chanel bag, anyway."

"You little minx! Come here." Ravi grabbed and smooched her right in front of the freezer.

She squirmed in his grip. "Ravi, the freezer door is open!"

"It can wait!"

And yet, the next day she found herself curled up in a foetal position, sobbing her heart out.

Mama, Mama, Mama.

How could she miss a mother who'd never been there? Why hadn't she cried for her grandmother as much as this? A grandmother who had substituted for a mother most of her life.

She pounded the ground with her fist, angry at her own outburst of emotion, glad that Neha and Ravi weren't around to see it. At thirty-six, she needed to have a better handle on her emotions. She was tiring of the constant roller-coaster of feeling happy one day and despondent the next.

She picked herself up off the floor and went to wash her face. Eyes swollen, face puffy, the stranger that looked back from the mirror was someone she was determined to change. And because she needed some tough love, she rang Nonita.

"Anu! Where the hell have you been?"

"Sorry, Noni, it's been mad. I've been meaning to call."

Nonita's voice softened.

"Have you been crying, *jaanu*?"

"Yes. For Mama, but mostly for myself."

"You are allowed, you know."

"Noni, sometimes I wonder if I'm just like her. Not in terms of the marriages and divorces, and all the lovers. But more in terms of searching for something that's unattainable. Is that why I feel so displaced, so out of sync with everything and everyone around me?"

"Only you know the answer to that, Anu. But I suggested counselling to you before and I'll suggest it again."

Anu carried on, only half-listening.

"The only time I'm ever at peace is when I'm painting."

"Then there's your answer! Paint more. Maybe that's what you've been missing all along. You're stifling a talent that's trying to find a way out. Maybe that's what all this searching is about. Listen, Anu, so many people would give their eyeteeth for what you have! Admittedly, you've just had a bereavement. But look at it as a fresh start, a way to finally break free from your past. Yes, you have your mother's genes, but you also have your father's kindness and sensitivity. Why not build upon those rather than focusing on the negatives?"

After hanging up, Anu felt better about herself, once again resolving to return to her painting. With two canvases done, one that she'd stowed in the attic, and the second that sat on the landing - the one that Cathy had so admired - she felt ready to start work on her third. Perhaps an ode to an absent mother. Yes, that is exactly what it would be.

❖

Recalling Mama through the medium of paint wasn't the easiest of tasks. How could she paint the many faces and facets of a chameleon-like woman? What colours could describe her sunshine smile or her stormy moods?

Starting with a yellow dot in the centre, Anu swiped her brush across the canvas. Then she took flecks of gold, sprinkling them liberally on top. Slowly she added turquoise and coral, marbling them together, creating a swirl that suggested beauty and confusion. From not knowing how to begin, it felt nearly impossible to stop. Hours flew by as she added more colour and texture to the painting, taking elements like gravel from the driveway or pebbles from the back garden, sticking them on the canvas with glue, painting on them, above them, around them. Using multiple elements was her effort to convey the multiplicity of a single life. Her mother's life.

When Susan came in to borrow a cup of sugar, she let her in wordlessly, still in a trance, her jeans splattered with paint.

"What is this about, Anoo?" Sue asked, circling the easel.

"My mother, mostly."

"I cannot pretend to understand abstract art, but whatever this is, it's very powerful."

"Do you really think so?"

Susan nodded thoughtfully.

"Cathy had told me about your paintings, but I never imagined they'd be like this. Does this have a name?"

"Yes, it's called Mama."

Susan kept looking at it.

"How long have you been working on it?"

"I started this morning. Still have a ways to go."

"This painting tells me that your mother was a complicated person. Am I right?"

Anu nodded.

"You are, as well. But in the most artistic way. I can bake cakes Anoo, but that's the limit of my artistic ambitions. This... this I cannot do."

Later that evening, Anu took the laptop to bed with her. Ravi was busy reading his reports while she surfed the internet, looking for ways to approach galleries.

"How much of a body of work do you think it'll take, Ravi?"

"Hmm?"

"To get displayed in a gallery?"

"Haven't a clue, Anu. I'd imagine at least ten, but I could be way off base."

She chewed on her nail, reading through an article detailing how to create a portfolio and email the lesser known galleries, asking if they'd be willing to display her works.

"This sort of thing makes me nervous."

"Why?"

"You know me, Ravi. I can't walk up to strangers and ask them to give me the time of day."

Ravi placed the sheaf of papers on his chest, then turned his head towards her.

"First off Anu, if this is something you want to take seriously, then you will have to put yourself out there. So all these qualms and inhibitions will have to go out the window. If you believe in your work, grab the bull by the horns. Go out, shout it from rooftops. Be loud, be proud."

"Oh Ravi, just the sound of it is exhausting!"

But secretly she felt thrilled that Ravi thought she had it in her.

In early June, while looking for a specific artist on Facebook, Anu stumbled upon it - a joyfully worded invitation to a summer barbecue at Louise's home. Almost half the village had been invited, Cathy from across the street as well. Likely in a hurry, Louise had forgotten that the event's settings were public, and that everyone could see when and where it was being held and who had been invited. Anu's name was conspicuous by its absence.

It stung. She chewed on the inside of her cheek, wondering whether to ignore it or to say something. This was the same woman who had come to her home, eaten several meals with her, watched movies, sung karaoke, shared a room on holiday, and today she didn't have the decency to issue her an invitation to her barbecue. Then again, it was her home, and she was free to invite whoever she chose. But to do it in so public a manner? Even if it was an oversight, surely even she would know that Anu would find out at some point, especially since Cathy would probably mention it to her?

Taking a deep breath, Anu decided that the best course of action would be to do nothing. She shut the laptop and made herself a cup of tea. But two minutes later, she was back on Facebook, posting a comment on Louise's barbecue page - "Thanks for the invitation, Louise. Sorry we won't be able to make it. Oh wait, you haven't invited us! Silly me."

With trembling fingers, she shut her laptop once again. There, she had done it. It was about time that things were finally brought out into the open. She was sick of the lot of them: the cliques, the insiders, the outsiders, the unknowable code of conduct, the inability to accept anyone different from themselves, the uniform conformity to some invisible barometer of suitability, the saying of one thing to your face and quite another behind your back. Something had to give, and today, she had snapped. Now, she wanted to see where the chips would fall.

Anu got to school early, waiting to see if any of them were around, but she only saw the usual clusters of early arrivals. Taking herself off to a side, she kept her sunglasses on, hoping no one would approach her. She lay in wait, hoping that today they would get to thrash it out.

As the playground filled up, she saw Jemima and Louise walk in together. Either they didn't see her, or they pretended not to as they turned their backs on her and talked to each other. Then Julie joined them, followed by Jill. It was clear that they had no intention of approaching her. As she walked towards them, the bell rang and the children were let out of their classrooms. Jemima grabbed Libby and Emily and scurried out. Louise took her children, said something to Julie and walked away from her.

Neha tugged on Anu's hand, asking her a question.

"Shhh baby, I need to do something first."

Julie watched her approach, her face grim.

"I'd hoped to talk to all of you together."

"That was uncalled for, Anu. Your comment really hurt Louise!"

"And I wasn't? I haven't been hurt by your behaviour over the past year? How do you think it feels to be cut out suddenly; cast aside as though I'm yesterday's news? No reason given, no explanation offered."

"I have no idea what you're talking about." Julie's voice grew even colder.

Anu was mortified to find tears running down her face.

Mothers walking by glanced at her, whispering amongst themselves.

"Why don't you just tell me what I did? At least with Zoe & Co.," she glanced at Jill, "it was obvious that they didn't want to make friends with the likes of me. But you, you were the one who approached me, who befriended me. All those times we spent together, did they mean nothing? Was I just an amusing plaything to be used and discarded when you were bored with me?"

"Please Anu, you're making a scene! Stop acting like a jilted lover. We didn't do something as dramatic as 'drop you'! Sometimes people drift apart. You just take everything so seriously."

"So, that's it? That's all I get by way of a reason?"

"I really don't know what you want from us. We've been nothing but decent with you. It's a shame that it's come to this, but you've certainly burned your bridges with Louise and Jemima."

"I see. So, a four-year friendship is over just like that." Anu snapped her fingers, then wiped the tears off her cheek.

Julie looked at her and said, "I think you need to take your daughter home."

Anger fuelled her as she drove home, barely listening to Neha. Her tears dried as she raked over her memories to see whether she'd made any of it up. But repeatedly, she came up with the same confusing scenarios. One minute they were friends, and the next she was nobody to them. The worst of it was that none of them had had the courage to speak to her, to tell her where things had gone wrong, given her a chance to fix it, or at the very least been Joe-blunt about the fact that they were no longer on the same page. Instead, it had been a blow-hot, blow-cold game, leaving her confused and wrong-footed. When she had tried to force a discussion, it had made her the villain of the piece.

A failed friendship was just as bad as a failed love affair. Time and emotions were invested in both because the people seemed worth the effort. Julie had said she was acting like a jilted lover, and she probably was, because her feelings were like a person who'd been dumped for no good reason. The 'dumper' rarely realised the damage they had done to the person dumped.

Neha had fallen silent, realising that her mother was in some kind of mood.

Anu parked in front of the house. As she opened the boot of the car to get Neha's bags out, she heard Cathy call out.

"Anoo!"

Not in the right frame of mind, she pretended not to hear, hoping Cathy wouldn't follow through, but today was just not her day. She heard Cathy's door slam behind her as she rushed towards Anu. Plastering on a surprised look, she turned to see Cathy standing with a large box in her hands.

"The delivery chap brought this over to me, asking if I'd hold on to it for you."

Anu took the box from her, wondering what it could be. She hadn't ordered anything.

"Thank you, Cathy."

"Hey, you okay? You look a bit… "

"I'm fine."

"Listen, about the barbecue - we weren't planning to go, anyway. We barely know Louise and her husband. I met her at the ball at your table. She's more your friend than mine, and I figured since you weren't planning to go... Oh my goodness, Anoo! What have I said? What's happened?"

The floodgates had opened once again, and as Anu stood on the sidewalk weeping openly, Cathy took the keys out of her hands and led her and a shocked Neha inside the house.

Putting the kettle on, she looked at Neha and said, "All right, pumpkin, go on upstairs for a bit. I need to talk to your mummy."

A stunned Neha complied immediately.

Cathy handed Anu a strong tea loaded with sugar.

"Right, you need to tell me exactly what's going on."

Out it came, in fits and bursts, until she had related the whole sorry saga. Cathy sat across from her, nursing her own tea; listening to her speak, gently encouraging her when she stopped, nodding in places, and frowning at others. When she had finished, Cathy set her tea down.

"I can see why you're upset, Anoo. They haven't played nice at all. I am rather perplexed by everything too. They seemed like perfectly lovely ladies. In fact, I've been out for a few lunches with Julie because she was so insistent. But if she makes a habit of 'collecting people' then I'm not interested either. It's shocking really that they could treat you so badly."

"You know, Cathy," Anu said between sobs, "if only they'd been upfront about it."

"Hey, just forget about it, okay! Why are you wasting your tears on them? You think they'd do the same over you?"

"Probably not." Anu sniffed.

"I must go now, Anoo. I'd put Mel in front of the telly and rushed out to catch you. You're going to be alright?"

"Yes, thank you. Sorry about the meltdown."

"Shush! That's what friends are for."

She gave her a quick peck on the cheek before letting herself out.

After Anu had settled Neha with a white lie about feeling sad recalling her mother, she remembered the box that Cathy had brought over. Wrapped in brown paper, it sat innocuously on the table where she had left it. As Neha sat bent over her homework, Anu took a pair of scissors and cut through the paper to reveal a shoe box inside. An old 'Clarks' logo was embossed on the cover. Curious, she lifted the lid to find a letter on top of several black-and-white pictures. Opening the envelope, she took out a single sheet with writing on it.

My dear Anu,

I've thought several times about calling you, but just haven't had the words to express how I feel. We were not particularly kind towards each other recently, and even though I heard out your apology, I think that perhaps you still harbour a lot of resentment against me.

To a large extent, that is my fault. In looking out for you, I ended up patronising you. Your breaking away from me has hurt me more than I can explain. When Ravi and you moved to England, I thought we could be close once more, but that never happened. Then all those accusations, and I just had to step back and reassess our relationship.

In the last month, I've come to realise that you do mean a lot to me. I cannot even begin to understand how devastated you must be feeling right now at the loss of your mother. I hope looking through these pictures might bring you some joy. Mummyji sent them over as soon as I requested for them. She'd held on to them because these were the few precious memories of her brother she had left. But we both think that you deserve to have them. I hope you see this as a peace offering. If you find it in your heart to forgive my thoughtlessness over the years, call me. I'll be waiting.

Lots of love,

Annie.

Black-and-white photographs of her parents when they were young and together. Her father, looking smart in his suit and narrow tie, his arm around his young wife's waist. Her mother laughing, her hair in a bouffant, a single rose adorning the side of it. Pictures of them on their honeymoon, candid shots of them walking in the snow, Mama still in saris but wearing a heavy overcoat and looking impossibly beautiful. Then photos of herself as a baby, a big black *kajal*[2] spot on her cheek to ward off the evil eye. Her father playing with her, throwing her up in the air, Mama smiling in the background. Pictures that showed a family that seemed happy, seemed complete. Nothing in here foreshadowed the sadness that would follow.

When Ravi came home, he found her sitting on the floor surrounded by the photographs, her eyes swollen from crying, her entire body trembling.

He scooped Neha up from the sofa where she'd been sitting and watching her mother.

"Have you been a naughty girl, Neha? Have you made Mummy cry?" He mock-scolded her.

She shook her head vigorously.

"Have you had any dinner?"

She shook her head again.

"Do you want pizza?"

Immediately her eyes lit up.

"Yes, Daddy!"

"Let's order Dominoes, shall we? Now, you go up and take your shower. By the time you're out, dinner will be here." He gave her a quick kiss on the cheek and sent her upstairs.

Then he knelt down in front of Anu, examining the pictures.

"How long have you been sitting here for?"

She looked at him blankly. His voice seemed to come from far away.

"Anu, it's nearly 8 p.m. - how long have you been sitting here?"

Snapping out of her reverie, she focused on him.

"I... I don't know..."

"Come on, get up. You need to get to bed now. I'm going to bring you a brandy, then you sleep."

"Neha... "

"Don't worry about her. I'll take her to school tomorrow. Just have a lie-in."

She nodded mutely, allowing herself to be led upstairs and tucked into bed. A few minutes later, Ravi made her gulp down some brandy, which temporarily halted the trembling.

"Sleep now." He kissed her forehead, tucking the duvet around her, before closing the door behind him.

The river was dark and malevolent as it rushed past her silently. Swollen and threatening to break its banks, it frightened her, but she waded in nonetheless. Voices called out to her from the distance, urging her forward. Unable to see in the pitch-black night, she groped her way one step at a time, her hands outstretched to feel for any resistance. The rocks on the river-bed were slimy with algae and she felt herself slip, righting herself before she slid into the sludge-like water. The voices were still too far away to make out what they were saying. Suddenly, she felt an overpowering need to be there amongst them, knowing she was missing something important.

She ran through the water, letting it splash up and cover her in mud and slime. Then she spotted a fire on the bank and waded towards it silently. A group of people sat around the fire, roasting marshmallows. She thought she saw Andy's hair, orange in the fire's glow.

"Anoo... Anoo..." The voices seemed nearer now, incredibly close, as if they were running next to her, screaming her name into the wind.

She crawled ashore, desperate to get away from them. The nearer she got to the fire, the colder she felt. There was no heat in the flames. Then she spotted Jemima sitting with her back to her, holding out a large stick over the fire with something at the end.

"J... Jem..." She tried calling out, but her voice wouldn't leave her throat. Suddenly, as if sensing Anu, Jemima turned around. But it wasn't Jemima. It was Mama. Mama staring at her accusingly.

"You left!" She screamed. "Look, look at what you did!"

Then she held up the stick with her own heart upon it. Charred but beating, it oozed blood, dripping down the sides slowly, the dark liquid making its way towards Anu. She tried backing away, but her legs would not move. Held hostage, she watched the crimson ooze reach her feet. And the voices screamed banshee-like into her ears once again.

"Anu, Anu, wake up! You're having a nightmare."

Her heart thudding, she sat up, her night clothes drenched in sweat.

"Ravi, it was awful... Mama's heart... she was roasting it... my fault... "

"Shhh, shhh. It was only a dream. Go back to sleep. It was only a dream."

CHAPTER FIFTEEN

Mid-July, Ravi finally confronted her.

"It's been a month, Anu. You can't carry on like this."

She was in her sweatpants, hair lank and greasy, face unmade, dinner hastily cobbled together, and the house worse than a tip.

Anu had not thought it possible that grief could sledge-hammer its way out of her in this manner. But her emotions had taken on a life of their own. Listless and apathetic, she lay in bed until 11 a.m. every morning, listening to Ravi getting Neha ready for school and preparing his own lunch. She heard them leave daily, barely responding to their goodbyes.

Hunger would drag her out of bed at noon, when she'd nibble on a toast and sit on the sofa staring out at her garden. If the doorbell rang, she'd ignore it. If someone rapped on the window, she'd sink lower into the sofa, hoping they'd leave soon, which they invariably did. The phone remained unanswered; the house remained dusty, and the clothes piled up in the laundry basket.

Nothing seemed worthwhile anymore. Grief, anger and

shame mingled into a knot that sat in the centre of her chest, leaving her inarticulate and frozen.

"Are you listening to me, Anu?" Ravi ran his fingers through his hair, looking harried. "Please pull yourself together. This is affecting all of us. It scares Neha to approach you, I'm at my wits' end, and honestly, I don't think I can carry on this way. It's taking a toll on my work and my nerves."

"I'm sorry." She responded tonelessly.

He sat next to her, taking her hands in his.

"You may not like this, but I've had to call Annie. She's coming tomorrow. I need the help, Anu, I can't manage on my own."

She looked at him and shrugged. What did it matter? All she wanted to do was crawl back into bed.

He sighed and pulled her towards him, planting a kiss on her head.

"Oh Anu, what's happening to you, my darling?"

"The first thing we are going to do is air this entire house out!" Annie said, flinging the windows open. She'd bustled in at 9 a.m. with Ravi greeting her quickly before leaving for work. Anu was still in bed, and when Annie drew the curtains back and opened the windows, she groaned.

"Right, Missy, you can get up now. Go take a shower while I vacuum the house."

Anu sat up in bed bleary-eyed, watching Annie use the kitchen cloth to dust all the surfaces. Her large figure filled the room, disturbing the dust motes in the light. She turned around suddenly.

"I'm not joking, Anu. I will physically yank you out of bed and put you under the shower unless you're out of bed in the next two minutes!"

Anu scooted out of bed, scared that Annie would follow through with her threat.

Standing under the hot shower as the water sluiced over her, she felt the grime of the past week wash away. How long since she'd taken a shower? Emerging from the bathroom, she saw Annie holding a mug of coffee for her.

"Drink this while you dry your hair. Breakfast in ten minutes."

Annie had cooked her a meal of poached eggs on English muffins with bacon on the side. Anu's stomach rumbled in recognition of the flavours that awaited, the smell of bacon tantalising her appetite. She reached forward to take a piece off the plate and Annie slapped her hand.

"Sit down and eat properly."

Anu sat down, feeling weak with hunger. The first mouthful was like biting into a slice of heaven.

"Mmmm." She couldn't help the moan of pleasure that escaped her.

"Look at how thin you've gotten, Anu! You need feeding up."

Anu nodded absently, tucking into the breakfast. From time to time she stopped and took a sip of her coffee, dark and sweet, just the way she liked it. When she'd finished, she pushed her plate away. Then she looked up at Annie and said, "Thank you."

Annie took the plate from under her, and as she walked to the kitchen she said from over her shoulder, "What for?"

What was it about having the familiar figure of her cousin around that made Anu feel better immediately? Yet, she eyed Annie warily, aware that she had not responded to the box of photographs she had sent her.

"Annie..." Her voice came out as a croak and Anu

realised that she'd barely spoken in a month. What kind of wife and mother had she been wallowing in her misery? "I meant to call, but..."

"I know. Ravi told me all about it."

"I've been selfish and stupid."

"Anu, you're grieving. It can take years to recover from a bereavement. Did you think you'd bounce back within a few weeks?"

"I should have made more of an effort with Mama. Reached out more often, visited more frequently."

Annie sat across from her on the sofa, tucking her feet beneath her as she regarded Anu carefully.

"You know I wasn't her biggest fan, but I really don't see the need for all this remorse. You did the best you could under the circumstances. Mala *mami* [1]was, ummm, a free spirit. As a mother, she should have been the one reaching out and making the effort, which she never did. So, grieve her as much as you like, but get rid of the guilt."

Anu picked at the fibres on the throw.

"You said I was like her once. Did you mean it?"

"Aren't we all like our parents in one way or another? But how much of that governs our behaviour is up to us. You called me bossy and patronising once. Guess where I get it from?"

"*Bua?*" Anu recalled Annie's mother, a large intimidating woman who had everyone quaking in her presence.

"Who else?" They looked at each other and started laughing, the unease between them dissipating.

"You do know that you have to get back into the rhythm of things soon? Neha needs a routine and a mother who is there for her, and you have a saint for a husband. He needs a break as well."

"I know." Anu sighed.

"I can only stay a few days before heading back, and far

be it from me to tell you how to lead your life. But I'm here to listen if you want to unburden. And I promise I'll keep the sarcasm in check."

Anu sank back into the sofa, smiling weakly.

On Sunday evening, as Annie was preparing to leave, Anu went up to her and handed her a parcel.

"What's this?"

"A little something as a thank you."

"Can I open it?"

Anu nodded, watching as Annie unfolded the brown paper. Her gasp of surprise was the reaction she'd been hoping for.

"This is for me?"

"For your home. If you like it enough."

"I had no idea... " Annie looked down at the painting - a swirl of the moss-like green dappling the background of anthracite and dove. "This is beautiful. So unlike what I remember you painting before. What's it called?"

"The Wall."

"I love it!" She reached forward and hugged her. "And I love you, Anu. Never forget it."

Standing together, holding Annie, the knot inside her loosened somewhat. Family, she realised, wasn't just about who was related to you. It was who was willing to forgive you your foibles and embrace you, regardless of your flaws.

Anu looked at her face in the mirror as she tied her hair back in a ponytail. She'd been giving herself a talking-to all morning, trying to psyche herself into taking Neha to school. Since her showdown with Julie, she hadn't been back at school, with Ravi doing the drop-offs and the childminder picking Neha up for an extra fee. Then Annie had come to stay, and somehow, shortly after, an entire Summer had just gone by in the blink of an eye. Now that Neha was in Year 5, she knew that in a few years' time they would be done with primary school. But right now she was worried sick at how people would react. What was the gossip doing the rounds? Would she be judged as needy, desperate or unhinged? She kept telling herself it didn't matter, but she knew that to her, it still did.

Dressing in a striped linen shirt and jeans, she put on a bit of lipstick and her sunglasses. There was no postponing the moment.

Downstairs, Neha looked at her and said, "You look pretty, Mummy."

"Thank you, baby!" Anu kneeled down and straightened Neha's collar, then looked her in the face as she said, "Mummy was not well for a while, but I'm okay now. I promise to take care of you, Neha, and not let you down again."

Neha's little hands cradled her face. "It's okay to be sad, Mummy."

Anu smiled shakily before getting back on her feet.

They were early at school, and she let Neha run off and join her friends, standing apart once again. Just a little while longer of coming to this playground and then, hopefully, she'd never have to see any of these women again. Six years of being overlooked and marginalised had created deep dents in her psyche. She recognised now how much she had craved acceptance, willing to change herself to achieve it. Yet, whilst she'd had it, it had been a hollow victory. One that self-combusted with the tiniest bit of dissonance. So, what did it matter what these people thought of her? Why did she still quake inwardly at the slightest sign of a smirk that showed disdain towards her?

She saw Julie walk in with Louise. They didn't spot her and instead joined another group of mothers chatting amongst themselves. Anu looked away. Just a while longer, she reminded herself, and then she would be done.

"You are a sight for sore eyes!" Helen came and stood next to her. "Have you been away to a spa? Looking amazing! New figure and all that."

Anu chuckled. "It's called the grief diet."

"Oh crap! I'm always putting my foot in it." Helen examined her face. "How are you feeling?"

"Okay," Anu shrugged. "Rubbish, actually. Emotionally, I've been a mess. And I guess you've heard about my little hissy fit before the Summer holidays?"

"Can't say I have."

"Oh come on Helen, it's written all over your face."

"All right, I may have heard something."

"And what's being said? Avoid the crazy Indian woman?"

"Actually, many people have said some very nice things about you, yours truly included." Helen stared at Julie and Louise. "Look, I don't know what went down between you women, and I don't even want to know. All I'm going to say is that there's always two sides to a story. You're justified in feeling how you do, and they might be as well."

"I don't want to gossip, Helen. All I wanted were answers, and I never got any."

"Sweetie, life's like that, isn't it? Sometimes you don't get answers and you just have to let it go."

"I was petrified to walk in here this morning. Thank you for supporting me, Helen."

"Hey, let me tell you something. All these women - all of us - are riddled with our own insecurities and anxieties. Just for a moment there, you let the mask slip. So what? It makes you human. Stop worrying about what the world thinks, Anoo. Just live your life."

Three days later Susan stood at the door, holding a lemon drizzle cake.

"I thought you'd let me in if I brought an offering."

"Come in. I'm sorry I've been a bit under the weather."

"The number of times I knocked and rang..." Susan walked in. "Finally, I cornered Ravi, and he told me you weren't well. What happened, Anoo?"

"Oh, just... you know... "

Susan set the cake down.

"Cathy wanted to come, but she had a dentist appointment, so she'll come by later. Any chance of a cuppa?"

Anu sliced into the cake, serving them both a portion with their tea.

"Did you get my flowers?"

"Yes, I did. I meant to ring and thank you, but I fell ill, and then, what with one thing or another, I just didn't get a chance. Sorry, it's been a lowkey kind of Summer. Just recovering, you know... "

"Are you better now? I saw you drop Neha off this morning and since you weren't in your running clothes, I thought of taking a chance and dropping in."

Anu took a bite of the cake, then set the plate down.

"Is something the matter, Susan?"

"Well, yes, and no," she answered cryptically. "Cathy already knows, but I wanted to tell you as well." She took a large sip of her tea, looking pleased with herself. "We had a bit of argy-bargy, Jan and I. She was around two weekends ago, having a right go at me for not releasing the equity from the property, and I just snapped! Gave her a piece of my mind. Oh, she wasn't happy about that, not at all. Stomped out of the house saying she'd never come to see me again. But two hours later she was on the phone begging forgiveness."

Susan sat back, looking smug.

"Wow!" Anu exclaimed, unable to believe her ears. Susan had always been so mild-mannered that she couldn't believe she'd finally given Jan the ticking off she deserved.

"And what's more, I rang Mark and told him that if he didn't want his sister to swallow up his entire inheritance, he'd better visit again, and bring my grandchildren along too. That wife of his can stay home if she wants. Never cared for her anyway."

"My! What prompted this change Susan?"

"Life's too short, Anoo. After my sister's funeral, I decided that whatever years I've got left, I'm going to live them on my terms. I've been held to ransom for far too long by my children. Not anymore. If I didn't want them trampling all over me, I needed to stop behaving like a doormat."

Neha had missed her dance lessons for an entire month before the Summer holidays, so when Anu walked in to explain the absence, she fully expected Mrs Madhok to be displeased. But she was taken aback when Mrs Madhok came over to her instead, asking how she was.

"I'm fine Romaji, but as you know, in a year or so, Neha will have her SATs. We are thinking of dropping dance now."

"But Mrs Dhawan, she is very good."

Anu smiled at her wryly, watching her daughter's lack-lustre spins in the distance.

"I think we both know that she's more enthusiastic than talented. But it has been a wonderful experience for her. She's made some friends here that she keeps in touch with. And through you, she's learned more about our culture and tradition than I could've possibly taught her at home."

Mrs Madhok held her elbow, leading her to one side.

"I hope you're not leaving because of what happened after the show?"

"My goodness, no! That was last year. Absolutely not. It's just that I was the one who forced Neha to take up dance, without even considering if that was something she would have chosen for herself. Neha has other hobbies and interests, and I'd like her to find what she enjoys without me forcing my opinion on her."

Mrs Madhok nodded in understanding before being called away by another student. Anu went and sat in the corner, wanting to watch Neha the last few times she'd be attending these dance lessons. The curly-haired lady came and sat next to her.

"I have not seen you around in a while."

"Yes, we've been busy." Anu smiled at her. "I've been carrying this around in my bag for you. It's a bit bent out of shape now. Also, I've never even asked your name, so I had to keep it quite generic."

Puzzled, the lady took the envelope Anu proffered, taking a stiff A5 size card out. Anu had painted the back-drop of the show in miniature upon the card and written a simple 'thank you' on the other side.

"This is for me?"

"Yes. For standing up for me all that time ago. I didn't forget, even though it's taken me this long to show my gratitude."

It surprised her to see the woman's eyes fill with tears.

"This is so unexpected. I didn't do it for any thanks, I just couldn't bear to see Jigna walk away with all the credit when all of us knew how hard you'd worked."

"Still, it takes guts to stand up for what's right and not everyone has the courage to do that. We won't be continuing with Kathak after this term, but I just wanted to say that it was truly my pleasure to meet you."

"You know that our daughters have become quite good friends?"

"They have?"

"Yes. I'd like them to keep that friendship going, if that's all right by you. And, if you're willing, maybe we could meet up for an occasional coffee or lunch too?"

"I would like that very much."

"Then you need to take my number down. Oh, and by the way, my name is Rani."

Life had a strange way of compensating for dearth. While some friendships had broken down, others had emerged unexpectedly. And strangely, it was where she had never felt the need to pretend to be anyone but herself that she had found people who liked her.

Most of Year 5, Anu parked in the playground car park and let Neha walk the short distance to and from school on her own, fostering in her a sense of independence in readiness for secondary school. Maybe that signalled to some mothers that Anu was a coward, but now, she didn't feel the need to reach out to anyone, retreat becoming her position of choice. For far too long, she had tried her best to fit in. But now, for some odd and inexplicable reason, that desire had receded.

Still, she was unfailingly polite to the few school mums she met at Parent-Teacher meetings or play rehearsals. She rarely ran into Julie or Jemima, almost as if the Universe was conspiring to keep them apart. Occasionally she spotted Louise at Sainsbury, but with her, it was a relief not to have to pretend anymore. They ignored each other as strangers would.

This time out was rewarding in its own way. She had returned to her first love - painting. Hours just melted away as she tried capturing the changing seasons and her own emotions on canvas. With art, it felt effortless. No one was judging her here, there was no standard to live up to. It was her, the easel, the paints and a vision.

Ravi had said little, watching the canvases stack up on their landing. One time he'd asked, "Anu, are you okay?"

"I think I'm getting there, Ravi."

"In your own good time, my love."

So she was taking her time to process her life - the last few years, a mother's loss, a child growing up and the friend-ships that had disintegrated. Where, she asked herself repeatedly, had she lost herself? And how could she find herself once again?

The school had booked the end-of-year show in the usual auditorium, and from her previous years' experience, Anu knew to get there early in order to get good seats. Ravi had finished in time too, so as they made their way inside, they could find seats in the fourth row from the stage.

"Neha is in the chorus, you said?"

"Playing a ragamuffin."

"And we're watching... "

"Oliver! ... Ravi, really, I told you already!"

He winked at her. Things had slowly started to return to an even keel, and in the past year, even though she had moments when she had felt despondent and alone, never again she had decided quite firmly would she allow it to impinge on her family life.

Her jaw tightened as she saw Jemima come in, chatting with a few other mums from their year. Ravi followed her glance.

"Remember what I said Anu. Act normal, be civil."

She nodded, swallowing. Jemima's eyes caught hers, but she looked past her as though Anu didn't exist.

"No need to act anything, Ravi. I've just been given the cold shoulder."

"Their loss, not yours."

Just then a mum leaned over from behind them to chat about the show. Anu turned and responded, setting the episode aside. She'd be damned if she was to let any of them affect her again!

The show was a success, and as they collected their children from the chorus line, Natalie came up to them.

"Hey Anoo! I'm having a little leaving-do at mine. We'll be moving to Edinburgh by the end of the month. Would you be free to come on Saturday?"

"Oh! That's come around quickly." Anu looked at Natalie. "Is it just mums?"

"No, everyone - husbands and children." She smiled. "The forecast is for a sunny day, and we figured we might as well get some use from our garden for the last time."

Anu met Ravi's eyes, and he gave her a slight nod of assent.

"We'd love to come! What time?"

As they discussed details, Neha came over and stood next to them, her face shining despite the mud marks they'd painted on.

"Did you like the show, Mummy? Was it good? Did you hear me singing?"

The sun was shining on Saturday, with the slightest of breezes proving it to be an utterly pleasant day. Anu chose a turquoise chiffon dress with a white belt and matching accessories.

"You look very summery!" Ravi remarked, grinning at her.

"So do you." She looked at her handsome husband in his linen shorts and blue linen shirt, wondering how on earth she had gotten this lucky.

"Are you ready for this?"

"I am." The irony was that after years of wanting an entry into the gilded circle of mums, now that she had it, she found she couldn't care less.

"And if you see Julie and the others?"

"Act normal, be civil. I remember."

"Good girl." Ravi kissed her on the forehead. "Oh, and before we get going - here's something for you."

He handed her a little key, with a keychain of two inter-linked hearts.

"What's this?" She looked down at it, perplexed.

"It's the key to your new art studio."

"What?!"

"Well, it's only one room that I'm renting in a larger establishment, but I thought it'd be a good place to begin."

"I... I don't understand!"

"Anu, sweetheart, you said you wanted to work. I think painting is your passion and your vocation. Now that Neha is older, you can really get stuck in and I thought you'd need a dedicated studio to get started. Besides, I'd really like to reclaim our landing."

Anu looked up at him, her love and gratitude shining in her eyes.

"I don't know what to say, Ravi. This is more than I could've hoped for."

"Nonsense! It's the least I could do for you after the year you've had."

"But the cost?"

"Is nothing. Now stop worrying, and let's go out and have a good time."

At the barbecue, Anu spotted several mothers who smiled and waved at her. She waved back, but went up to Natalie with a bottle of wine and flowers first.

"There is something else I've brought you, but it's a little bulky and I didn't want to bring it out into the garden."

"Ooh, now I'm curious," Natalie followed her to the gate.

Anu had propped up the canvas against the fence, and as Natalie came up to it, she turned it around. It was a charcoal sketch of Rebecca and Neha blowing dandelions, which she'd had framed as a leaving present for Natalie's family.

Speechless, Natalie stood back looking at the picture. Then she reached forward and squeezed Anu's hand.

"I'm going to cherish this forever."

As Anu mingled amongst the guests, she was relieved to see that aside from Louise, no one else from her former group had made an appearance. It was easy enough to give Louise a wide berth as she chatted with mothers she had never had occasion to get to know. The last year had liberated her of all desire to belong, and that in turn had allowed her to be herself and mix with no expectations.

Zoe was there with a new boyfriend. She looked as chic as ever, dressed in a white waistcoat and narrow knee-length white shorts, gold bangles clinking on her wrists, her blonde bob as sleek and shiny as always. She gave Anu a small smile of recognition before turning back to her partner. Anu noted how little Zoe's lack of interest bothered her now. Some people were just not meant to be in her life, and it had taken her several years to realise this. Nevertheless, she was glad it was a lesson she could now pass down to Neha.

"How's Dawn?" She asked Helen as they queued up to get their hot dogs.

"Jeremy's taken her to the US for some experimental treatment. We're all praying it works."

"I hope it does too."

"And how are you doing, Missus? You look really well, even though I haven't seen you around much in the last year."

"I am well." Anu said. Then she realised that she actually meant it too.

"And what I hear is that he's drinking himself into a stupor every day. At this rate he won't last long." Kriti was filling her in on all the news during their monthly chat. Abhishek invariably featured in those, although Anu had lost interest in him long ago. But a sense of betrayal and desertion still lingered in her brothers and sisters.

"Nitin *bhaiyya* says its guilt. If he really killed Mama, he's doing a pretty fine job of killing himself too."

"But what if it's because he misses her?"

"Anu *didi*, don't be so naïve. He was only with her for the money."

Anu stayed silent. Who could understand the inner workings of anyone else's relationship, let alone their minds or hearts? Only Abhishek and Mama knew what their dynamics were, and if she'd learnt one thing, it was to take a step back before judging anyone.

"So when are you coming to India? We were thinking of organising a getaway to this resort in Manali. All the families and kids, and we want you, Ravi *jiju* [2] and Neha to join in too. It's Nirav *bhaiyya*'s 40th birthday. You have to come!"

Laughingly, she agreed, promising to come back with dates. After she'd hung up, Anu mused that in the last year or so they had grown so much closer as kith and kin. Scattered and fractured as they had been in their younger years, age and losing the one common denominator in their lives had bound them together in the most unanticipated and astonishing way. Suddenly, she didn't feel like she was on her own, a single child between two sets of siblings, forever standing apart. Instead, she felt comforted being cushioned between them, knowing that she belonged there, in that warm circle, in that elusive thing she had hunted for all her life: her kindred.

That summer, Ravi finally took them to Dubai after years of promising.

"What a month to pick!" Anil *bhaiyya* greeted them at the airport.

Truly, August was one of the hottest months in Dubai, but Ravi had convinced them by saying that since they'd spend most of their time indoors in air conditioning, it didn't really matter.

As Anu relaxed on the couch with her cup of tea, Smita turned to her and asked, "How have you enjoyed living in the UK, Anu? I envy you your seasons and all that lush greenery. The heat here is so oppressive at times that I don't even want to step out of the apartment."

"But don't you feel closer to India, *bhabi*? After all, you're only a few hours away by plane."

"That's true, it is convenient in that way. Someday soon we'll be back in India too. After all, we'll never become citizens here, the law doesn't allow it."

"How do you feel about returning to India?"

"I'm looking forward to it, honestly. I've never felt at home here. It's hard to establish roots in a place that doesn't treat you as one of its own. There is also the revolving door of expats in and expats out. Just when I think we've made friends, they move on. And don't even get me started on the super-wealthy Indians here..."

As Smita *bhabi* talked, Anu had a sudden realisation that this feeling of being alone, being a foreigner in a strange land, wasn't unique to her. Nearly everyone who had left their homeland for a different place faced similar challenges of finding themselves incompatible with their new environs.

That night, after making sure that Neha had settled in with her cousins in the adjoining room, Anu said to Ravi, "I'd always thought that Anil *bhaiyya* and Smita *bhabi* had a huge social circle, but in some ways she is just as lonely as I am. She can't wait to go back to India once and for all."

Ravi propped himself up on the pillow and looked at her.

"That's odd, because Anil *bhaiyya* is applying for jobs in the US at her behest."

"Then why would she say that to me?"

"Anu, it's normal to feel nostalgic for home and a certain way of life. But once you've lived abroad, it's hard to go back to living in India. Most of my colleagues who have tried have invariably ended up returning."

"Why is that?"

"Not sure. Maybe it's the recognition that there are greener pastures outside, or that all the necessities we take for granted living abroad are still luxuries for many people in India."

"Does that mean we'll never return either?"

"Never say never. Right now, we have the best of both worlds. Why not enjoy that?"

"Ravi?"

"Hmmm?"

"You know the new art studio you've rented?"

"Yes?"

"I haven't even seen it yet. I thought I'd go before we left for this trip, and then got busy packing. I'm sorry, I must seem so ungrateful." Anu smiled ruefully.

"You can go once Neha starts school in September. Just relax and enjoy the holiday now."

And that is exactly what they did - eating, shopping and watching lots of Indian movies together. Neha loved spending time with her twin cousins, holding on to them just a little too tightly the day they were leaving.

"It's your turn to visit us in England now, *bhaiyya bhabi!*" Anu said in the car on the way to the airport.

"Of course we will! You live in such a beautiful area, and our girls can't wait to go to Legoland with Neha. She's told them so much about it." Anil *bhaiyya*'s eyes crinkled at the corners as he smiled at her in his rear-view mirror.

❖

That first day of September, when Anu walked into the studio space, she wasn't sure what to expect. A large barn conversion had been subdivided into one large shared studio, several mini-studios, a gallery and a workshop. On a big wooden table in the centre of the shared studio stood several containers with brushes. Tubes of paints were piled up in the middle, with graphite pencils in jars and stacks of drawing paper next to it. Some people were leaning over their sketchbooks, while others had propped up their easels in different spots to catch the light. The mid-morning sunshine streamed in through the floor-to-ceiling windows, highlighting the paint-splattered walls. Large, overhead ceiling lamps were left mostly unlit, and a transistor radio was tuned to Classic FM in the corner. Around twenty men and women were working silently on their respective paint-ings, occasionally stopping to make an observation or comment to their neighbour. The room smelt of wet plaster, turpentine, canvas and sodden rags. It smelt like home.

A tall Afro-Caribbean lady came up to her, all smiles.

"Welcome! Are you one of our new artists?"

Anu smiled back at her.

"I'm Anu Dhawan. I've rented one of your mini studios." She looked down at the key in her hand. "Studio 7, I believe?"

"Ah, yes. Follow me this way."

Anu followed the colourful kaftan-clad lady down the

side of the room. As she passed, several people looked up and smiled, some carried on working with an intensity and concentration that was all too familiar to her.

Studio 7 was a small but beautifully lit room in the corner.

"Your husband insisted on this one. As you can see, it gets a lot of light because of the windows on both sides. It is a smaller studio than the others, but you'll still have plenty of room for stacking your canvases and art supplies in the corner."

Anu looked around, immediately enchanted by the potential of the room.

"My name is Yolande, and I'm an artist myself, and also the owner of this space. You saw our communal area outside, and you're more than welcome to join us if you ever feel lonely here on your own. There's a small kitchen on the other end with a kettle, a fridge and a microwave. Tea and coffee supplies are always in there. I just ask you to replenish whenever you see supplies running low. No rota or anything. Just of your own free will. It's surprising how generous people are if they're not forced." She smiled kindly at Anu. "Do you have questions?"

"Just one," Anu said, "When can I begin?"

CHAPTER SIXTEEN

"Two gin and tonics." Simone placed the drinks on the table. It was a balmy summer's evening, and they'd chosen to sit in the outdoor garden area of their local pub. Luckily, they'd gotten there early enough to nab a nice table.

"It's filling up, huh?" Simone nodded at the new group that had just arrived.

"How's Kayla's foot now?" Anu asked, sipping on her drink.

"Much better. The cast will be off next week, just in time for school. Only my daughter would break her foot on vacation!"

"Must have been stressful for you both!"

"But Steve was a star! Any other man would've run a mile in the opposite direction."

"How are things working out between you two, Simone?" Anu looked at her friend's glowing face and didn't really need an answer.

"Early days Anoo, but I am happy. I never thought I'd meet anyone, let alone anyone as nice as him."

"Sometimes things are just meant to be. I'm really

pleased for you, Sim." Anu reached forward and placed her hand on Simone's.

"And how are things with you? It's been hard pinning you down between your travels and your work. Is Neha looking forward to secondary school?"

"Haha. Yes, I know, the last few months have just flown by, it's been crazy busy! Neha is super excited to start secondary school. She was sad to say goodbye to so many of her friends as many of them are heading off to private schools now. But she's got a few going up with her, and of course, plenty of opportunity to make new friends too."

"And the painting is going well?"

"The third show is in a few weeks, in a gallery in London. I'm really quite nervous about it."

"Don't be! You're fantastic. I wish I'd nabbed a work of yours before you started getting famous and all. Then I could sell it at some silly price in the future and make a killing from 'an Anoo Dhawan original'!"

"Ugh! So not true. I'm still relatively unknown."

"It's only a matter of time, Anoo. I've seen your paintings."

It had been a year since she'd first walked into the art studio. A year of discovering herself through the one medium that had never let her down. She'd plunged head-long into her journey, expecting only to produce enough work for a showing or two. But Yolande had teased her out of her little studio, asking her to display her work in the in-house gallery, with the other talented artists working there. When Anu's first painting sold, she was stunned. Then she was invited, along with four other artists, to exhibit her work at two different galleries, one in Le Marais, Paris. From there, the buzz had built.

Ravi had designed a website for her, and she'd started finding different exhibitions to display her work at. Nonita had connected her to a professional photographer who had helped her build a portfolio of her paintings. Slowly, and with word-of-mouth, knowledge of her was growing in the art world.

But for Anu, it had never been about the fame or the money. Art had rescued her in her darkest moments. It gave her joy; it gave her purpose, and it allowed her to express herself in a manner that she could never have in person or in words.

"You were a million miles away there. I've ordered a bottle of rosé now, and two fish and chips. I'm starving." Simone sat down opposite her once again. "Guess who I spotted inside?"

"Who?"

"Your old favourite friends, the holy trinity of JJL."

"Oh, them."

"Want to go in and say hello?"

"Not really. I'm just relieved I'll never have to see them again now that Neha's going to secondary school."

Simone twirled the straw in her glass.

"You never told me what that entire brouhaha was about."

Anu stared into the distance thoughtfully.

"You know, for the longest time, I didn't know either. But now I think I needed that phase to happen in my life to discover who I am and what's really important to me. If they hadn't put me on that roller coaster of emotions, I wouldn't have gone back to my painting. If I hadn't painted in a frenzy like I did, I would never have discovered that I truly have a passion for it, and that I am pretty good..."

"Bloody good," Simone interjected.

Anu smiled shyly. "If you say so. But really, I think everything in life happens for a reason. Look at us. A few years ago I'd given up on our friendship, yet here we are."

"And I'm glad that we could look past our egos and salvage it."

"Yes, I'm grateful for you, and for every single person who spotted something redeeming within me. I wasn't a pleasant person back then, was I?"

"Rubbish! I always liked you. But Anoo, do you resent them for what they did to you? I know I'm still mad at the mothers who treated me like poo."

"Honestly Sim, I don't have the energy or capacity to harbour any resentment against them. A long time ago I read that holding a grudge is like drinking poison and expecting the other person to die. Why would I want to do that to myself? I've exorcised all my demons on canvas, and thanks to all my experiences, I have a body of work that means something to me and that is being recognised in the art world. If that's not a positive outcome, I don't know what is."

Just then the waitress brought over two glasses of Prosecco to their table.

"We didn't order these," Simone frowned.

"It's been sent by that couple over at that table. They said to tell you "congratulations and drink up!""

Anu peered into the dusk to see Cathy and Andy giving her the 'thumbs up' sign, and grinned. "Just my crazy neighbours."

"My dears, it's been a marvellous year, hasn't it?" Susan poured out the tea, handing one cup over to Cathy and one to Anu.

It had been more than marvellous for Susan. She was not just happier but also more sprightly, with Mark visiting regularly with her grandkids. Even Jan had stopped pushing her mother around.

"It took me years," Susan said, dipping the digestive biscuit in her tea, "but I finally stopped bending over backwards for my children. You know," she looked at Anu directly as she said this, "the moment you develop self-respect, everyone else starts giving you the respect you deserve."

"I have a bit of news of my own," beamed Cathy, setting her teacup down. "We will be adding another bubba to the brood." She patted her tummy and looked around in satisfaction.

"Took you long enough! What is it, five years between the two?" Susan chuckled.

"Mmmm, I thought I didn't want any more, but Andy kept saying how nice it would be to have another baby, so I finally relented. I'm happy I did, though. This pregnancy has been easy so far, touch wood!"

"Congratulations!" Anu came over to Cathy and gave her a little hug and kiss. "I'm so happy for you guys. This baby will have wonderful parents. But why were you in the pub the other day? You shouldn't be drinking!"

"I wasn't, it was just club soda. We were discussing how far to postpone the wedding again!" Cathy winked. "And you, Anoo? Are you happy with how things have worked out?"

Andy and Cathy had been more than supportive after her friendships had disintegrated. Even though they were always diplomatic in their dealings with all the other parents, Cathy had made no bones about the fact that her loyalties lay with Anu and Ravi. And because of her natural charm and affability, people were unwilling to believe that Cathy would associate with anyone who was awful or ill-mannered, stopping a lot of the nasty rumours in their tracks.

"It's been a steep learning curve for me as well. You saw how it was, Cathy, and I've unburdened myself often enough to you, Susan. But I can say now, hand on my heart, that I'm in a much, much better place. Ravi and I would have loved to have had another baby, but that was not meant to be. Instead, I have my painting, a lovely child who occasionally drives me bananas, and a husband who has put up with so much from me that, as my cousin keeps pointing out, he deserves sainthood! What else do I need in life?"

"Hear, hear!" Susan lifted her cup as a toast.

Anu looked at the two women and considered how different they were from each other in age and background, and yet the three often found themselves sitting together like the unlikely friends that they were. She closed her eyes momentarily to thank whoever it was up there who had sent them into her life. Then she lifted her cup in response to Susan, and took a large, happy sip of her tea.

Neha's first day at secondary school was so different from her first day at primary school. This was no cowering child, but a confident, enthusiastic pre-teen ready to begin the next chapter of her life.

"Mum!" She complained as Anu fussed over her collar, insisting she stood still outside the front door as Ravi took a photo.

"Someday you'll thank us for preserving these moments. I have the same picture of you at age five and now look at you!"

"I'm going to be late, Mum."

"No, you won't. Give Daddy a kiss before he leaves and get into the car."

Their route took them past Neha's old school, and as they stopped at the traffic lights, Anu watched the new mums walking their little ones to school. She remembered the wide-eyed wonder that Neha had first exhibited before the nervousness had taken over. She remembered her own trepidation as she had first walked into the school, holding on to her child's hand. If she could rewind the clock, she'd tell them both to relax and let time take its course. But she also hoped that the new mums and children would encounter more kindness and acceptance than Neha and she had.

"How little they are, Mum! Look at that one, she's so cute."

"Neha baby, don't forget that you'll be the little ones at your new school. You've gotten so used to being the big fish in the little pond."

At this Neha quietened down, realising perhaps for the first time the jump she was making from a three-hundred-strong student population to one that was over twelve-hundred-strong.

Year 6 had seen her excel in her academics, just the way Mrs Pellow had predicted back in Reception year. Neha was neither the sportiest girl nor the most popular, but she was kind and gentle, and had made other friends over the course of the last two years. Although her friendship with Libby had never recovered, there were no more accusations of bullying and no further drama from either side. With the typical resilience of the young, she had rebounded from that time to emerge stronger.

Even so, she could not hide her nervousness and chewed on her lip as the enormity of starting secondary school dawned on her once again.

To distract her, Anu said, "You'll be okay walking back home?"

Neha rolled her eyes, immediately camouflaging her apprehension.

"Of course, Mum. I'm not a baby, you know."

"But you'll always be my baby..." Anu started singing.

"No, stop! That's awful. You can't sing; don't even try, okay?"

Anu sang louder, and Neha sighed in mock-irritation, putting her hands over her ears.

As they drove up behind the long queue of cars lining up to drop their children, Anu suddenly sobered up.

"You know I'm really proud of you, baby, don't you?"

Picking up on her mood, Neha turned towards her. "I know, Mum. And I'm really proud of you too."

"This is the best time for us to go to India," Annie said before Anu lost her again.

"Where on earth are you? I keep losing you."

"In the car, sweetie, driving to the supermarket. Sorry, the signal's crap, but keep talking because now I'm stuck in a jam. What on earth...?"

Anu heard some rustling and conversation before Annie came back on the line.

"Just my bloody luck! Roadworks! Anyway, I have some minutes to kill now. Tell me, how did Neha's first week at school go?"

"Great! She's really loving it. And after the first few drop-offs she's insisted on walking to and from school."

"Less of a headache for you."

"Yeah, but I miss that little bit of time with her in the

car. Anyway, you were saying how this is the best time for you to go to India?"

"Yeah, because the school rush is done. Tickets are cheaper, and the weather's not too bad. All that monsoon stickiness is over. I can't wait to eat my favourite *chaat* [1] and *golgappas* [2]."

"Stop Annie! My mouth is watering at the thought... "

"Don't complain! I saw all those fabulous pictures on Facebook of you and the family eating at the roadside *dhabas*. The food looked amazing! How is it working out, with the extended family stuff? Your second vacation with them, right?"

"Yes. Manali was the first, and this time we took off for Shimla. It's actually been great. I mean, I try not to get involved in the family politics, but above all else, it's been wonderful for Neha to get to know her cousins from my mum's side of the family. They've been getting along really well. Reminds me of us when we were that age."

"Who's the bossy one, then?"

"Do you know what?" Anu said, truth dawning on her slowly. "I think it might be Neha. Oh, gosh!"

"Mmmm, better nip that in the bud!" Annie giggled. "By the way, did she like the books I sent her?"

"My goodness, she devoured them over the weekend. You need to stop!"

"If I don't spoil my favourite niece, who will?"

Anu laughed. Her own prickliness with Annie had slowly vanished as she understood that even though neither of them got it right all the time, they meant well and genuinely cared for one another. That alone was fuel enough for a steadfast relationship.

"How's my painting coming along?" Annie asked.

"To be honest, it's on the back burner right now. I'm trying to get myself sorted for the exhibition in October."

"Oh yeah, I forgot about that! No, you concentrate on that, but then get back to mine ASAP. I've saved pride of place for it over the fireplace."

"What did you do with 'The Wall'?"

"That's at the entrance. Everyone keeps asking me about it. I'm gathering up a list of future clients for you here."

"Right!" Anu chuckled.

"Okay, they've opened things up. Gotta go. Let me know if you need anything from Delhi?"

"Will do. Travel safe and give our love to Richard."

"Bye, hun!"

Anu disconnected with a smile on her face. If *bua* had anything to do with it, Annie would go back to being Antara for the duration of her stay in India, while Richard would get the traditional pampering a son-in-law got in Indian households. She couldn't wait to hear all the stories Annie was bound to return with.

Pulling out an old folder in the storeroom, she inadvertently knocked over a few boxes. As she was replacing them, she spied the Clarks shoe box that Annie had sent her over two years ago. Ravi must have put it out of sight and forgotten about it, as had she. Now, she pulled it out again.

Making herself a cup of tea, she went through the old photographs. This time there was no stabbing pain in her chest, and she looked at them as one might old flowers that were pressed and faded but still held a slight fragrance within them. Then she selected the one of her father throwing her up in the air, with Mama smiling in the background, and put the rest back in the box. Someday she would set herself the task of placing them all in a photo album. But not today.

She got into her car and drove to the nearest town centre. Her mission was a simple one, and in no time at all she had found exactly what she was looking for.

Back home, she took the silver frame out of the box, and placed the old photo reverentially within. She was done with hiding her damaged past. It was time to acknowledge that she was who she was because of, maybe even despite, what had transpired back then. She had never known her father, but she hoped that he was looking down on her with pride.

As for Mama. She sighed as she examined her beautiful face. Who knew what demons she'd fought her entire lifetime? Anu did not want to carry those demons into her own. Maybe she had not been blessed with Mama's looks, but her blessings were plentiful, regardless. She stroked the surface of the glass, letting go of the remnants of animosity and grief within her.

"We journeyed together for a while, Mama," she whispered at the photograph. "Then you had to journey on. Maybe we'll meet again, maybe not. Wherever you are, Mama, I wish you peace."

She picked up the frame, placing a kiss on its surface, and then put it on the mantelpiece with all the other family photographs.

"Anu, come here, I want you to look at this." Yolande had her back to her, but as she turned Anu glimpsed the portrait behind her and gasped.

"You like it?" Yolande looked amused.

"I'm not sure 'like' is a word I'd use for it. Is it one of yours?"

On a white background, a woman lay with her legs akimbo, the head of one baby emerging from her vagina, while another was being pulled out of her stomach. The image was vivid and provocative, shocking to a casual bystander. But it drew Anu in, and she walked to one side, then the other, observing it from all angles.

"It's the one I'm planning to send for the exhibition. What do you think?"

"What's it called?"

"The Birth of a Woman."

"Ah!"

"Now, I need one of your stronger works. Something to complement this."

"I thought 'Mama'?"

"No. I like it, but it's not strong enough. What about the first one? The one you said your husband found frightening?"

"Oh, that." Anu bit her lip. She'd put that one away in the attic, only briefly talking to Yolande about it once. As she kept looking at Yolande's painting, she noticed that the mother's expression wasn't one of pain or suffering. Instead, her eyes and her smile were knowing, as though containing age-old wisdom; knowledge that said, "Look at me. I am woman, and only I can do this."

For an exhibition entitled 'Woman Power' perhaps Yolande was right, she needed to pull out her most visceral work yet.

She got Ravi to bring it out of the attic, and as he unwrapped it, her heart thudded unevenly. Unfinished, she'd abandoned it all those years ago, scared to face the raw savagery of it. But as she looked at it within a new context, she realised just how powerful it was. Whilst there was rage and agony within it, there was also a recognition that a heart that full would tolerate darkness for only so long. The smoky greys and the blacks of her oil paint wound and stretched out to the edges of the canvas, grooved with the scratches she had inflicted upon their surfaces. But in the centre lay a crimson heart, exposed and palpitating, asking for love, and more than willing to give it.

"She wants this one?" Ravi asked incredulously.

"She hasn't seen it yet, she might change her mind." Anu answered lightly, knowing in her heart that this would be the one going to the gallery.

If art was meant to expose the truth within, then it was this work that spoke of a particular time in her life with a verisimilitude that could not be forced or faked. She examined it with fresh eyes, finding beauty in its imperfections and comfort in its fury.

"Yes, I think Yolande will like this," she said with a sudden certainty, proud that her work reflected an unexpected power and strength instead of the weakness she had experienced back then.

The exhibition was in a small gallery in Shoreditch, London. Twenty-five new artists, all women, had been chosen to exhibit their paintings on the theme of 'Woman Power'. When all the paintings had been mounted up on the walls, Anu walked around in a daze looking at them. From stark cubic outlines to intimate realistic portraits, colourful pop art to surrealist juxtapositions of objects on human forms, there was a breathtaking diversity of talent on display. Compositions that captured the subtle and the overt, the everyday and the extraordinary. Art that celebrated womanhood, paintings that stripped down facades to the bare minimum, exposing vulnerability and grit.

"Amazing, isn't it?" A grey-haired lady stood next to her,

looking at the cartoon depiction of a famous pop star, a thought bubble with a feminist manifesto in it.

"Yes. Extraordinary."

"And yours is...?"

"That one." Anu pointed to hers, hanging on the wall to their left.

"Are you one of Yolande's then?"

"I am." Anu smiled. "There's three of us here today."

"Yes, I met Yolande already. I'm Joan Harrison, the curator."

"Pleased to meet you, Joan. I'm Anu Dhawan."

"I have to say, I really liked your contribution. Quite unlike anything I've seen before. Very abstract surrealist but with a twist. Who are your influences?"

As Anu chatted to the curator, she realised how completely at home she felt in this environment. There was no need for her to pretend to be anything other than what she was. She belonged in this world much more than she had ever belonged anywhere else.

The exhibition lasted a week, with Yolande's work getting a lot of attention.

"There's been a lot of interest in 'The Birth of a Woman'. I'm really pleased for Yolande. She's been working so hard and for so long, and if this piece sells well, her back catalogue might get some attention too." Joan said, while handing Anu a glass of red wine.

Dressed in a simple black jumper and jeans, Anu nodded. Today was the last day of the exhibition, and most of the paintings had sold. She refused to feel a twinge of envy just because hers hadn't. Yolande deserved every bit of the limelight.

"She's been a sort of mother hen to us all by housing us

and giving us space and encouragement. You should come by our little gallery sometime. It's a fantastic atmosphere, so creative and freewheeling. We've also got lots more work there, including some sculptures. Yo's rented out a few studios to sculptors and multimedia artists too." Anu said.

"Yolande is truly a wonderful mentor to have, you're all very lucky to have her." Joan smiled at her.

Right then, Yolande came up behind them.

"Did I hear my name being mentioned?"

"Just saying how lucky we are to have you, Yo!" Anu gave her a quick side-hug.

"All right, my little Indian Princess, you might want to speak to that couple looking at your painting. They've been asking too many questions I can't answer."

"It sold, Ravi!" She squealed down the line, standing outside the bar.

"Well done, babe! Now it can give someone else nightmares." He laughed at the other end. "What time are you coming home?"

"It'll be a bit late. The entire crew is celebrating, and we're heading out for dinner after drinks."

"Are you rich yet?"

"Not rich. But even after the gallery takes its commission, it's not too shabby a sum."

"I'm proud of you, Anu! Don't rush home. Enjoy yourself, let your hair down. You deserve it."

When she crawled into bed, she could hear Ravi's soft snores. She'd already checked in on Neha, tucking the duvet around her gently. It was nearly 2 a.m. and she was dog tired but happy. It had been an intense week, but one that she'd learned so much from. Yolande's toast was still echoing in her mind - "When one of us succeeds, all of us succeed. When one of us fails, the rest of us pick that person up. This is a collective as well as an individual journey. Art is our ship and our anchor, and we are voyaging together. Here's to many more adventures!" They'd whooped and shouted and drunk down their shots, in celebration of their success. Tomorrow, she knew, they would return to their work with renewed energy, their passion fuelled by the recognition they'd received. But tonight, she wanted to snuggle into her man and tell him just what he meant to her.

She curled her leg around him, knowing her cold feet would wake him.

"Anu," he groaned, turning in his sleep.

"Hi," she kissed him softly, her arms travelling under his T-shirt.

"So tired," he mumbled.

"I know... " She carried on kissing him. He opened one eye and peered at her.

"Getting frisky?"

"Mmmmm."

He yanked off his T-shirt and pulled her on top of him, wide awake. She laughed softly, then reached over for the box she'd wanted to give him.

"What's this?" He sat up, turning the bedside lamp on.

"Open it."

"Hey! Not fair. I thought you woke me to... "

"I didn't say we wouldn't, just open this first."

"Okay." He tore open the wrapping in haste, flinging it to one side. Then, as he registered the name on the box, his eyes widened. "You didn't!"

"May I?" She asked, taking the Rolex watch out of the case and putting it on his wrist. "I know how long you've wanted this, and I'm so glad that I could buy it for you."

"But Anu, how? Why?"

"How? With the sale of my paintings. Why? Because, you, Ravi, mean more than anything in this world to me. I haven't said it or shown it enough, and this is my way of making it up to you. Every day when you look at your wrist, I hope you'll remember that your wife loves you very, very much."

Then she leaned over and turned off the bedside lamp before kissing him slowly, leaving no doubt as to just what she meant to do.

"This really is the best view you can get of London, especially on a clear day like today." Anu said to Nonita. They were sitting in Hutong restaurant at The Shard, the tallest building in London, and Anu had got them a table right next to the floor-to-ceiling windows.

Nonita's work visit had coincided with the school Christmas break, and since Yolande had shooed everyone out of the studio telling them to enjoy the festive season at home, Anu had brought Nonita out for dinner at Hutong, leaving Ravi and Neha to vegetate in front of the television. Mama, she thought wistfully, would have enjoyed the food here.

"This is a treat, Anu! I'm so glad you persuaded me to come up here. I thought my vertigo would kick in, but nope, I feel fine. And it is a fabulous view!"

They both watched the orange glow cast upon the London landscape by the setting sun. Anu pointed out The London Eye, St Paul's Cathedral, London Bridge and other landmarks to Nonita.

"For the number of years I've been coming here *jaanu*, I can't say I've ever had a better view of London. What a magnificent city!"

As the lights of the capital city lit up one by one, Anu nodded happily in agreement.

"What better way to celebrate the end of the year than with you here, my darling Noni!"

"Hang on! We're still a few days away from the 31st."

"I know, but you'll have left for Mumbai by then. So this is our advance New Year's Eve celebration."

Right on cue, the server arrived with two glasses of champagne.

"Anu, you are positively blooming. What's the secret?"

"No secret. Just contentment, I guess."

"You're in a good place now?"

"Don't get me wrong, I still have days when things go wrong, I feel upset or generally listless... "

"We all have those... "

"That's the thing! It's taken me all this time to recognise that I'm not alone in feeling blue occasionally. But you know what, that daily dose of Vitamin D supplements is also helping loads." Anu laughed.

"What else?" Nonita's eyes narrowed speculatively.

"What's this, an interview?"

"No, I'm really curious. Over the past year I'd picked up on subtle little things on our phone calls, but now, seeing you this way, I want to know what brought about this change."

"Gosh, you want me to break it down for you? I wouldn't know where to begin... "

"Okay, how about telling me how you went from being someone who wouldn't say boo to a goose to this strong, assertive, *happy* woman."

Anu thought back to the last few years of her life and smiled.

"I think it happened when I stopped looking for external validation. My problem, Noni, was that I always wanted other people's approval. The day I stopped needing that, the day that I realised that the only person who could make me happy was me, everything changed. It was like a mental shift - a clarity of sorts. Suddenly things started falling into place, my life pivoted and I wasn't lost anymore."

The server came to take their order.

"You have to try the Peking duck here. It's delicious!" Anu said.

"Go for it, sweetheart, you choose. I'm all yours this evening."

After the server had left, Nonita moved the chopsticks to one side.

"Anu, you are my dearest friend, so don't take this the wrong way. You've always been on a roller coaster of emotions. How do I know that this isn't just one of your 'happier' phases? Please don't be offended."

"I'm not! You have every right to ask. For a while I wondered that too. But you know, unlike the previous occasions, this time the happiness isn't illusory. It isn't bound up with what's happening around me, the people I'm surrounding myself with, or the activities I'm throwing myself into. It feels stronger, more grounded. This time it's about me choosing what's good and right for me - my family, my work and a few genuine friends. It's a deeper happiness, something that's springing up from inside of me. Something that cannot be corrupted from the outside."

Nonita nodded thoughtfully.

"Then this may be the right time to tell you my news. I... I'm going to be a mother soon."

"What?! You're not pregnant, are you?" Anu eyed Nonita's slender frame in disbelief.

"No, no, not pregnant at all." She laughed. "Not even a steady beau in my life. I'm adopting a little girl from an orphanage in Mumbai, Anu. Something I've wanted to do for years, but haven't had the courage until now."

"Noni, really?"

"Yes. I think you hit the nail on the head when you said that happiness has to come from within. Sure, I've led a glamorous life - partied, had fun, had... have a great career, but there's always been something missing. Something solid, something more substantial, something that fulfilled me at a deeper level. Watching you make a change, I felt that I needed to think of something... someone... beyond myself. What could be more meaningful than being a mother?"

She looked at Anu, her lovely face filled with apprehension.

Anu observed the elegant woman across from her, the pixie cut, the shift dress, the nude heels. She remembered them growing up together, doing each other's homework, lending each other romance books, talking about their first crushes, sneaking their first drinks, heading off to separate universities, falling in and out of their friendship but never letting go. Nearly thirty years of watching each other grow and transform from silly young girls to the mature women they were today. She held out her hands and Nonita took them.

"My darling Noni, I couldn't be happier for you! You are going to be an amazing mother."

"You think so? I've had so many moments of doubt, so many sleepless nights, but something within me tells me this is the right thing to do."

"Then you must absolutely do it!"

"If I need advice... "

"I'm here. I'll always be here, just as you've always been there for me."

They smiled into each other's eyes. The server came over and refilled their glasses.

Nonita raised hers and looked at Anu.

"Cheers! Here's to you, here's to us, and here's to the future!"

They clinked glasses, but before they took a sip, Anu raised her glass once more. Nonita's eyebrows rose questioningly. Anu took a deep breath and exhaled slowly. She looked at her friend, looked around the busy restaurant, looked out at the lights of her adoptive city twinkling below and smiled with the pure joy that flooded her.

Then she said, "Here's to life!"

THE END

What next?
A new novel about love, loss, and the deeply complex
nature of female friendship:
Intersections - A Novel

AFTERWORD

Word-of-mouth is crucial for any author to succeed and if you found this book interesting *please* do leave a review on your preferred retailer. Even if it's just a star rating or a sentence or two, it would make all the difference and would be very much appreciated!!

If you enjoyed this book, you can sign up to hear more about my new releases and any special offers!

Do visit www.poornimamanco.com to keep abreast of all my news.

GLOSSARY OF TERMS

Chapter 1

1. Grandmother from the mother's side
2. Brother or brother-in-law
3. Sister-in-law
4. Aunt, typically father's sister

Chapter 2

1. Lentil curry
2. Small bowl
3. Indian dish of rice cooked in stock with spices, typically having vegetables.
4. An Indian side dish of yogurt containing chopped cucumber or other vegetables, and spices.
5. A pancake made from rice flour and ground pulses, typically served with a spiced vegetable filling.
6. A village, typically in rural Punjab
7. Sikh temple
8. A Sikh place of worship
9. Lentils

Chapter 3

1. An expression of mild annoyance or mild impatience
2. Grandmother-Grandfather (from the mother's side)
3. A mixture of ground spices used in Indian cooking
4. Small cup-shaped oil lamps made of baked clay
5. A Hindu religious ceremony that is considered as the main festive day of Diwali
6. A full ankle-length skirt worn by Indian women, usually on formal or ceremonial occasions.
7. Devotional songs
8. Vegetable fritters

Chapter 4

1. A respectful greeting
2. A term of endearment

Chapter 5

1. An ornament made of bells worn around the ankle
2. "That's it! Finished."

Chapter 6

1. A roadside food stall
2. Indian breakfast/snack made out of flattened rice, vegetables and potatoes
3. Fashionable

Chapter 7

1. A rustic or unsophisticated Indian
2. The tenth and final day of the Hindu festival of Navaratri, usually in October
3. Lord Krishna's childhood town
4. Indian flatbread
5. Carrot pudding

Chapter 8

1. Aunt (mother's sister). In this instance used to denote closeness, even though there is no blood relation

Chapter 9

1. Lentil curry
2. A suffix to denote respect
3. Uncle (typically mother's brother)

Chapter 10

1.   A triangular savoury pastry fried in ghee or oil, containing spiced vegetables or meat
2.   A piece of vegetable or meat, coated in seasoned batter and deep-fried

Chapter 12

1.   The origin of Kanjeevaram sarees is from Kanchipuram village in Tamil Nadu
2.   Elder sister

Chapter 13

1.   Father's sister (or, in this case, father-in-law's sister for Anu)
2.   Child
3.   Prayer
4.   Utensil
5.   Temple
6.   Slipper
7.   Contractor
8.   Loose shirt and trousers
9.   Elder sister
10.   Brothers
11.   Homespun cotton shirt
12.   Chicken drumstick
13.   Custom/Tradition
14.   Fatso
15.   An abusive and extremely offensive term

Chapter 14

1.   Grandmother (mother's mother)
2.   Kohl

Chapter 15

1.   Aunt
2.   Slang for brother-in-law

Chapter 16

1. A savoury snack that originated in India, typically served as an hors d'oeuvre at roadside tracks from stalls or food carts
2. A round, hollow puri, fried crisp and filled with a mixture of flavored water (pani), tamarind chutney, chili, chaat masala, potato, onion and chickpeas

ACKNOWLEDGMENTS

If it wasn't for NaNoWriMo (National Novel Writing Month) in November, I may not have had the courage to attempt writing a novel. Breaking the goal of 50,000 words into bite-size chunks of writing, I soon surpassed the word count, surprising myself by settling comfortably around the 80,000 mark. The result was a novel that I had long wished to write, but never known quite how to.

As an Indian living abroad, I was keen to explore the dichotomy of straddling two cultures and environments. Not everyone's experience is the same, but maybe, somewhere in this story, certain elements resonated with you too. If they did, I'd love to hear about it. Email me with your thoughts at:

poornima@poornimamanco.com

My acknowledgements wouldn't be complete without expressing my heartfelt gratitude to my ART team. Without their feedback, picking up of errors in the initial drafts, and also being frank about what wasn't working, this book wouldn't be what it is.

A shoutout to my lovely friend, artist Patricia Maneim, for talking to me about her journey in the art world, and allowing me to take inspiration from her life. You can follow her on Facebook , Instagram and her website is: **patricia-maneim.wordpress.com**

Thank you for reading this book and being a part of my journey. As a writer, there is no better reward than knowing that someone gave your book the time of the day.

Many thanks and happy reading!

Editor : charu.dpp@gmail.com

Book cover design: team@miblart.com

ABOUT THE AUTHOR

With a voracious appetite for reading and an unbridled imagination, Poornima started writing stories at age eight. Newspaper in Education, The Times of India supplement, published several of her winning entries. Over the years, family and career took over and writing took a back seat.

In 2009, when a short story of hers placed in an online competition run by The Guardian newspaper, she once again found her writing voice. Subsequently, she started an online blog where she continued to write articles and stories. Nine years later these stories appeared in two separate books as a part of the India trilogy. Since then, she has published the third book in the trilogy, a novella and another book of short stories, and is working on her first novel.

Born and raised in New Delhi, India, Poornima graduated from Delhi University with a degree in English Literature. She lives in the United Kingdom with her husband and two daughters, and remains an avid reader. She also loves travelling, baking decadent cakes, celebrity fashion faux pas that make her laugh, old black and white movies, all kinds of art and music, and Nature walks with her family.